Mayhem in Melbourne

Juliette Davis

First published by Juliette Davis in 2019
This edition published in 2019 by Juliette Davis

Mayhem in Melbourne

EPUB: 9781925786842
POD: 9781925786859

Cover design by Red Tally Studios

Publishing services provided by Critical Mass
www.critmassconsulting.com

This **is a work of fiction**. Names, characters, businesses, places, events and incidents are either the products of the author's imagination or used in a fictitious manner. Any resemblance to actual persons, living or dead, or actual events is purely coincidental.

Monday

Chapter 1

Monday's a crazy day at Caruthers Real Estate. Action on Saturday means mayhem on Monday. As if to prove this point the phone is calling for attention as I approach my desk. I grab it and slip into my chair and the day is off to a racing start.

It's Lauren.

'Hi, I saw you come in. Why didn't you stop at my desk? I've got a couple of applications for Bruno's property. You need to get on to them. He's already rung this morning.'

'Bring them down,' I say.

'Too busy. It's flat out here.' And she has gone. I raise my eyebrows. Then I remember Monday Mayhem. The name I have given this day.

One of my Monday Mayhem jobs is to help Lauren with her applications for the properties she has vacant. She is on my team. Before I can dwell on 'too busy to bring me the applications' the phone goes again.

I recognise Lisa, our receptionist.

'Bruno's on the phone. Lauren said you're dealing with him.'

'What?' I say.

'Bruno. He's on the line.' Lisa has gone and I have a Bruno's voice in my ear.

'Who am I speaking to? I want Lauren.'

'It's Juliette Davis. We've spoken before.' I begin to sigh then I stop myself and swallow it instead. Bruno is the last person I want to deal with first thing on a Monday.

'Oh, yes…yes…but where's Lauren? Why isn't she taking my call?'

I'm wondering that too. 'She's not available, so Lisa put you through to me.'

'Well, what I want to know is, are there any applications on my property? Two people went through on Saturday. I got the text. They took applications. It was in the text.'

I turn my mouth into a smile. 'Yes,' I say, lips stretched. 'You got two applications, they both applied so that's good. I'll check them and get back to you.'

'No. No. I want to know who they are. You can check them later.'

'I can't tell you that. They're on Lauren's desk.'

'Well, wouldn't you think I'd be interested in the applications? What good are they on Lauren's desk if you're dealing with them?'

He had me there – what good were they on her desk?

I say firmly, 'When I've checked them, I'll get back to you.'

'Yes, check them now, I'll want to get moving on them. I'll have my phone with me all day.' He always says this and he always answers on about the second ring. It is as if he has the phoned taped to his hand, or hung around his neck.

I sip my coffee. This is the beginning of Monday Mayhem. It's good to take five, to sip my coffee.

Caruthers Real Estate has a busy property management office which I joined as the senior property manager about four years ago.

For Monday Mayhem I think carefully about what I wear. It helps me with the all the action. I like to dress for the weather, too – today I am wearing my favourite turquoise top and my summer boots. They have a pattern of pretty cut-outs along the side and at the toe – no good in the rain, but they are boots and they give me a feeling of power – 'these boots are made for walking' sort of power. Power and confidence.

My top matches the cloudless sky and looks good with my blue and white striped skirt. It is cheerful and uplifting. I like the look and it goes with my blue eyes. If you look around, you'll see lots of people have brown eyes so I'm very pleased with my dark blue. My mother says it is the Irish coming out in me; black hair and blue eyes. I'm happy with that.

I used to be a school teacher but I got over that. The job became more and more stressful and exhausting. At the end of each week I would throw my hands in the air and announce to anyone who was listening that I needed the next week in bed with several bottles of wine. What I really needed was to move on.

Where to move to was the problem. A friend suggested veterinary nursing because that is what she would like to do. Another idea was the police force. I am not keen on uniforms but I added that to the list. A teaching colleague said, 'Why don't you drive a tram while you think of something permanent? That'd be fun.'

I love Melbourne's trams but that's another job with a uniform. I kept these suggestions, and others that came my way, tucked into the back of my mind and went on teaching.

One morning a voice in my head said, 'property management'. I was surprised. I hadn't given that suggestion much thought. But the universe had spoken so I went with it.

I have been in the job for a number of years and now I work at Caruthers, in one of Melbourne's inner suburbs.

* * *

On Monday, there is no time for a chat over a morning coffee. I grabbed mine as I passed Café Yellow and took care not to slop it on my beautiful turquoise top as I pushed through the heavy glass doors into our stylish reception area. I gave a quick greeting to Lisa and a nod and a pat to the aged and huge do-it-all photocopier that is positioned behind her desk as if it was her assistant. It has a habit of playing up and we call it The Monster.

Lisa was on the phone so she ignored me, and The Monster appeared to be asleep. I am not sure how The Monster feels but Lisa, who has been with the company for years, believes she is the pivot that the office revolves around. She would notice if I didn't greet her. Receptionists can wield a lot of power, and Lisa wields that power and she has broken us into her way of working.

Through reception is the comfortable shabby office where the real work is done. I marched down to the very end of this long narrow building to my desk.

I like it here by the back door. When the last incumbent moved out I threw my weight around as senior property manager and grabbed the desk.

Despite the occasionally cranky or stressed landlord, I am happy I chose this as my new career. There is no timetable to stick to – I can arrange my own. Monday is Mayhem but it is quiet down here at the end of this old building and it is seldom quiet in a school classroom.

I push Bruno's applications to the back of my mind and look at my emails. There could be something there that is more important than Bruno although I doubt he would think so. I'm also hoping Lauren will get sick of them on her desk and bring them down. It's not that I'm making a point. Well, perhaps it is but I *am* helping her out by checking them.

I scroll through my inbox. The emails are never-ending. A lot of junk of course. How is it that even with the filters Caruthers has in place, I get emails on how to enhance a penis and pictures of sexy Russian girls looking for husbands? I had two like that last week. I forwarded them to our IT company. These emails are more use to them, as they are an all-male organisation. They assured me they had the problem under control. Whatever 'under control' meant. Perhaps it is under control because my junk today is about courses on how I can become a better property manager, up-skill myself on dispute resolutions, or be more effective at time management. There are a couple from a fashion outlet called Corporate Dressing and others of the same style. Not a penis in sight. I go through trashing them and the list becomes manageable.

Nerida, a tenant, has written half a page complaining about how the junk mail is distributed in her apartment block. She missed out on a free gift of Twinings teabags. *We should have some rules for distributing whatever arrives. The mail is just dumped on top of the boxes and we help ourselves. There's got to be a better way.*

Her complex must be full of tea drinkers. If you are a tea drinker, why wouldn't you grab more than your share? And why does she think I care about her not getting her free teabag? The junk mail and its distribution is nothing to do with me. I email back and ask her if she has any ideas and to come up with a solution and I will look into it. I wonder if she will bother, or will she disappear into the background.

Tenants see us as the answer to everything that goes wrong in their lives. A while ago, a tenant rang and asked me what I could do about an old flatmate she had fallen out with. He kept coming around and harassing her about some money he said she owed him.

'This is very distressing,' she said. 'You should be able to do something to stop him.'

'Why?' I asked.

'You're managing the unit and he's not on the lease. He shouldn't be here.'

'You could go to the police,' I said.

She came back with, 'What are they going to do?'

'I'm sure they can do more than I can. I'll put that suggestion in an email to you.'

She slammed down the phone.

Does she think I am some sort of miracle worker? I always confirm my telephone calls in writing – it takes away any confusion.

There's an email from Tom. He is a complainer. He lives in a top-floor unit and finds a myriad of things that need attention, which he fires off in regular emails. Over the weekend he heard a noise in the roof.

I bet there are rats up there, he writes. *Well, it could be a possum. But I'm sure it is rats. The couple next door put their rubbish on the landing. Sometimes it's there for the whole weekend before they take it to the bins. That's going to encourage rats.*

Personally, I do not see how a rat in a roof cavity, however brave and athletic, is going to make it to the hallway to rat-around in some rubbish. If it managed the feat, it would be spotted and the whole building would be up in arms. An animal in the ceiling is an owners' corporation matter. I smile as I flick the email on to them; something to add to *their* Monday workload.

If I check the dates, I can see most emails are generated on Sunday. What is it with Sunday? It appears that most tenants in this beautiful city sit around doing nothing. Then to break the boredom, they decide to report issues to their property manager and so add to the flow of emails waiting for the week to begin.

Most people hate Monday but in an oddly masochistic way, I like it. There is drama and action. The week begins with a bang and it is like being in the centre of things. There are issues to sort and problems to solve. I wonder if this is a hangover from my teaching days, where Monday has the energy of the students arriving at school after a two-day break and there is a sort of excitement in the air. Of course schools and property management departments are both places of action. Neither is a 'kick-back and relax' sort of job. Action is something I am used to.

There are bad days in this job when I come home and slam my door and never want to open it. Those are the days when I can't believe I chose this career. That I studied to get my agent's representative's licence and paid to do it. The bad days can be bad, but I always bounce back for more. I can't get it out of my system.

Some offices have a meeting about 9.15 am on Mondays, where they review the properties that were opened on Saturday. This doesn't work because everyone has that, 'I'm bogged-down-I've-got-too-much-to-do' look about them to pay attention to the manager, who's making a show of being in charge.

Caruthers doesn't do this. On Saturday, the staff who open the properties for inspections fill out a running sheet for each property. At some point during their hectic day they text the owners with an update – how many people looked at the property and how many took applications.

The effort we put in encourages landlords to see Monday morning as a time to check if they have applications on their property. Bruno was one of the first off the rank. These calls add to Monday Mayhem. A call comes from a landlord whose property was opened by Lauren on Saturday. She sent him a text to say two people viewed it.

'I hear two people came through the open. Did you get any applications?'

I think, give them time to get their act together, but I say, 'No. Not yet.'

'Well you've got their names and numbers haven't you?'

'Yes,' I reply. I smile again. Have you noticed that when you smile you lift your voice and you sound bright and on the ball?

'Can you give them a ring? See what they think and if they're going to apply, then get back to me? I'll have my phone with me all day.' The whole world has their phone with them all day – why do people keep telling me this?

'Yes. I'll try to get some feedback,' my carefully red-painted-lips are still stretched over my teeth.

'Yeah, do that,' he says. 'Get back to me by lunch time if you can. I've got to get the place let. It's been open three times now and not a sausage. I can't afford to be waiting around.' I make a note on my to-do pad just in case I forget, and he rings again. I will email him so I have a record of what I have said. It's quicker that way too, as I won't have to discuss it with him.

I hope the people who visited are happy to have me call. Prospective tenants can sound annoyed when they are phoned after an inspection. Their frustration at being disturbed can make them short and at times rude.

As a tenant, you should think of it from the owner's point of view. You may have hated the place you viewed or thought the advertising was misleading, and you would not live in it if you were paid to. If that's what you think, be kind. Keep it to yourself. Visualise the anxious landlord hovering near the phone and say something positive. Being a landlord can be stressful.

This is not the time for me to tell this stressed landlord that a sausage has not applied for his property because the place is too expensive. That conversation is better left to later in the week, when I am speaking to him again about the lack of sausages and what we are going to do to get more of them through at next Saturday's open.

With all this going on, you would think it would be the last day of the week a property manager would call in sick. Yet, every Monday our manager of property management, Emily, emails a list of the names of the poor souls who have identified themselves as being sick. There is at least one, and sometimes two or three, who are taking a sickie.

Today Kylie, who is in my team, is on the list.

I wonder about her. She likes a good time. Perhaps she called in sick because she is so hung-over, she can't lift her head without throwing up? Perhaps her alcohol level is so high she cannot risk driving. Real estate people know how to drink. Maybe, just maybe, she has been struck down with a nasty strain of flu. Or perhaps Emily has shared her bugs with her.

Emily's emails never give the reason for the staff member's absence. When the missing people turn up on Tuesday, they usually answer our concerned questions with, 'Much better. Thanks'. If they mention the cause of their absence, it is likely to be 'gastro'. Too much action at a night club can cause that and those Champagne brunches on Sunday that spill over into the rest of the day can encourage a tender tummy to rebel.

Today we can access our emails from our iPad or phone. If you can raise your head off the pillow even for a moment you can leave a message about returning calls and emails on Tuesday. If you don't do this, people who view themselves as 'a-very-important-person' will contact you several times, leaving more and more angry and frustrated messages. That means more to wade through on Tuesday.

As Kylie's manager, I will make time to check her emails. I want to look as if I am on top of this job.

Chapter 2

Bruno! He won't stay buried in my mind.

It looks as if I will have to collect his applications myself. I am starting to worry he will call again before I have got onto them.

I ring Lisa. 'If Bruno calls, can you take a message? I'm not available.'

'Don't be unavailable too long. He won't give up.'

'Thanks,' I say. 'I have to check his applications before I talk to him again.'

'Well, hurry up and do it. I don't want him having a go at me,' she says and she's gone.

I head off to get the applications. I want to buzz Lauren and ask if they are still on her desk. But I don't. I tell myself it is good to get up and walk – it is healthy. I am always reading that.

I collect them and the running sheet from the edge of her desk and she has the grace to say, 'Sorry. I've been flat out.'

'It was good for me to have the walk,' I say. 'We all need to move around more.'

She picks up the phone and begins to dial without a comment.

I glance at Bruno's applications. One couple has put themselves down as having two dogs. They're not going to be suitable. Bruno will not have a dog near the place. His no-dog policy is set in concrete.

I ring them and tell them, so they can move on to another property.

Checking Bruno's applications finds me caught up in a strange, rather surreal game that I have played before. Seeing this situation as a game helps me to cope with it, and in a bizarre way, to enjoy it. It must be something about chasing a ball and a desire to win; perhaps just the desire to win.

I regularly check applications for this two-bedroom villa unit in a beachside suburb. It's usual for one or two applications for the property to be waiting for me on Monday. I ring the references and confirmed the information the tenant has given us is correct. The next move is to take the applications to Lauren the property manager. Then we really begin the game. Kick off goes like this:

'This application on Princess Street checks out. The other one's no good – two dogs,' I say.

I wave the good application. 'This guy sounds fine. All you have to do is put it to Bruno.'

Property managers are the contact for landlords, regardless of what goes on behind the scenes.

'Oh god! Bruno!!' A large sigh. 'I don't want to ring him.'

There is a pause. I wait.

'Could you ring? I'm so busy this morning, just look at my desk.' Her desk certainly looks like it is shrivelling under stacks of paper, but then her desk always looks like this. Invoices disappear for weeks in there. It's as if they have been eaten.

'I'm sure he would rather talk to you,' I try. 'You're his property manager and he wanted to talk to you this morning.'

No one wants to talk to Bruno. We are into our fourth month of having this property vacant. There have been a number of applications for it. Some have checked out very well and some tenants have seemed keen. There is a catch to closing the deal.

'No, you ring.' Says Lauren, 'Give him some excuse; say I'm out at an appointment. Anything! Say I've drowned myself. He's already rung twice and Lisa said I wasn't available. I'm still not available.'

I wait.

'And really, I think I am sick, I'm not up to it today.' She stops again and I wait.

'Just the thought of ringing him makes by stomach churn, and I want to throw up. I can't do it!'

'Okay! Okay, I'll ring him.' I pick up the application and walk back to my desk.

This is part of the game plan. In the end I do this for almost every application. I am not keen to ring Bruno either, but then I don't deal with him on a regular basis. What is hard for us and upsets Lauren is that we really want to let his property. That is our job and we have worked hard at it. To have it empty for so long gives us all a feeling of failure.

I have tried to tell Lauren about seeing it as a game and a challenge, but she doesn't get it. She is too emotional about it.

After we have been through this, I dial his number. I am playing the game, and remembering that it is a tough one. I play often but I have never got the ball into the goal. For three months we have been lining up our shots. Each time the goalkeeper is too good. In my mind Bruno is the goalkeeper. This is the wrong way around because Bruno should be on the same team as us. It does not make sense. Sometime I find myself getting really angry, but the game scenario lets me detach from the emotion.

Bruno of course picks up on the second ring. I bet he would pick up even if he was underwater discovering a lost treasure.

'Well, at last someone's returning my call. I've been waiting all morning,' he says, as soon as I say who I am. He doesn't have my direct line in his phone or he would have answered with those exact words. He likes to get to the point.

He is off again before I can tell him that Lauren has drowned herself. 'How did the applications go? You said there were two. I want to know the details.' I open my mouth to start but he hasn't finished. 'You know I'd be interested in these people, but I have to wait and wait to hear anything.'

'One's no good. Two dogs.'

'Why didn't you tell me that earlier? Wouldn't you think I'd be interested to know that? I've been thinking about two applications!'

I don't remind him that I didn't know when we spoke earlier, although Lauren would have known if she had glanced at the applications.

We move into the next stage of the game. In the office, we wonder if he is using the property for some sort of classy tax dodge. Every tenant we think is suitable has to be checked by him.

Definitely no pets of any sort. I believe he once turned down a bird. There is a reasonable sized outdoor area leading off the lounge and the place is not pristine. You could call it lived in and you could think it was ideal for a pet but you would be wrong. The subject is best avoided. If there is a badly behaved dog or cat or bird or even fish out there they have crossed Bruno's path at some time, and the experience has not been a happy one for him. We have yet to find out how the animal viewed the encounter.

Once, earlier on, I mentioned an applicant who had a dog with references for good behaviour and he asked me to find out what sort of dog it was. It was a kelpie.

'Fancy anyone living in the city with that type of dog, and why would they think I would want it in my property?' I wanted to ask him if he had seen the Australian film *Red Dog*, where the main character was a kelpie-cross. I'm glad I didn't, because when I thought about it, I saw it proved his point. Red, the dog, did not live in the city. He lived in the Outback. We have 'no pets' in the advertising, but people try anyway, especially those who can't read an ad properly or have a reference for their dog or cat.

Bruno also needs to meet his prospective tenants face-to-face.

In his words, 'I need to know what sort of person I am going to deal with. Will we get on? This person may grate on me. You know you can never tell exactly what a person's like on paper. I need the meeting to get the feel of them.' The excuse for this is because Bruno does his own maintenance.

Today's prospective tenant is a single older man. Unfortunately, the Privacy Act does not allow us to ask him whether he has been married or has a girlfriend or if he has any children who are not going to live in the property but will visit. This disappoints Bruno, and I imagine he will ask when he meets him. Bruno is not worried about the Privacy Act.

I fax the application through to him and arrange a meeting with the guy and Bruno at the property for the end of the day. Some people do not want to meet the owner and be shown around the property again by him and be asked personal questions. They pull out at this stage.

Kylie once said, 'For god's sake, he's looking for a tenant not a best friend.' I wonder if that is a good thing. He is very attached to his properties and if he has personal difficulties with the tenants we could all suffer.

I am surprised he has not taken this property away from us. Many owners would have done that long before we reached the four-month-vacant mark.

While I have been doing this I have had several phone calls. I don't mind the interruptions but phone calls like this one on Monday annoy me.

'I put in an application for 3 Railway Avenue on Saturday. When am I going to hear something back?'

'Did you give it to the property manager at the property?'

'No, I came into the office and dropped it off, so I know you got it.'

'Right. What's your name and I'll let the property manager know you called. I have to tell you, you won't hear back until we have contacted your references, and that could be later to-day or tomorrow.'

He knows we got their applications, so why call so early?

Vince manages that property. I email him to check that the application has reached his desk.

Another interruption is from one of Kylie's tenants.

He starts with, 'At last someone's taking my call. I've been put through to a voicemail three times.'

'Right,' I say, 'talk to me.'

'We've got a dripping tap we want fixed.'

'Right,' I say again. 'Have you emailed your request to Kylie?'

'No! I'm talking to you now.'

'We need all our maintenance in writing. Then we have a record of it.'

'You mean that if my hot water bursts and the power goes off, I'd have to send you an email before you'd take any action?'

'No, that's an emergency, so you should contact us immediately.'

'Well, what about my tap?'

'It's not an emergency, so you have to send your request in writing. That way we can keep track of it.'

'What do you mean track of it?'

'A paper trail. A record. How long has the tap been dripping?'

'On and off for a few months. So we want it fixed.'

'Right.' I am getting good with 'right'. 'Email it through to Kylie and she'll get onto it. I'll let her know you're doing that.'

'Well, I suppose I'll have to do that.'

'Yes. The sooner you do it, the sooner it'll get fixed.' I can hear him draw breath, so before he says anything else I say, 'Thank you for calling. Have a nice day,' and disengage.

It's frustrating to have to waste time on things like this. Kylie should have trained her tenants better. If the maintenance is not an emergency, we require it in writing. We put that in the documents we give a new tenant. But then who reads those? Not this tenant or he would know that a tap that has been 'dripping on and off for a few months' is not an emergency.

Chapter 3

Bruno's applications, even the unsuccessful ones on his property are carefully filed away. Normally I would shred the unsuccessful ones after a few days. We do not want people's personal details floating around the office. But not Bruno's. He is likely to ring up and ask about someone he turned down weeks ago or even how many people went through on a certain date. I have no idea why he wants this information and I can't see how it can be of any use to him. I wonder if it is just to catch us out. I file his running sheets too.

The running sheets are my bible on Monday. Prospective tenants must have been through the property before I consider their application. If their name is not on the running sheet I put the application aside to follow up later. If you are someone who refuses to give your name at the open for inspection, beware. Your application does not take priority. We need proof that you visited the property. I also check for any comments, good or bad, that are beside the names.

Good comments go a bit like this: 'Lovely to deal with.' 'Liked them.' 'She's really keen.' 'They have a dog.' 'Nice.'

Positive comments are the most usual ones, but there are the negative ones. I have seen 'No! No! No!' and 'No Fucken Way!!!' written on a running sheet.

Why would anyone go to an open and behave so badly they get 'No fucken way' written beside their name? It's beyond me. Often the property manager conducting the open will also manage the property. Are they likely to put someone in who they think will make their job harder? If you have 'No fucken way' against your name you are not going to be accepted as a tenant. No one is going to want to deal with you.

Then there are the time wasters. A year or so ago I showed a couple through a property that belongs to Bruno's daughter. It has an aubergine coloured feature wall. Aubergine painted on by the fair hands of Bruno's daughter. It is not a large wall, so not a lot of aubergine, but definitely aubergine. It helps divide the half-formed dining alcove from the kitchen.

The couple looked through every cupboard and robe, they flushed the toilet, turned on all the taps to check water pressure and asked about the neighbours (not that I knew anything about them). They stood on the balcony and gazed at the unit's car park – a space along the drive below – and discussed its location and convenience to the entry door. It was opposite. They asked if the landlord would consider a lower offer for the rent. The answer to that was 'no'. They took applications. When they were leaving she turned to me and said, 'The landlord will have to paint out that dreadful colour if we take it. We couldn't live with that!'

I have no idea what Bruno thinks of the colour but his daughter is very pleased with it. She thinks it gives style to this very ordinary two-bedroom apartment.

How can it possibly matter how the toilet flushes to these people, when they cannot live with the colour on the feature wall? Wouldn't their first utterance be, 'Oh my god, I can't stand that colour! I couldn't live with that. Will the landlord get rid of it?'

With the answer, 'No, she likes it,' we could all leave and get on with our day. Actually, the colour shows on the internet advertising, but I guess you have to see it to get the full effect.

Bruno is allowed to do the maintenance on this property but his daughter selects the tenants. A wise move on her part and I wondered at the time how she kept him from meddling in her decision.

Shortly after the 'I-couldn't-live-with-it-inspection' we found tenants who paid the asking rent, and never once mentioned the feature wall. I have no idea if they liked it, hated it, were colour blind or just did not care. I was careful not to ask their opinion. Lauren manages it, and now I am thinking about it I wonder if they have discussed the colour in the negative with Bruno. I am sure he would complain to Lauren. He is very proud of his daughter, who is overseas, and her taste in home decoration. Not so pleased that he has given her free rein in his Princess Street property. That is very bland.

An email from Lauren pops onto my screen. It is addressed to everyone.

Has anyone seen an application from Trevor Walker for 10/22 Railway Avenue? He said he dropped it off on Saturday.

There, what did I tell you? However annoying it can be for a property manager, tenants should follow up on their application. I wonder how Trevor's application travelled from reception. There are a number of routes and many hazards along the way.

I'm tempted to ask Lauren if she would like me to look through the stuff on her desk for it. But it is probably tactful to wait a while and see what happens.

Instead of ringing Lauren I ring the people who went through Sausage-Man's place on Saturday. Neither of them answers their phone and I leave a message asking them to ring back if they are interested in the property or have questions about it. Then I email my lack of results to Sausage Man.

My screen pings and there is another email from Lauren.

You can stop looking for Trevor Walker's application – I know that's what you're all doing. I've found it!!

As she doesn't say where she found it, I deduce that it was on her desk the whole time. It is nice to be right sometimes.

Now that I've got Bruno sorted out I move onto other applications. Monday is all about applications.

I have a good application on a property in Barkly Street that I had trouble with last week. The tenants who applied last week added extra stress to my Monday by making an offer on the rent.

At Caruthers the rent is what's advertised. Sometimes if the property has been on the market for some time, we may be able to persuade the landlord to take a slightly lower offer, but we advertise the rent the landlord has agreed on.

If the property is advertised for $650 per week, as the Barkly Street property is, the landlord is not expecting to receive $620, which is what this prospective tenant offered.

She explained to me, 'When we saw the property we discovered it was smaller than we thought it would be.' She enlarged on that, 'Therefore, being smaller it should command less rent.'

'Smaller than what?' I asked.

'Smaller than we thought it would be. It's not as big.'

'Not as big as what?' I couldn't resist. It was such a ridiculous thought process.

'Well, we thought it would be bigger. If it was bigger we would pay more.' Of course this sort of conversation goes nowhere and it's not one that is wise to pass on to the landlord.

I said, 'The landlord is not going to be interested in your offer. If you want the property, you'll have to pay the full rent.'

'I'll talk to my boyfriend and I'll see what he says. But he thinks $620 is what it's worth.'

'Right, do that! Come back to me if you're happy to go ahead at the advertised rent.'

Her boyfriend wrote the following email:

We are writing to say that we like your property but we think it is too expensive. We have been looking at properties in the area for some weeks. We have got a very good idea of what rents should be. We are making an offer on the rent. We think it is only worth $620 in today's market.

You'll find us very good tenants. We have excellent references and we will look after the property as if it was our own. Please call any of our references. They will be expecting a call.

Please pass this email onto the landlord.

We look forward to hearing from you.

As I was asked to pass it on to the landlord, I forwarded it to Barbara.

She was on the phone immediately.

'I'm offended. This is an immaculate apartment with two great bathrooms and two off-street car parks. Do they think I don't know what it's worth?'

'I thought I should forward their offer to you, as they asked me to.'

'You should be offended too, because they're telling you that you don't know your job...you don't know what a property is worth. How dare they?'

As a property manager I have a thick skin that I've developed over time. I can't afford to be offended so easily.

Barbara is a great landlord and very good to her tenants. She gave her previous ones a Christmas hamper. They moved out a couple of months later. Funny they did not want to stay for another hamper. It was a good hamper.

I emailed the new applicants with her refusal and left it at that.

They came back two days later with a higher offer – almost the full rent. Barbara had taken such offence; she didn't want to discuss it. It was all over for them.

I'm sure this couple felt in command of the situation when they decided to put in the offer. I can see them sitting round a computer starting to fill in the online application.

'What do you think? We'll go for it. Right?' says Gung-Ho who later writes the email that loses him any chance of the place.

'Well! It is a bit small. We wanted something bigger,' replies his partner.

Gung-Ho looks for other problems. 'The carpet in the bedrooms has had a bit of wear but I could live with that. And you won't notice when the furniture's in there.'

'No, you won't but did you see that stain on the carpet in the robe?'

'Yes, I wonder what caused that. It didn't look too good.'

'Our shoes will cover that, so it'll be all right.'

Gung-Ho goes on, 'The light fittings are the ones that insects die in. You know the ones. The cover clips on.'

'It's hard to get it off to replace the globes. Mum had some like that but she changed them for those hanging ones.'

'They're not that bad. I could change the globes. That's not a big deal. Let's make an offer.'

Gung-Ho's partner is a little doubtful. 'Do you think we should? I really like it. I don't want to miss out.'

'We'll make an offer. They can always come back with another offer and we can negotiate. Let's knock it back by, say $30 and see what happens.' Gung-Ho turns back to the computer.

'No. No, that's too much! We don't want to miss out. It's the best we've seen.'

Is this person less greedy or is Gung-Ho one of those people who have an almost pathological desire for a bargain?

'Trust me. We're good tenants. We've got good rental references. They'll want us.'

They send off their applications with Gung-Ho feeling pleased with himself. It doesn't occur to either of them that if they like it, there are sure to be others that do too; other people who won't make an offer. It doesn't occur to him that working in the industry, we have some idea of the market and what people are prepared to pay. Gung-Ho is in for a surprise and a letdown.

I'm glad the next applications on Barkly Street check out well. The owner deserves better than Gung-Ho and his partner.

This week's applications are from a couple in their mid-twenties who are moving in together. That can be tricky. They have to sort out the irritations of day-to-day living for the first time. Some couples can't do this and we hear about it when they break their lease.

These tenants have not made an offer on the rent. They work in different areas of the city so the two car parks will make their lives easier. There is street parking but to have secured off-street parking for two cars is always a bonus in this city. Barbara approves them and I ring and confirm it with them. They are happy and I send them off our confirmation letter that tells them how to pay the first month's rent and the bond to secure the property. I arrange to have it marked 'under application' on the internet. So far it's been a good morning. One property leased and Bruno's under offer.

I have not given another thought to Gung-Ho and his partner, although I see by the running sheet that they had another look on Saturday. For their sake, I hope they found it even smaller than they remembered from their first viewing.

Chapter 4

I'm heading to Kylie's desk when my mobile rings. Mother flashes onto the screen. I have asked myself a hundred times why I don't change the word to Mum. I thought it was funny when I first put 'Mother' in but it always throws me. She is not 'Mother'. She's definitely 'Mum'. I have to make a mental switch every time I answer.

'How are you darling?' She always asks that with a voice full of concern as if I've been sick for years.

'Fine,' I say, 'And you?'

'Oh fine too but I won't be coming down this weekend. It's going to be too hot. 37 degrees has been projected. I'll wait until it cools down a bit.'

Mum lives in a hamlet in the Wombat State Forest. She likes the rural, laidback lifestyle. She and her partner Clive have a sort of market garden where they grow produce they can sell at local markets. They have to grow their vegetables under a huge netting frame because wallabies come and eat them. As I'm not working this Saturday she was driving down here and we were going to meet for lunch.

'That's fine Mum,' I say. 'I think you're right. Too hot. Another time.'

'Do you want to come up here? You could come up on Friday evening and stay over.'

'No, but thanks,' I say. 'Too hot to drive.'

What I really mean is that in this hot weather I'm afraid of bush fires. Mum says they have their evacuation plan so there is nothing to worry about. From my bedroom window up there I can see rows and rows of pale grey trunks of gum trees. They are beautiful, but too close for comfort in this weather is my thinking.

'Yes, you're probably right. Even on Friday evening it will be hot.' I know she knows it is because I am anxious about fires but she doesn't say so. She goes on. 'Darling have you seen Tim's latest Facebook post?'

Tim is my ex.

'Mum you know I'm not interested. I don't follow him anymore.'

'I don't know why you let him go. He's such a nice man. He's posted some great pictures. I've told you before you should've followed him overseas. You could've done that. You didn't need to buy that apartment.'

Mum and I are different. Very different.

I don't want to discuss Tim so I say, 'I have to go Mum. It's very busy today.'

'Well don't wear yourself out. Have some fun too.' She's always saying that. She thinks I don't have enough of what she calls 'fun'. She and Clive often kick back and smoke a joint or two and sip beer or their homemade wine on their veranda. They do a lot of 'letting life just drift by'. Vegetables do not need constant attention.

While I have been chatting to Mum I have been booting up Kylie's computer and checking her emails and any applications that have been emailed to her.

No sooner have I disconnected from Mum than Kylie's phone rings. I hesitate, but feel driven to answer it.

'What's this about my rangehood? I want to know what my tenants have done to it.' The voice is angry. I know nothing about his rangehood but this is part of the job; trying to work out what someone is talking about. This rangehood hasn't come to my notice before, but I'm sure I'm going to get to know it.

'Who am I speaking to?'

'Who are you?' It sounds rude the way he says it. Little things like that don't bother me anymore and I answer with my lips stretched into a smile, the physical symbol of putting warmth into my voice.

'Juliette Davis. I'm Kylie's manager. Tell me your problem and I'll see if I can help you. What's the address of the property?'

He tells me. While we talk, I find the property on the computer so I can take a stab at helping him.

'Kylie sent me an email to say the rangehood needs to be repaired. I want to find out what the tenants have done to it. It's always been working. There's no problem with it. Do they know how to use the thing?'

Why does he think tenants would request maintenance if there was no problem? I keep this thought to myself and say, 'I see they have been in the property for six months so I'm sure they know how to use it.'

'Rangehoods don't just break down. Have they unplugged it? Did they try to clean it and break it that way?'

'Let me ask them those questions, but if it has just stopped working are you happy for me to get a tradesman to attend to it?'

'Get a quote! Don't let anyone do anything without me agreeing to it.' His voice is hectoring.

'How about I give the tradesman a spend-limit, say $150, and if it goes over that he can quote?'

'What do you mean?' I wonder what he thinks I mean. It sounds clear to me, but then it is Monday and it can take a while to get with the play.

'I'll get him to go and look at it. If he can fix it for under $150, let him go ahead. If he can't fix it for that much, he can quote.'

There is a silence on the line. I'm good with silences. I wait. He comes back with, 'Why do you want to do that?'

'Well, he has to come into the office to get the key to go to the property to quote. Why not let him fix it if he can within the spend-limit? Then he won't have to go again. If it is going to be more than $150, he can quote.' With a flash of inspiration, I say, 'That'll keep the tenants happy. They just want it fixed.'

There's another silence and I think he is going to refuse then he says, 'Yes, I can see the point in that but if he charges more than $150 inclusive of GST – notice I said inclusive of GST – I'm not going to pay. I'll want a quote.' I wonder if he cares about keeping the tenants happy, or has he just seen sense?

'Right,' I say. 'I'll make that clear on the work order.'

Thinking of the rangehood makes me remember my toilet at home. The flush is broken. We can push the button as often as we like, but no water gushes forth. We heave a bucket of water from the bath into it to flush – or at least, I do. My roommate Amy went to stay with her boyfriend, Brett.

How could I have forgotten that? I've been so busy, and it is the rangehood-landlord who brings it to mind. He gets me wondering what I could have done to have caused the problem. Did we push the button incorrectly? I have been pushing it the same way since I bought the property about a year ago, but you never know, it could be the wrong way.

I'm with the rangehood landlord here – flush systems do not just break down.

I grab the plumber's number. I don't want to continue pouring a bucket of water down it every time it needs flushing and I have Amy to consider. I dial the plumber and it goes to voicemail. I leave a message.

I like the space here that Kylie has created for herself. I study her pinboard. Most of us use our pinboards to display printouts of the properties that we have up for lease. This way we can see them at a glance. Kylie has her properties interspersed with fashion pictures. Mainly pictures of shoes. She has a passion for shoes. This is a good city to live in if you have an on-going love affair with shoes. Every shopping strip has a profusion of shoe shops; Chapel Street in South Yarra and Acland Street in St Kilda just to mention a couple and then there is David Jones and Myers. Kylie has a picture of a stunning yellow shoe that looks as if the heel is made of glass. I am sure I saw one like it in David Jones, but there are so many beautiful shoes it could have been in any one of the hundreds of windows I have browsed. Then there is the retro shop Shag full of eye-popping stuff. I am more a boots person and boots that have a solid heel for stomping about. Even these pretty summer ones I am wearing have what my mother calls 'a sensible heel'. There is nothing sensible about the heels Kylie is displaying or that she wears.

Sitting to the right of her computer is a large noticeable mauve mug, sporting a picture of a red shoe with a spiked heel. At the moment it is also sporting some old milky tea that only needs a dead fly floating on it to make it really gross. No one else is allowed to use this mug, so the revolting tea is Kylie's. Most of us don't have a special mug, so new people can think this one is for general usage. Kylie immediately points out their mistake and they never use it again.

Her inbox is flooded with emails. Many of them dated yesterday and today. I scroll through. Some of them are personal.

I try not to have too many personal emails coming through the office except perhaps from friends or previous colleagues making lunch or drinks dates. I don't know why anyone would make their office email their personal one – you can set up any number of free email accounts and access them from your phone. There is no need to let the office know your life and the problems with it.

Once I took over the portfolio of someone who had been sacked. I'm not sure why but she was asked to collect her things and depart. It is often done that way. The real estate company decides they can live without your services and you are gone. Here one minute and gone the next. I sometimes remind myself of that when I am getting too comfortable or complacent.

This property manager had no chance to delete emails or even clear out all the food and snacks in her drawers. Perhaps she didn't care about the food, but if I had been her I would have wanted to organise my emails. What an interesting collection – I began to know her whole life. Family matters, like a row with her mother about attending her grandmother's birthday, a message from a bank about a mortgage application, contact with friends and an acrimonious discussion with an old boyfriend about some DVDs she had 'stolen' from him. I loved it.

After a few days she rang to say she had set up a Hotmail account and could I forward all her personal emails there? I did that but I couldn't resist reading them first. Eventually, the personal ones ceased to arrive. I missed them.

Kylie's emails appear to be more of the lunch and drinks variety.

She has a few minor maintenance requests. They do not seem urgent so I leave them for her. The guy with the dripping tap has not emailed yet.

There are two applications to be printed off and checked, and a very long, detailed and angry complaint from a tenant who has just vacated his rental property about the final inspection and the release of the bond. I notice he has copied in everyone he can think of including our two directors, Emily and for some reason the trust accountant. I cannot see her caring about this issue. She has no involvement.

As I read the complaint, I find it far too complicated for me to want to follow up. I will leave it to one of the people copied in to respond. It is a good example of how things can go wrong.

The owners of the property have been living overseas and we were leasing out their house for them. They have just returned to take possession of it.

Kylie did the final inspection for the release of the bond. She asked the tenants to go back to do some extra cleaning in the bathroom and to wash down the kitchen benches and the floor, as well as some extra outside garden maintenance. They returned to do the interior clean and asked Kylie if they could clean up outside in a couple of days because of time constraints with moving into their new place. She agreed. This is all outlined in the email.

When they returned they found painters on ladders and trestles scraping and chipping away at the house. They went inside and found more painters and ladders. The bath they had done extra cleaning on was full of venetian blinds, dust was everywhere and the drop-sheets left areas of the carpet they had paid to have steam cleaned covered in dust. The lawn and garden were decorated with chips of paint. They took photos of it all including a large pool of paint on the edge of the lawn and the front path.

As I was reading, Emily came by the desk. She has been away sick lately which is unlike her. Today she is clearly unwell, pale and with shadows under eyes, but still looks elegant in a loose shirt-dress in rich cream that comes just below her knees. The colour is a little paler than a lemon. It is a good colour for a sunny Monday morning. Clear and positive. She is tall, willowy, with light brown hair, a beautiful smile and wears elegant and sexy clothes. There are no dreary charcoal suits for her. The day she interviewed me for the job, she wore a clinging red dress and her hair was held up with a large flower clip. She smiled a welcome smile and I was blown away. My immediate thought was, let me work for this woman.

I had worn my lucky stone; a piece of nephrite jade and I put my hand to my throat and stroked it. It worked or something did. She hired me. And here I am, three years later and still admiring her.

At the moment, though, I am not admiring her quite as much as usual. She has been sick for several weeks now and is soldiering on; coming in and spreading whatever bugs she has got around the office. I want to tell her that she is not doing us any favours by being noble. She should stay home until she is cured. Of course I don't tell her that, but I often think it when I see her pale washed out face and she says she has got an upset tummy and she is dealing with it – whatever 'dealing with it' means. She needs to add the words 'curing the problem' in there somewhere. I am not impressed with noble. I wish she would take her bugs somewhere else.

She looks at what I am reading and says, 'I should do something about that.'

Then she gives a sigh, 'I can understand these tenants being angry. It's a wonder they're not asking for a refund for the steam cleaning. It'll be easier if I respond and copy in the directors. I remember these owners. They were never good communicators. I bet they've hardly spoken to Kylie. And I'm sure they won't have said anything about painting.'

They may not be good communicators, but is it not a courtesy to tell your tenant you plan to paint and there is no need to get the carpets steam cleaned? There should be some thought for the tenants who cared for your property and paid rent and consequently your mortgage while you enjoyed yourselves overseas. It smacks of arrogance to me, but then I don't know the owners. There may have just been a misunderstanding. I feel sorry for the tenant. I'm on his side.

'He wants his bond.'

'Yes. Can you process the form for me and I can attach it to the email? I'll be full of apologies. We don't want them claiming any money back.'

Emily troubleshoots and generally manages the department. She is also our BDM (business development manager), and pitches for new business. She gets the new business and her trouble-shooting usually prevents a disgruntled landlord from taking business away from us; in this case, a tenant claiming a refund from us.

There is just one thing to remember about her. She holds a grudge. If someone leaves, she won't hire them again. She believes under her management, Caruthers Real Estate is the best and there is no need to leave to find that out. With this attitude she can lose good people who left for a legitimate reason and now want to return. She has taken a stand and that's that. It's a silly stand in my view – pigheaded. That's not a word I would usually use for her.

Despite this, Emily is one of the best managers I have had. It is like her to see instantly see the mistake is likely to be the landlord's and not Kylie's. In some companies if someone complains, it is always the property manager's fault. Property managers don't last long in those companies. It is probably one of the reasons some people who have left here apply to return.

The bond is held by the Residential Tenancies Bond Authority or RTBA, as it is called by its friends, customers and just about everybody. In the last few years they have upgraded their website so all forms can be filled out online. It is so much easier than working with the paper ones, and harder to make a mistake. So many forms used to be filled out incorrectly, with names misspelt and incorrect maths for deductions. Now all this is part of the online claim form and mistakes are rare.

I email a couple of Kylie's landlords to get their approval for maintenance repairs and I reply to a couple of emails saying she will contact them tomorrow. I work from Kylie's desk so her name is on them. Then, I collect the applications and head to my desk to check them out. I can create the bond claim from here, too. This way I cannot see what is dropping into Kylie's inbox and be distracted by it. I call it time management.

Emily's desk is upstairs where Hayley, the administration assistant, and the accounts department are located. The residential sales people in our company have an office down the road but we hardly see them. Emily is a sort of buffer between us and them and the directors. I like it that way.

I email the bond claim form to her so she can attach it to her email to the tenants.

She comes down to thank me. She is looking very pale. She should have called in sick.

'Are you okay?' I ask. 'You don't look well.'

'No, no. I'm fine. I just need some food. I didn't get break-fast this morning. Got up a bit late.'

I look at my watch and find it is lunch time. Obviously this is not a day for a leisurely 60-minute relax in a café.

'I'm going to get some sushi. Do you want me to get you some?'

'No. No, I think I'll go home.' Emily lives about a ten-minute drive from the office. 'I'm thinking of something set-tling like Weet-Bix.'

'Weet-Bix?' I couldn't help myself.

'Yes, something that is easy on the stomach. I should have had it for breakfast. I got it out but then I noticed the time.' She glances at her watch now.

'I'll be on my mobile if you need me.' She is another one who always says this.

She heads out presumably thinking about her Weet-Bix. Weet-Bix?!! Each to their own, I suppose.

Chapter 5

As I wait for my sushi I remember Kylie worked on Saturday. I worked too. It was hot and busy. She could have picked up a bug. I think Saturday is the day we property managers really earn our money.

It is a day of challenges. The biggest is to get from one open for inspection to the next, and stay on time. We have fifteen minutes at a property, and about ten minutes to drive between properties.

The routine goes something like this:

Find the property. Find a car park, get into it and notice the number of people waiting. Find the right bunch of keys, get the right running sheet onto the clipboard, grab a handful of applications and rental lists and get out of the car. Jam the applications, clipboard and rental lists under one arm, haul the pointer board out of the car with the other hand and assemble it. Assemble it so it is pointing the right way, and not blocking any access to prevent a complaint. Take a firm grip on the stuff under your arm, and head for the door.

Place everything on the ground while you find the right key in the bunch to open the door. If it is the front security door of a block that instantly tries to close again, hope someone volunteers to hold it while you pick up everything and get inside. That person is going to get a tick against their name on the running sheet.

Head to the apartment. Get ready to put everything down again so you can get the key in the lock, the person who volunteers to hold your stuff will get a tick.

You're in, and if it is a popular property, you're almost crushed by the surge of viewers. Place rental lists and applications on the bench and you're ready to fill in your running sheet with names and numbers and explain the advantages of the place and answer questions.

Closing up. You reverse the process; grab the rental lists and applications that are left, check windows, balcony and courtyard doors and head for the front door. Does it need the key to lock it? Put everything down while you do this. Where is that helpful person to hold the stuff for you this time? Down to the main door, open that while you clutch everything to your person, find your car keys, try not to drop the property keys while you are doing this, open your car, put your stuff in, get the pointer board and load it, check where you're going next and head in that direction.

Last Saturday, I did this eleven times.

Many prospective tenants have a time schedule, too. They need to view the property then race off to their next open, find it, get a park and see it before it's closed. These people usually understand the need to lock up right on time and disappear.

Saturday opens challenge our patience. Keeping calm is a skill I have learned. Once the property is open, the questions flow.

'How long is the lease?'

'How much is it a week?'

'When is it available?'

'What's the bond?'

The answers to these questions are on all the internet advertising and the rental list that are handed out. I often wonder why you would go to an open for inspection if you didn't know the weekly rental.

There are other questions too. I have stood by an electric stove top and been asked if there is gas cooking. Conversely, I can be near a gas stove top and be asked if there is electric cooking. I am not that bulky that I hide these things.

People can look through all the cupboards in the kitchen, then come and ask if there is a dishwasher. They may want to confirm their eyesight is okay but I often wonder if it is a subtle way of pointing out an omission on the landlord's part – people do want dishwashers these days, and many a good tenant has moved on because the landlord has not installed one.

Thirteen minutes of this and the property manager needs to push everyone out the door ready to close up. It is time to load up with the applications and rental lists and exit. A tenant who tries to stop the property manager from leaving with questions, or just wanting another look, is likely to get a bad mark against their name.

It is very easy to forget a pointer board when you're in a hurry. You will only notice this at the next property when you begin the routine again and it is not in the boot. It is too late to go back. That has to happen at the end of the day.

Saturday traffic can cause delays. At the next place, another park has to be found, another key to be sorted, another running sheet put on the clipboard, the pointer board taken out of the boot and assembled.

'You're late!' is not music to the ear of a harried property manager as he or she pounds up to the top floor, arms full of applications and rental lists. You know you are late, and as you are opening up you are wondering if you can get everyone through in ten minutes to give yourself a chance to be on time at the next place.

When a property is popular, all the parking spaces have been taken by the crowd milling around the gate. These are times when you pray you will not get a parking ticket. Fifteen minutes is not long to park somewhere, but it can be long enough to get a ticket. The company does not pay our tickets.

No wonder Saturday night can be a big night flowing into Sunday. Winding down is essential. It also makes some sense to spend the occasional Monday in bed.

These mornings are hectic and I think back to my teaching days when I had the whole weekend free – although not really free as there is always lesson preparation. But when you are over something you are over it – there's no going back even if it is for free weekends.

I did my first Saturday opens in the city in summer and I loved them. I liked the fact the people wishing to view were all adults. In those days, I basked in this new world of adults that I had found.

Of course not all tenants and landlords behave like adults all the time.

At busy opens there is often some pushing and shoving at the head of the queue just as there is when a class is waiting to go into the gym.

At one popular open a guy came up to me and said, 'See that woman there? She just pushed in front of me. I want a fair crack at this place so I'm not letting her go in before me.'

The woman turned to me. 'I didn't push in. I had to park the car. My partner's in the queue. I just joined him.'

'There's no way I pushed in,' volunteered her partner. He turned to the guy making the fuss. 'I was in front of you as we walked up the path. You can just wait your turn.'

As I listened to this I had a flashback to a school group waiting for something to start. There is always a bit of argy-bargy in a queue.

There was a big demand for rental properties in my first summer on the job. Sometimes there was a queue waiting when I got there and I had to send people in batches. Like a traffic cop on point duty or a school teacher sorting seats for an assembly.

'Next please.'

'Are you together? Then of course you can go in together.'

'No, you can't go in yet. There are too many people inside already.' Few people argued or objected. They did as I told them! I felt I had a skill that I brought to this new job – crowd management.

* * *

Saturdays can be gruelling, but it can be fun – laughing with a couple who appear at open after open describing themselves as a bad penny that keeps turning up; people who I want to have as tenants and who I hope apply; the guy who said he used to conduct opens and how nice I was. He said he was always grumpy. Friday night was a big night for him and he invariably had a hangover. I glowed in the praise. Praise doesn't happen much in teaching.

Most people I meet are helpful and friendly, and of course most of them want me to see them as great people who are going to be great tenants. There are always a few who do not take on board that being rude to me is not going to secure them a place to live.

* * *

I munch my way through a shrimp and avocado and a teriyaki chicken sushi and send a work order to our appliance repair person regarding the rangehood, making sure I put the spend-limit on it. Rangehoods often have to be replaced once they break down. One appliance repair place we sometimes use told me they were disposable and they would only quote to replace. I cannot see this landlord seeing his rangehood as a disposable unit. I can sympathise with that. There is too much 'throw it away and get another one' in this world. What is wrong with trying to fix something? I don't use the disposable repair guy unless I have to, as I wonder if this attitude is because he hasn't got the skills for a simple repair.

Sending off work orders is almost a full-time job. There's so much maintenance. I once met someone who worked for a large construction company that leased apartments and his job was maintenance, that's all he did, just dealing with repair problems. That could lead to many stressful phone calls and hellish days. I always wondered how dedicated to the job he was – did he allow himself to be called after hours or did he turn off his phone? I wish I had asked him. I like the idea of turning off my phone after hours. We have a list of tradesmen on call. It is their job to answer their phone at 2 am. They get after-hours call-out fees.

I have just finished when Vince comes by with a toasted sandwich.

'You've finished your lunch?' he asks, leaning on the wall by my desk while he chews on his sandwich.

'Only just. I see you brought your lunch. I didn't manage that this morning. Sushi instead. Emily's gone off to eat Weet-Bix.'

'I bet she's pregnant.'

'What? No!'

'I've seen a couple of signs.'

'What sort of signs? You don't mean because she's sick?'

'Well, there's that. But it just came to me when she was talking to me.'

'Talking to you. What about? Her health?'

'No. Have you noticed she's careful not to talk about her health? She was talking about a landlord wanting to attend an inspection. She was explaining something about him and it came to me – she's pregnant. I suddenly knew. I know I'm right.'

'She's getting thinner not fatter.'

Vince just looks at me and munches away at his sandwich. The smell of the toasted cheese makes me hungry all over again. He always has cheese and something. He swallows and grins.

'Take my word for it.'

'What does everyone else think?'

'I haven't mentioned it to anyone else. So keep it to yourself. We should respect her privacy.'

'I agree. It would be a stupid rumour to start.'

'Mark my words,' says Vince again.

'Haven't you heard her talking about not wanting children and that her nieces are enough for her? She doesn't want children!'

'Mark my words,' repeats Vince, annoyingly, as he wanders off.

My inner voice says, 'Who'll do her job if she is pregnant?' I try to push the voice down but it bobs up again saying, 'You, you could do the job'. I could, I think. I'm good now, well, better than I was and manager is the next step after senior property manager. I let myself smile as I think about it.

Chapter 6

I have learned a lot over the years, but one thing I am still learning is to keep my emotions out of it. That's easy to write and to say, but not so easy in practice. Take Bruno for example. He's a nice man and kind, but he has this odd quirk of being ridiculously anxious about the tenants he will put in his property. If I knew him better, I might understand it. I used to feel frustrated and angry with him but now I have found myself caught up in the game we play – it's a challenge and in an odd way I enjoy it. Can I get the ball into the goal this week?!

Early in my career I did get my emotions tangled up with the business side of it. I would have been offended and upset over the Barkly Street property because I liked the owner.

One property in particular where I allowed my emotions to get the better of me serves as a sort of benchmark to my professional progress.

I got a call from a prospective landlord who said, 'Would you come over and take a look at my place? I want to rent it out?' I was new to the job then and I wanted to be a success.

One way to be successful in this business is to bring in new business, so I dropped the phone, leapt into my car and drove to the property.

Joe greeted me at the entrance with a wide grin on his round, cheerful face. His eyes met mine and passed on his sense of excitement.

He was so likeable and happy; I let my initial reaction to the property drift away. I looked around and thought, perhaps I can get this to work.

I misjudged the situation.

The first time you look at a property, you can see if letting it is going to be a struggle, especially at the price the selling agent has given to a new investor. Real estate sales agents can develop a form of blindness to the location in their eagerness to sell.

Many people who buy an investment property do not look at it from a tenant's point of view. Tenants have any number of properties to choose from, so why would they choose yours? It's a question that needs to be asked. The thought of a capital gain can also create a blind spot for the investor.

Joe's house was pleasant enough; two reasonable sized bedrooms, a modern eat-in kitchen, a large lounge with picture windows divided into small panes. These gave it a certain style and charm when you drove up. It had street appeal. The main bedroom along with the lounge opened onto a private lawn, with a high fence that divided the property from its neighbour.

Joe was chatty and friendly. He was delighted with his purchase. He had been working at two jobs and saving hard so he could start a property portfolio.

'Even cut back on m' beer,' he said, with his engaging grin. 'I want to get somewhere in m' life. You know what I mean?' I nodded. 'So what's a few beers, eh?' I agreed with him.

We all want to get somewhere in life even if we are not sure where that is.

This place was one of the few properties in the area in his price range and he saw himself on his way to great riches. Perhaps he was, and perhaps now he has a huge property portfolio and is enjoying the fruits of his hard work and the effort it took to cut back on his beer.

I liked him, so it was easy to enthusiastically pitch my services to him. I did that well because he chose our company over a couple of others. I was as pleased with my success at listing the property as Joe was with his ability to purchase it. We became a sort of Silly Grinning Club. A Silly Grinning Club that lost sight of the battle it had on its hands.

The selling agent had given Joe a rent he should be able to achieve. The agent did not have the job of letting it. After settlement, he moved on.

'Great place to rent,' he had told Joe. 'All this local industry brings people into the area. You'll have no trouble.'

This was an area of light industry with a few houses dotted about. Some houses were now used as offices.

Joe did not go with the rent I suggested. He waved that aside as if it was an annoying mosquito. He went with the rent the selling agent had given him. This was the rent he had done his figures on.

A mate of Joe's came and took photos and I listed the property on the internet. The photos were great and at the first open there was a sizeable crowd, including the energetic and chatty Joe, himself.

During the open he asked questions of the prospective tenants. 'What do you think? Great outdoor area for barbecues isn't it?' he would say as he swept his arm around the area behind the high unpainted wooden fence.

Then he would rush inside and sweep his arm around the lounge area, 'What do you think? Great space! Great windows!' Some people feebly agreed with him. I kept up the Silly Grinning Club's reputation by praising the gas hot water for being very cost-effective and pointing out how useful a separate laundry was.

The Silly Grinning Club got little response for their sales effort. Most people were non-committal.

No one took an application. I took everyone's name and number and Joe was eager for me to contact them all. He could not believe that no one wanted to apply for his property.

The reason hit you in the face the moment you drove up; a large and flourishing petrol station hiding behind the board fence. Because of the fence Joe could not see it as a problem. And as part of the Silly Grinning Club I had lost sight of that difficulty in my initial euphoria of having beaten other agents to the listing. I was so pleased with myself, I let my judgement fly out the window along with common sense. Who wants to live next door to a 24-hour gas station, especially at the rent Joe was asking?

I liked Joe. I worked hard for him. When someone showed interest in viewing the property I rushed over to show them through.

Whenever I was there, the petrol station was doing good business with vehicles continually driving alongside the dividing fence. I would try not to mention it to the prospective tenants. When someone brought it up, I would pretend not to notice the noise. I would say something like, 'Yes, it is there, but the fence cuts down any noise.' As I said this a huge truck would grind in and I would have to raise my voice. It was the owner of this petrol station who was on the upward trajectory to wealth, not Joe.

After a couple of weeks, we dropped the rent and Joe ceased to smile. He wanted to blame me, but he was too nice. The Silly Grinning Club ceased to exist.

After it had been on the market for what seemed like a lifetime, we found two guys who were housemates. Their rental references were not good but they had not shared together before and we were hoping for great things – although I must confess I would not have put them in if I had not been getting desperate. Joe just wanted them in there so he could get some rent.

I asked them to pay their rent in a lump sum instead of separately every month. They said yes but they never did. They paid separately and at separate times so they were always in arrears.

This affected Joe's mortgage payments. When he rang me about the rent, he would sort of threaten me that if I could not get it together and get them to pay on time he would have to take a third job. He was wise not to have given up his second job.

I drove past sometimes to check on the place. It began quickly to look run down with bits of litter blowing around. A car died on the front lawn, and became a feature like a piece of modern urban art. The grass grew around it giving it an air of permanency.

At the first routine inspection we could see things were not as they should be. They had a mate staying, making three of them. He looked settled in but we were assured he was 'just visiting'. None of them was good at housework or mowing the lawn.

The rubbish lying about the kitchen and wheelie bin suggested they had forgotten collection day or perhaps they imagined the rubbish guys would wander round the side and collect everything. They ate a lot of pizza, KFC and Chinese take-aways. This had the advantage of keeping the stove clean but at the same time increased the litter waiting for collection.

Their dirty clothes were all over the bedrooms and not in that useful laundry.

Joe was distraught, although he must have had some idea of what it could be like. He drove past often enough. He had complained about the car and I referred his complaint to the council who said they could not do anything about it as it was on private property.

'How can they live like this?' Joe sort of wailed as we did the inspection. 'How can they live like this? How can they do this to my property?' The only answer was that not everyone lives the same way and it was not their property, so their attachment to it was unlikely to be the same as Joe's. That was not the answer I gave him. I made sympathetic soothing noises and pointed out there did not appear to be any actual damage. Joe was not soothed.

Their rent became more erratic but they were never over fourteen days late so we could not give them a 'Notice to Vacate'. Joe found it hard to understand that we had to follow the law here and not just evict them because we didn't want them anymore.

I had a complaint from the petrol station. Our tenants were throwing empty beer cans over the fence. I tried to rectify these problems as much as I could.

Then Joe felt that as an agent, I was ineffective. I felt that too. I had no idea what to do to change the situation.

He moved the property to a new agent that his friend recommended.

I hate to lose a property and I was upset. Well, gutted would be more accurate. I had put so much effort into Joe's place. Yet, amongst all the angst there was a small chink of light. I did not have to hear Joe's hurt and disappointment on the phone and feel I was responsible for it. That was something of a relief.

I drove past one day and saw another car had died there.

It should have been a consolation to find the new agent did not have any more success than I did in keeping the place cared for, but it upset me. Joe was a lovely person and deserved better from his tenants.

The tenants' names are burned into my brain. There is no way I would put them into another property that I managed. A few years have passed and they may have turned over a new leaf but I would never give them the chance to prove it.

Over the years I have learned to be a little more detached. Well, I think I have. I did not know Emily then, and since I have worked here I have watched her and learnt. She always appears calm and keeps her distance. She listens, gives the person all her attention, but doesn't emotionally engage. I sometimes channel her when I feel myself getting too emotional. I draw down her image and pretend it is her speaking. It helps. I believe I have come a long way since those early days.

Chapter 7

The wonderful thing about this Monday is a routine inspection booked in with a tenant, Simone, who likes to be there and is only available on Monday. I am going to my favourite house.

When I first saw this house, I stood in the entrance and thought, 'I could live here. I could thrive here.' It's like a dream house. There's magic there.

From the front, it is modest. A very modest brick terrace squeezed between two others. There is not much land between the gate and the front porch and the little bit there is has been paved with grey slate. On one side is a white rose bush. It seems to flower constantly, as if it is happy and smiling on the world. On the other side is an old lion seated by the front steps, watching the street and the passers-by. He is a weather-beaten concrete lion and is growing a little moss. He does not see much sun as he gazes towards the south. If he was my lion, I would move him to the sunny back.

These terrace houses are often dark inside with no windows on the sides – just at the front and the back. This house is different.

Simone opens the door for me without me knocking, 'Hi! I've been looking out for you. I need to go back to work today so I'm glad you're on time.'

'Hello,' I say. 'It's such a lovely day. It is nice to get out of the office.' I give the lion a passing pat and step inside. Once again I am stunned by the light shining on me.

The owners renovated before they went overseas. The architect managed to put in a light-well with sliding stacker doors that can be opened on two sides to let the outside creep in. Simone has put a large feathery fern there that adds to the being-outside effect. Two bedrooms and a bathroom lead off to the right, and the kitchen, living room and a lovely curved pale-wood staircase are past the light-well. The kitchen is white and glass and the living room flows into a partly covered courtyard.

Simone and her partner have a house in Sydney but work has brought them to Melbourne. They came with an old dog and there was great doubt on the owners' part as to whether the dog would damage their beautiful house.

It is the opposite. Their beautiful house damaged the dog. Two weeks after they moved in he got his leg caught when the front door slammed on it. He now manages on three legs. He greets me in the hallway and I think he believes he has always been on three legs. He is amazing. After greeting me he heads for the courtyard that has a Balinese look and a bed he has in a sunny corner. The Balinese ambience is due to the tenants. It was rather plain when they moved in. Now with the aid of planters and pots, it is lush.

I check downstairs and then Simone leads me upstairs saying, 'I want to show you our new painting. I just love it. The moment I saw it I knew it was right for this place'. We arrive at the upstairs landing and there in front of me is a large colourful painting.

'Don't you just love it?' asks Simone. I study a vibrant splash of yellow and some exotic birds on a flight of the artist's imagination. Beside it, through the floor-length window, I can see grey slate roof-tops and a neighbour's tree that is casting delicate shadows on the balcony.

'It's perfect here,' I say as I study it. 'All that light from the window gives it a glow. It's wonderful.'

'Yes I think so too. Pierre, you know my partner, was unsure. He thought it was perfect for here but he kept saying, 'How will it look back in Sydney?' I said I didn't care and even if it is no good there it will always remind us of Melbourne. It'll be our Melbourne painting.' She laughs.

'I think it should look good anywhere,' I say and I believe that. It would look good in my apartment but I don't mention that.

The light pours in up here too. I catch sight of myself in a large mirror and realise my clothes are right for the house and the painting. I am part of the beauty. I keep smiling.

The place is spotless, the paintings and furniture just right, minimalist and gracious. I take some photos for the landlord and pat the old dog. He heaves up and comes to the front door with me. A quick pat for the lion and I am on my way. The day has developed a sparkle and a bit of wishful thinking. I love the way in this job I can leave the office and enjoy the summer. I am free to make these appointments whenever I please.

As I head back I think about how owners respond to pets in their property.

Some landlords, like Bruno, are anti-dogs. They are so anti-dogs they become quite stressed if they even think a dog is in their property. I am puzzled as to why this is. When I have asked the question, the answers are something like this:

'I've had a bad experience with a dog and I don't want to repeat it.' This does not really answer my question. Did they have a bad experience when they were a child and a dog attacked them or tried to do so? Perhaps they were chased by a dog and the humiliation of streaking down the street with a dog at their heels has never left them? Did they have a dog as a pet and when it died they were so bereft that they have avoided them ever since? No, I do not think it is any of these. This feeling comes out as a hate for the dog itself.

Francine is anti-dog. She owns a rather pretty Victorian terrace house that had been her mother's. The floors are polished, and the kitchen and bathroom upgraded. It was tenanted by a professional woman when Francine had her incident of the dog.

Francine drove past often to check that everything was up to scratch in the front, which was all she could see from the street. The inspections that she attended with me and the tenant showed that everything was up to scratch inside too. She could relax, but she did not. Relaxing did not seem to be in her nature. In fact, I would say she went out of her way to cause stress to herself, as if she liked to have some drama in her life and therefore something to stress about.

One bleak, cold winter's day I arrived back in the office to find her voice on my message bank in a state of agitation, demanding I ring her immediately. I was curious, so I did as I was told.

Her first words were, 'Has My Tenant got a dog?'

She had met her tenant at the inspections and knew her name was Trish but she always called her My Tenant.

'No. I don't think so. Why?'

'I saw her in that pet shop down by your office buying a pet toy. I am not having a dog in my house.'

'Did you ask her about the pet toy?' I queried.

'No. That's your job. I didn't let her see me.' I had a sudden vision of Francine sneaking behind shelves and sidling unseen out the door; rather like a thief.

'Have you driven past to see if you can see one?' I asked knowing that she would have done so.

'I couldn't see a thing from the front, but then I wouldn't, would I, if she had it in the back?'

I rang Trish and no, she did not have a dog. She was buying a present for a friend.

'I travel so much, there is no way I could have a pet.'

I reported this back to Francine, who did not believe that Trish was telling the truth and we arranged an inspection.

We were all there, Francine, Trish, me and the invisible dog. As we walked through the house Francine sniffed and took deep breaths. She announced she had a cold which was why she was sniffing. I knew she was trying to sniff out a dog. She admitted that when we left.

'I couldn't smell anything, could you?' she asked. 'I thought the laundry may be where she kept it, but nothing there.'

There was no trace of dog. No digging in the back yard, no muddy paws prints on the polished boards, no scratches on a door, not a whiff of a canine body anywhere in the house. No dog.

In parting outside, Francine said, 'I'll keep driving past to see if I see anything.' She never reported anything to me and the issue died away.

I do not understand her hatred of seeing little paws going up her front path, even if it was only in her imagination. Actually, it was Trish's front path, as she was on a lease and had possession of the house.

Trish was a very patient and understanding tenant. I was sad when she finally vacated to move to Sydney.

* * *

I get back to the office to find Vince preparing for an early hearing at The Victorian Civil and Administrative Tribunal (VCAT tomorrow. He is hoping to claim cleaning expenses from a bond.

'Have a look at these photos. They're crystal. My new camera's a cut above my iPad,' he says as he waves them at me.

'Look at the gunge in the plug holes. And in this photo there's a couple of old socks and thick dust in the robes.'

I study the photos. 'It looks as if they could've given the kitchen a good going over,' I say. 'It's a great photo of crumbs and splashback marks. What are the bits of paper?

'Rubbish.'

'Good photos of squalor Vince, you could exhibit them,' I say laughing.

He laughs, too. 'I don't know what they're thinking. I told them I could send Wyatt in to give it a good vacate clean. And do you know what they said?'

I just raise my eyebrows and look at him.

'We've cleaned and I don't know what you mean by 'a vacate clean'. A clean is a clean.'

'That proves they didn't read their vacating pack,' I say. 'It's clear in there what a vacating clean is.' This is one of my bugbears – the lack of reading.

'Definitely didn't read it. Anyway, I'll be at VCAT first thing so I'll be in later.' Vince disappears with his remarkably clear and sharp photos.

Our company files are full of tenants who don't read. When a tenant gives us written notice that they are vacating, we send out a letter confirming the date and the rent owing to that date. Attached is information about our cleaner, someone who will remove old furniture, people who remove general rubbish and the council's waste removal. All this work on our part is usually wasted. If the tenants can read they keep this skill hidden when they are dealing with us.

We hope they will use our cleaner. He is good and the place is spotless when he has finished – so less stress on all of us.

It is 'his' services. Our cleaner is a man. Of all the cleaners I have used for vacate cleans, this guy, Wyatt, is the best. Reliable, thorough, and if he has missed something he will go back to attend to it. He does not carry on if we don't think something is clean enough. Some cleaners do. Some immediately take on attitude and getting them back to redo whatever it is can be a bit of a battle. Strange the way they can take on like this. Something is either clean or it is not. We can all do a slip-shod job once in a while. We have eliminated those cleaners from our list.

My phone rings and it is Lisa asking if I can come out to reception. She has one of Kylie's tenants insisting on seeing someone.

'What's it about?'

'Something to do with their bond. I'm too busy to go into it.' She disconnects.

I get up and head to the front of the office. I don't need this in the late afternoon. My thoughts about Kylie lounging in bed or winding up an elegant lunch are not positive.

Lisa waves her hand towards a couple standing near the door. The phone is going and she has her hand up holding a group at her desk at bay. I can see she is a bit stretched.

I approach the tenants and they both start to talk at once. I wait. Eventually he fades away and she says, 'We've come in to get our bond.'

'How do you mean?'

'We've vacated and we want our bond back.'

I can see why Lisa didn't want to get involved in this.

'When did you hand back the keys?' I ask.

'Last Thursday and we want our bond.'

'Have you signed the bond claim form?'

'No, we haven't signed anything. We can sign now.'

'Kylie is away today and she's dealing with this. Do you know if she's done the bond inspection?'

'I don't know anything. No one's telling us anything.'

I explain about the process for releasing the bond and that we have only had two working days to check everything is okay in the property. The legislation says Kylie has another eight workings to complete the bond inspection and send out the claim for their signatures.

'Eight days?' Her voice is rising. 'We can't wait eight days. We need the money now.'

The group waiting for Lisa have become interested. They are no longer bothering to get her attention.

Lauren, who is standing at The Monster photocopying, stops what she is doing and turns to watch.

The guy with Rising Voice is starting to shuffle around and I think he is going to add something, but he decides not to.

'Eight days!' she screeches again. 'You can't keep our money. We've vacated.'

'We don't have the money, it's with the RTBA.' The screeching makes me talk more slowly and at a much lower level. 'Give me the address of the property you were in and I'll leave a message for Kylie to contact you tomorrow.'

I wonder if I should look into it and do the vacating inspection. I notice it's almost 5.30, and as there is no need to do this, I decide to put it out of my mind. I'm not that helpful.

Rising Voice says rudely, 'Well, if you don't have the money, what's it got to do with you? Why can't we just get our money?'

A guy in the group waiting for Lisa raises his eyebrows in a sort of startled way. Lauren watches more intently from her position by The Monster.

To my surprise I'm still calm. 'When we are happy that everything is as it should be in the property you have just vacated, we sign the bond claim form so the RTBA can release the money to you.'

Before Rising Voice can say anything else I continue, 'If you give me the property address, I'll leave a message for Kylie. We're hoping she'll be in tomorrow. If she isn't, I'll look into it.'

He gives me the address. It is a place just round the corner, and I wonder if Kylie has already inspected it.

'We're going to take this higher,' Rising Voice is still screeching, 'You can't keep our money.'

I continue to be calm, and I'm surprising myself. 'I'll give you the number of Consumer Affairs and you can ring them and they can explain the Act to you. I'll get it for you.'

'We'll do that. You won't hear the last of this.'

I move towards Lisa's desk where she has the number on her list of useful numbers. She's ahead of me and hands me a post-it note with it written on, proving again that she's the linchpin of the place, and our lives are easier with her at reception.

The man takes it from me and manages to say, 'Thanks.' They reluctantly leave with him sort of pushing Rising Voice out the door.

They leave a silence behind them with no one knowing what to say. The phone rings and Lisa attends to that while the group at the counter turn back to get her attention. Lauren is back working The Monster. She raises her eyebrows at me as I head past her on my way back to my desk. I check out the tenants on the computer and find they still owe $110 in rent to their vacating date. Had they forgotten this? They made no mention of it. Did they think I would refund the bond on their say-so and they would not have to pay the $110 – just walk away and someone else will pay? I am curious now as to whether they have cleaned properly and removed all their stuff.

I send an email to Kylie and mark it high priority. I hope she is really sick.

* * *

The work day finishes and I arrive home to my north facing unit, pour myself a glass of red and sit on the balcony with my feet on the railing, watching the sun catch the wine and show off the depth of its colour.

Amy is not home so she must be waiting out the toilet repair at Brett's – sensible of her. One person using the toilet is enough.

When my last relationship finished and, as Gwyneth Paltrow put it when she broke up with Chris Martin, we 'consciously uncoupled', my ex-partner Tim took off to roam the world. He is having a mid-life crisis in his mid-thirties. It may be a teenage crisis, but it is more than just a gap year. He is still out there somewhere. Occasionally I check his Facebook page and there he is, like an old-fashion hippie living on the edge of civilisation. I don't get it. There is a world of people scrambling and fighting their way out of squalor – why join them and add to the numbers without running water? What is it about a rickety little hut on the edge of some beach? When Tim and I were together, I was the one happy with cheap and cheerful. He looked for tablecloths and fabric napkins.

I don't use Facebook anymore because I get tired of friends – and Mum of course – contacting me with, 'Have you seen what Tim's up to? Have you seen his latest Facebook page? Great photo! Beautiful beach! He's certainly living The Life!'

There would be a photo of Tim sprawled in a chair somewhere, grinning and looking far too relaxed and sexy.

We had been together for two years and I thought we might make a go of it. He did ask me to go with him – but there was no way I could do that. I could not get my head around it and understand what it was he wanted. It still puzzles me.

After Tim left, the boron effect clicked in – I will explain that sometime – and I organised my money, and with lots of mortgage I bought this unit. I saw myself living by myself with the second bedroom as a study. I could just afford it. I thought I wanted to live alone when we uncoupled but I found I got lonely. I didn't expect to, but if I am honest with myself, I have to admit I missed Tim. I thought I was showing him how well I was coping by giving him the finger and saying something like, 'See, I'm fine by myself. I'm doing great without you'. It didn't work. I didn't feel fine. I needed someone so I got Amy. I'm not ready for another man – what I wanted was a companion for slow Sunday mornings and dark winter nights.

Amy is easy to live with. She is relaxed about a lot of things, including cleaning. I used to feel annoyed about this, but then I realised I should relax too. She does not notice if my things are spread around the living area or if she does, she does not comment. It is strange that as she is not into cleaning, her things stay neatly in her room. Relaxed is good I decided. I have been wondering whether I would talk to her about getting a cleaner once a fortnight. That would be even more relaxing.

Recently she has been spending more and more time with her boyfriend, and I suppose she is there tonight. Maybe tonight is because I told her the plumber would not be coming until tomorrow, and this evening we would continue to heave buckets of water from the bath into the toilet to flush it.

If you own your home, you have not got a property manager to ring and go nuts to when there is a problem. What tenant would wait another day to get the toilet fixed without screaming about it? I'm waiting because the plumber said, 'Sorry, I can't make it today. I've got my back to the wall dealing with tenants' plumbing problems. It'll have to be tomorrow.'

I am not complaining. When he fixed my tap last month, he didn't charge me so I am hopeful this time.

I am not a great cook, so I order-in Thai. Pad Thai is one of my favourite meals. I have to order-in two portions and some spring rolls to spend enough to get it delivered free. I can freeze the extra. I'm not sure if this is a saving or whether it would be better to just order what I want and pay the delivery cost. A dilemma I haven't solved. I resent paying for the delivery.

The last rays of sun linger on my balcony as I wait for my food. It gives me a feeling of wellbeing, as if everything is right with the whole world. Of course I know it is not. And when I look down I see that somehow I have scratched the side of my beautiful summer boots. When did I do that? So annoying. Finding that scratch has taken some warmth from the sun. I wonder if I can fix it with a marker-pen. I have a pack of these magic marker-pens. Name a colour and it will be in there.

My mind drifts to Emily. Pregnant? No. Not a chance. How many times has Emily said, 'I love my nieces, they're enough for me?' Too many times to hazard a guess at a number.

Despite myself I start to draw down pictures of me doing her job. It would not hurt to be thinking about it. I do want to advance in this career. If there is something wrong with Emily and she has to take time off work I need to be The One. The one who is the obvious choice to step up and fill in. Not that I want anything bad to happen to her. Still, I will be on my game and keep all the balls in the air and prove I am a leader. I will keep this in mind tomorrow.

The door bell rings. Thai has arrived and I shelve these thoughts and prepare to hoe into dinner.

Tuesday

Chapter 8

It's nine o'clock on this warm Tuesday morning, and the pace slackens from yesterday's sprint to something more like a power walk. I'm wearing emerald green today. Not grass green or olive green but a clear brilliant emerald loose fitting top over a black skirt. I have managed with the help of a magic marker-pen to doctor-up my boots, so there is no sign of last night's scratch. I think I have done a good job and I thought I'd wear emerald to celebrate. Emerald is said to be a calming and inspirational colour. I'm not sure why, because this emerald is flamboyant. I like that about it.

There is a group of us from the office grabbing a coffee from Café Yellow and chatting with Jono the barista. It is more like chatting to ourselves with Jono listening in.

This busy, funky café, charges locals – that is, people working on the strip – $2.50 for a regular coffee. It's not the greatest coffee but it is the same coffee Jono is charging everyone else $3.80 for, so it's a bargain and we never complain about the quality.

Jono greets me with the word, 'Skinny?' This doesn't mean I have lost weight – I am still my usual 71 kilos aiming for 65. In this pursuit, I have changed from full cream milk to skinny. I say 'yes' and I know my order is on the way. His memory is another thing that makes this a busy place in the mornings. It's flattering to have our preferences remembered, along with any little changes and foibles we have. I grin at Jono. I'm with the action.

We cluster at one end of the long bar. Kylie is here, looking perfectly healthy with her long curly, chestnut hair pulled back with a scrunchie that allows some bits to escape. It is shining as if it has new highlights. Her eyes are shining too. Not sick. She explains why she was on sick leave yesterday.

'I needed time out to absorb it all. I couldn't have come in and faced a Monday of people complaining and all wanting something. I needed time to luxuriate and get my head around it.'

She scored on Saturday with the handsome, charming and flirtatious Nic, from the sales department of our Dennison office further up the coast. Nic has been in her sights for a while.

It was at our drunken Christmas party a couple of months ago now that she first made out with him, but to her regret, nothing has happened since.

Our Christmas parties are lunch-time affairs with no thought that anyone will return to the office. We don't invite partners and a directors' partner takes over the job as receptionist.

We start at noon and leave the restaurant and the open-bar tab at 5 pm. Some people head home while others move to the rooftop bar where we pay for our own alcohol. This doesn't deter consumption. It was up here that Kylie and Nic got together when they were returning from their respective toilets.

A romantic moment in a not-so-romantic spot, but a spot that has a history of drunken romancing.

Kylie and I were the only ones working in that dead time between Christmas and New Year when she described the encounter 'One glance at each other and it just happened. It felt like the right thing to do. We fell into each other's arms.'

The back corridor of this bar has high traffic flow and it has been the kick-off point for many a Christmas romance.

One property manager I know, who now runs a very large rent roll, told me, 'It was in that back corridor that Joe and I pashed for the first time. I hadn't known he liked me until then.'

They're married now, with a toddler.

It is early days for Nic and Kylie, so I haven't told her yet that the spot has a good track record for a lasting romance.

If there was anyone in the company I had wanted to pash at Christmas, I would have done so at this unglamorous spot. I would want the positive vibes. Sadly, there is not, and Kylie and Nic occupied the corridor for some time. It's hard to know if they knew why they were there or whether they were just propping each other up as people climbed around them.

They did drift away eventually and left the restaurant carrying their Kris Kringles.

Last Saturday Nic and Kylie turned up at the same birthday party.

A grinning Kylie says, 'We got together almost straight away. He hardly talked to anyone else. It was just me.'

'Who's this guy?' asks Jono as he starts to line up the coffees. 'Do I know him?'

'He's in our Dennison office,' chips in Lauren. 'Good looking. Blond with the latest hairstyle. You know, sort of swept up in the front.'

'No, can't place him.'

'Really, really good looking,' adds Kylie. 'You'd remembered him if you'd seen him.'

We all raise our eyebrows.

Jono turns back to the steaming milk.

Kylie continues. 'After a while he suggested we leave and go to a night club. He thought the party was a bit tame.'

'Was it?' I asked

'Well, when he mentioned it I could see what he meant. We went to Queens, you know right on the beach. It was great. I've only been once before and I'd forgotten how amazing it was.'

'I know it,' Lauren says, 'it overlooks the sea. I've been there a few times – amazing place!'

Kylie gives a sort of grin or perhaps it's a smirk.

'So, why didn't you come in to work yesterday?' I ask. I like to get these things clear and I'm feeling tetchy about it. Obviously she was not sick.

'I hadn't slept. He came back to mine and well…you know.' She gives a giggle, 'I can't believe it really happened. I needed time to absorb it. I spent most of yesterday in bed.'

'By yourself?' I ask.

'Of course. Nic was at work.'

'Right,' I say and I don't say anything else. I'm absorbing the fact that Kylie was lying around in bed or getting highlights in her hair while I did some of her work. I'm wondering if I should point this out to her. If she gives any thought to it, she'll know that I had her back but I can see she is not giving a thought to it. The only thought in her head is Nic.

We head back to the office and Lauren says to me, 'Kylie's dreaming if she thinks she's the only one. Nic's known for trying it on with anyone half decent that he gets in his sights.'

'Yeah,' I say. 'I can't see him being the faithful type.' This makes me feel a little better in a sort of mean way. Let Kylie have her moment and enjoy it. I willn't expect any thanks – after all it is my job to help her out. Why should I care if she doesn't thank me? And it is a beautiful morning and I am wearing emerald green.

I look at Kylie swaying ahead of me. She is wearing black strappy sandals with silver heels that glint in the sunlight. Very stylish, and I wonder if there is a picture of them on her pinboard. She has got style. Her style will enhance Nic's image. Perhaps he will go for her.

She turns as if she has heard me but we are too far behind her and Lauren's voice was low.

'He sent me a text yesterday morning that just said, 'Thanks'. Then another one later to say he hoped I was feeling better. He'd heard I was away.'

If she keeps this up everyone in the company will be talking about why she called in sick yesterday. I wonder how that will sit with Nic or with management if they get to hear. She needs to shut up but that could be difficult for her.

We head into the office, and at reception Lisa introduces us to Vicky, her temporary replacement. Lisa is on leave from Wednesday. Vicky is learning the ropes.

As we reach Kylie's cubicle I tell her about the tenants who came in yesterday wanting their bond. She has not read my email, but she knows who I am talking about. She did the bond inspection there on Friday.

'The place was filthy. Well, not filthy exactly, but not clean enough. They haven't cleaned the oven and there is a piece of old cheese toast in the grill. It's got tomato on it and the tomato's growing that long black hairy mould. Gross.'

'I notice they owe rent too.'

'Yeah, I was going to ring them yesterday and get them to do more cleaning. I guess it's a job for today. It makes me glad I took yesterday off!'

'Well, good luck,' I say. 'Rather you than me.'

'I've got photos and a good one of the piece of cheese toast. I wonder why they didn't eat it. Why make it and not eat it? God, what a way to start the day. If they make too much fuss, I'll tell them they can take it to VCAT. If I'm lucky they'll let me get Wyatt in to give it a once-over.'

'Pigs might fly…she's desperate for the money,' I say.

'Then they can go back and do it themselves. I've got a list of things they need to do. I'd better get onto it. I was feeling so good after the weekend. Sun, warmth and Nic, and now these two.' She turns towards her desk.

'I suggest you ring him,' I say as I move off towards my desk. 'He may be more reasonable. She was dreadful yesterday.'

I have an email from Bruno's prospective tenant. I hesitate to open it. Sometimes it's good to remain hopeful and not know an outcome. I take a deep breath – a 'be-prepared and be positive breath'. I click it open.

The will-not-be-tenant is such a nice man. He thanks me for my trouble but he is withdrawing his application for the property. He does not give a reason and he does not need to. He met Bruno yesterday. That can be reason enough. The legislation says tenants must have quiet enjoyment of the property they are leasing. If this looks like a problem at the beginning, the tenant is best to withdraw. Easy at this stage but difficult later on when things start to go wrong. Bruno needs to know everyone's business and in my view, he would be a damned nuisance popping around to do repairs or to see if anything needed to be done. I wonder if he would expect a cup of coffee for his trouble. Perhaps he would want a biscuit and the tenants would need to have a tin of stale Anzacs waiting for him.

I ring Lauren to tell her.

'Are you going to ring Bruno?' she asks.

It's a beautiful morning and there is a tang in the air, so I say yes without any discussion.

Bruno is pretty philosophical about it.

'He was an odd sort of guy, didn't have much to say for himself. Just walked through the place and didn't want to chat. I asked him all the questions I usually ask. He didn't answer some of them. Just didn't say anything. He didn't ask me anything either. Said, 'Thanks', and left. Oh well, I don't think he'd be suitable. I want someone who has something to say.'

Kylie hit the nail on the head when she said Bruno wants a best friend. What does it matter if his tenant 'didn't have much to say for himself'? He is applying to move his gear into a property and make a home. He is not applying to join a cocktail party where conversation is required. Besides Bruno could talk for both of them, I guess he did that yesterday.

We missed the goal again.

I find I am not as philosophical as Bruno sounded. When it sinks in that we will be playing again next week, I want to get my teeth into it. I want to kill the defence. I want to score this goal. The more I think about it the more I feel myself taking on the persona of a terrier after a rat, rather than a sleek and energetic netballer shooting for goal in emerald green. I do love the colour.

I ring Lauren. 'If you get any enquiries on Princess Street flick them through to me. I'll take them through myself. They needn't wait for an open. I have to get the place let. I'm beginning to feel like a failure and I'm going to make it my mission.'

'How do you think I feel? All these months and still we're doing a Saturday open there. If you want to do that, it's over to you. I'll send you anything that pops up,' says Lauren from her desk, which is the first one back from reception at the front of the office. A little bit of a walk from mine.

I like this old building that has been turned into an office. It rambles around and has individuality but I wonder too if this is why Lauren can't control the papers on her desk. The place does not look sleek and efficient and 21st century. It is more of a 1920s 'let's kick-back and have a cup of tea' sort of place.

An email from reception pops up and shows a photocopy of two bunches of keys. The text reads; *These keys were pushed through the door last night. Both these sets of keys have no tags as to what properties they are. Can anyone help identify them please?*

I am sure the temp, Vicky, has written this. Lisa is more abrupt and to the point. She deals with this sort of thing on a regular basis. It's amazing how many people shove their keys through the door with no address or identification.

What are they thinking? We manage about 1500 proper-ties, so their property is not so special that we will instantly know some unlabelled keys belong to it. Often a vacating ten-ant will return keys this way.

When the vacating date has passed and we ring them and mention we have not got the keys and they owe more rent they get very excited and insist they returned them.

That is when we find out that their set of keys is one of those held in Lisa's unidentified box. If there is not a tag you can write on, what is wrong with putting them in an envelope with the property address? Why would anyone just shove a bunch of keys through the door of a real estate agent with nothing to identify them? We deal in keys.

I asked Vince once if he thought some tenants did it to annoy us or because they hate us, a sort of 'here's a challenge for you'. He thought I was nuts – he thinks it is just stupidity, or ignorance.

I discover that one of the unknown sets belongs to tenants of mine. They have been difficult throughout the tenancy. Now they have proved difficult to the end. I ring them and carry on about the extra day's rent just to get a bit of my own back.

We don't have a new tenant for the property and I will delay my final inspection until later in the week or possibly next week. I know this sounds mean, but sometimes you have to get a bit of revenge.

I shove their file down to the bottom of the pile.

Chapter 9

'That was a good outcome,' says Vince as he arrives at my desk. I'm getting good at the mind reading business. It takes only a moment for me to realise he is talking about his tribunal hearing and not keys.

'The tenants didn't turn up,' he goes on. 'I was sure they would because they argued about whether it was clean or not. The hearing was over in a flash. I showed my stunning 'not clean' photos and the order was made in the landlord's favour. I had the cleaning costs and I was on my way before I could finish my coffee.' He waves the tribunal order at me. 'I am off to fax this and organise Wyatt to go out to clean. If only all hearings were like that.' He laughs and disappears.

A ping on my computer announces the arrival of an email from reception: *The Monster's playing up. The repair man has been booked. I'll email you when it's fixed. Don't ring me about it.* This has to be initiated by Lisa. It is her style.

Not everything is going well for Vince – The Monster is also our fax machine.

An email attachment is often as good as a fax, but then The Monster is our scanner. I thought when I first met The Monster how clever it was of someone to combine so many functions in the one machine. That someone, I have learned since, was not so smart after all. When The Monster has a problem so do all those small machines that have been so cleverly mixed in with it. Of course that is the trouble with every machine – when they break down we are helpless. All we can do is curse and whinge and wait for someone to fix it. I try to leave the office when that happens. To wait around for some unknown person to repair it makes me feel inadequate and frustrated.

Lauren's at my desk.

'Bruno's rung. Thank god I went to the bathroom and missed him.' So she is not complaining about The Monster.

I look up and I can see she's quite agitated. 'What about?'

'I've no idea. His voice message said, 'This is Bruno. Ring me urgently.' It must be something about the tenant that pulled out.'

'Can't be. He was fine with that. He wasn't keen on him. Not talkative enough. Ring him back and find out.'

'I can't.'

'How do you mean?' I love asking 'How do you mean?' because the other person has to answer. Emily taught me that. If someone says to her, 'I think your fees are too high,' she comes back with, 'How do you mean?'

Lauren comes back with, 'I mean that I can't ring him. It makes me sick even thinking about him. I'm just over it. That's all.'

She has told me this often enough so I should get it. And I do. Some landlords can twist you up inside and 'sick' is the feeling you get.

'I'll give him a ring,' I say. 'Let me find out the problem.'

I think Lauren will wait while I do this, but she disappears.

'Right,' I say to myself as I look up the number. I wish I could stop saying right. I need a notice by the phone with 'right' written in 100-point letters then crossed out in red.

Bruno answers on the first ring. 'Hello. Who's that?'

'Juliette from Caruthers.'

'I rang Lauren. Why isn't she ringing me back? I'm not getting much satisfaction from her.'

A lie is needed. 'She's not well.' Although perhaps that is not a lie. 'How can I help you?'

'Yes, someone at your place will need to help me. I want to know what has happened to the lock on the door.'

This is another moment for mind reading but I'm not successful, 'What door?'

'I'm trying to get it open and my key won't work and I want to know what my tenants have done to it?'

'At Princess Street?' I ask and my voice rises with surprise.

'No, no. Why do you think that key wouldn't work? I was there yesterday with the tenant you sent me. I'm talking about the unit in King Street. My daughter's place. I'm asking what has happened to that lock? Have the tenants changed it?'

'Why?' I ask, as I search in the computer for the property.

'When I called Lauren I was there – at the property. I've left now because she hasn't called me back. I can't wait around all day. I have the new part for the heater I need to fix. How can I get in if my key doesn't work?'

How indeed? And I wonder if he tried the windows, then I remember it's on the first floor. Of course there is no need for Bruno to 'get in'. In fact, he would be better off not 'getting in' if that is what he is trying to do – even if he is fixing the heater.

I check the notes on the computer. There is no mention of a new key.

'Have you used your key before?' I ask, which when you think of it is a pretty silly question and I'm waiting for Bruno to tell me so but instead he says, 'Not recently. I ring and get a time then I go. It is not always a convenient time for me but I go when they say. If I don't speak to them I leave a message and they ring me back with a time and they let me in.'

These are the tenants who live with aubergine feature wall.

'Why aren't they there today?' I'm confused.

'I phoned last night. I left a message to say I'd be there this morning. I didn't ask for a time but I told them I would come. No one rang me back to say don't come. When I got there, no one was home. I said I would be there so I tried my key and it wouldn't work. It used to work. No trouble.' I can hear agitation in his voice. 'I can't fix their heater if I can't get in. If it gets cold, they'll have no heat. So it's no good them complaining to me or to you if they've changed the locks.'

I draw in my breath to speak but he goes on. 'If the lock breaks I am to fix it, not them. If they change the locks I want to know. But why would they change the locks? It's only my daughter who lived there. She's overseas. She's not going to be using her key. Anyway I've got all her keys.'

There is a brief silence while I process this. Bruno is not good with silences.

'You need to find out what's happened to the lock. I've made a useless trip over there and I want to know why. They have no right to change my daughter's lock.'

Actually, they do have every right to change the locks. I don't mention this to Bruno. They should give us a key but I can see why they wouldn't do that. And I can even see why they wouldn't tell us. This is a property that involves Bruno. I wouldn't tell anyone either.

'Leave it with me,' I say. I want to hang up. I want Bruno's voice to go away. Not that it is a bad voice. It could be a pleasant voice in other circumstances. 'I'll ring you back.'

'Yes, do that. I'll have my phone with me all day.' That is a piece of information I do know. I buzz Lauren who doesn't know anything about the key either. She says the tenants thought Bruno went into the place without telling them, but they couldn't prove it.

Lauren says she didn't follow this up. 'The less I get involved with Bruno the better.'

I say, 'Bruno wants some action here. I don't understand what the big deal is. He goes round with a part for the heater and he can't put it in. It's the middle of summer for god's sake. I don't get the urgency.'

'I never get Bruno.'

I'm not getting him either. I'll ring the tenants,' I say.

The mobile number I have makes that international calling sound. I hang up and email.

I update Bruno.

'Don't they have to tell you when they go overseas?'

Who does he think we are – their mothers? Of course we could employ a full-time person to keep track of every tenant's movements. That would be a point-of-difference for Emily when she is out pitching for new business. Some landlords would love it. In real estate we are always looking for 'the point of difference' – something other companies don't do.

I assure Bruno that this is not what managing his property is about. 'It is nothing to do with us when they go on holiday. So long as they pay the rent, they can go on a holiday whenever they like.'

'I'm fixing their heater, so wouldn't they think I'd be interested? They're strange tenants. My daughter chose them. She wouldn't let me have my say. That was a mistake as I keep telling her. When I go there, the girl is always in a different room. She hides away. He stays with me and we talk. That's okay, but he doesn't always answer my questions. When I asked what his job was, he said he did 'this and that'. What sort of answer is that? I wonder if it is something illegal and that's why he didn't want me to know. You could find out for me. I need to know he has a proper job. This and that is not a proper job.' He gets me wondering what 'this and that' is, too. He can't shut up.

'I told them I had to order the part for the heater. Why not tell me they're going to be away?'

I agree. Why not tell him. It would have saved this problem.

I butt in and say, 'I'll let you know when they respond to my email.'

'And find out what he does. Find out what 'this and that' means!'

'Right,' I say and hang up. 'Right' can come in handy.

Chapter 10

Lauren and I have a final inspection at a property I used to manage. The time is flexible as Ralph, the tenant, has already left and handed in the keys. Now would be the time to go, and get out of the office for a bit.

We are going together because it's nice to have company, and because I know the place – Ralph was one of my favourite tenants.

We head off. I bury my curiosity about 'this and that' and say to Lauren, 'Let's not talk about Bruno or even think about him. There is nothing we can do but wait for the tenants to email us.'

'That's fine with me. I'd be happy if I never heard his name again.'

We sit in silence as if there is nothing else in the world to talk about. I start to think about the place we are going to.

I liked doing the routine inspections there when Ralph was in residence. He was always home and I enjoyed my conversations with him. I felt we had a certain connection and he made me laugh.

A few weeks ago, Ralph rang me to say he was moving. He's always energetic, chatty and friendly. In this phone call he was euphoric – lit up.

'I'm moving. I've bought my own place!' His excitement was catching and I began to grin. 'Mum's always saying I should do this. She says I shouldn't pay rent and make someone else rich. So I've taken the plunge.'

'Wow,' I say, inadequately. I didn't know he was thinking of buying. Though there is no reason why I should know. It is not the sort of thing you ring your property manager about, but I felt slightly put out as if he should have told me.

'Yeah! I've done it,' he says. 'It's a bit scary, really.'

'Where did you buy?'

He lived in an un-renovated two-bedroom downstairs apartment with the lounge opening onto a sort of terrace beside the driveway for the block. The rent is cheap, but higher than it should be because it is in a good area.

He named a place, and said, 'You know where it is? Further east from here. It's a two-bedroom town house. Only a couple of years old. Great bathroom and kitchen.'

'That will be a change,' I say trying to find the right words.

'No bath, though. I rather like that old bath. A good place to soak on a cold winter's night.'

This comment made me remember that there is no heating in his rented unit. He must have supplied his own. Ralph chatted on.

'It's a bit further out but it's near a shopping strip and there is a good café. I went there after the auction. I was shaking. I needed coffee, badly. It was good coffee, so that's okay.'

'Congratulations,' I said a bit belatedly. We are always saying congratulations in the real estate world. Not only in sales. In property management our confirmation letter to a new tenant starts with 'Congratulations, you have been approved for…' A bit silly really. It is not a race or a lottery. You haven't really won anything. You may be the only tenant who applied. Of course it is a feel-good word. I say it to Ralph hoping he will feel good.

'Yeah, thanks. It's a great feeling, but scary as I said. I woke up in the middle of the night on Saturday really worried. All these thoughts went through my head. What happens if there's something wrong with it that I didn't notice? What happens if there's a lot of maintenance? I'm at the top of my budget, not much spare cash. All this kept going round and round in my head.'

'Lots of people feel like that,' I said. 'That's why it's got a name – buyers' remorse. Regretting what you've done and a feeling you may have been swindled. Sort of panicking.'

'It was a bit like that,' Ralph enthused sounding relieved and eager at the same time. 'The worry about the money and the maintenance and being afraid I'd been suckered in. I drove over on Sunday and looked at it. There was the For Sale sign with a big 'Sold' on it. I took a selfie with the board. I made sure I got myself right in front for the sold sticker. I didn't do that on Saturday. Then I walked up and down the street and had coffee in the café. I was excited then. It was as if I was already living there. Now, I feel it's the best thing I've ever done. Forget buyers' remorse or whatever it is.'

While he was talking, I was visualising the last time I was in his unit. As he liked to be there for an inspection we arranged it for the end of the day.

I would arrive and he would be brewing coffee.

His interior decoration made this nothing-unit into something else. It's one of those old places that still have pelmets and curtain rods in place. He had put curtains over the white plastic slim-line venetians that were supplied. His curtains in the lounge were deep red, almost burgundy, with a green pattern. They looked a bit exotic against the yellowing off-white walls and his pictures added to the exotic vibe.

He had a couple of large pictures, one with a scene of a lake at dawn and the other was a skyscape of a large city, probably New York but I wasn't sure. I think I saw one like it in IKEA. It took up most of the back wall of the lounge. I visited several times and for some reason I never asked where he got it. It just never came up.

A large black and white cow skin hid some of the tired carpet and half a dozen lamps glowed. Perhaps these were from IKEA too, but the effect was about as far away from Scandinavian as you could get and light years away from this dull 1960s block.

One of the bedrooms was set up as a study with a lot of dark wood and more of the same curtains. The other bedroom, where he slept, had the windows closed off with gun-metal curtains. A king-size bed took up nearly all the floor space. It was something of a miracle that he got it through the door.

After I had trotted through and checked everything was still as immaculate as it was at the last inspection, he poured coffee and I sank into his squashy leather couch and we chatted.

He travelled a lot for business and told interesting and funny anecdotes.

I imagined when he got home after a long plane ride the apartment was like his cave. To my knowledge he didn't ever open the curtains or the venetians. Strangely, it didn't smell stuffy or shut up so he must have aired it sometimes. Having it so closed up was a recipe for mould, but it never smelt mouldy. It smelt of freshly brewed coffee and the sofa gave off a light and pleasant leather smell. It was hard for me to leave – to heave myself out of the deep squishy sofa and into the old, grey concrete foyer and head off down the grey, cracked, concrete driveway, and of course, into reality.

I will miss him and these visits.

The landlord insisted that we arrange opens for inspection there before Ralph moved out. I was dubious. What tenant or anyone for that matter could look at Ralph's exotic and so-phisticated world and picture the shell that would be left after the world had been picked up and transported 'Further East'? I found it hard myself and I am familiar with the units in this building and dozens just like them in similar buildings.

Ralph agreed that we could show prospective tenants around although he insisted on being present. He lit a couple of candles and played his jazz softly during the opens. The place had a sort of magic. I liked his jazz.

At the inspections the tenants walked in and their mouths fell open.

'Wow! This is great.' There was definitely the wow factor.

To bring them back to earth I would say, 'Try to think what it would be like without the furniture and the rugs. It is very basic really. Try to imagine it with your furniture.' I'm not sure anyone heard me or if they did, saw their furniture and not Ralph's. It was a hard call.

One thing that was admired greatly was the picture of the city view. I was waiting for Ralph to say he got it at IKEA. He said little during the opens except to confirm he was taking everything with him.

After the first 'wow' I could see that no one liked the curtains. When they asked if the curtains were staying it was because they didn't like them. They wanted them gone. Ralph's taste is not everyone's taste.

I wondered how the curtains would fit into his new place 'Further East'. He had insisted several times that I should visit, and I was looking forward to it. Even if it was only to check out what ambience he thought was appropriate for 'Further East'. More sky? More light? More sun?

When he handed in the keys at reception he gave me a leather document case with a very discrete company logo in one corner; very in keeping with Ralph. I'm waiting for an occasion important enough to show it off.

We have a new tenant and I'm anxious to see the place after Ralph. It will no longer have expensive appliances in the un-renovated kitchen, or a big mirror reflecting light in the bedroom. The worn cream carpet will be on show in all its glory. No Ralph and no glamour.

I wish Lauren had seen it when Ralph was living there.

We open up and walk into nothing, just yellowing, off-white walls and an exhausted carpet. The curtains have gone and the venetians are pulled up to give a view of the driveway from the lounge and the road from the bedrooms. The place looks dreary, almost as if it is exhausted. The kitchen is dark, as is the bathroom, and I remember Ralph had used lamps there too.

Wyatt has been, so there is the smell of cleaning products. I miss the smell of coffee. It's a different place. No magic.

There are dark shadows against the ceiling in the corners of the lounge and in the main bedroom. Wyatt said this was mould that he had tried to wash off with something like a window washer. He hadn't taken his ladder! How did he expect to clean the bathroom fan and the light fittings without a ladder? This was not one of his finer moments. It's hard to know what sort of effect a window washer on a long pole would have on any mould. None is my guess.

Lauren takes photos but it is difficult to take photos of a dark shadow. The wall doesn't co-operate, or try to adjust its angle so it is easy to capture. Empty units don't have things to stand on, and short of hoisting each other up we don't have much luck recording these dark marks to look anything like mould. Or like anything really. It is just a dark shadow from where we stand on the dreary carpet. Lauren takes Wyatt's word that it is mould.

We head back to the office in Lauren's car. After a couple of minutes Lauren gets a call from the landlord of the property. He has some position in a church and is generally known as The Rev in the office.

I am not sure that I am in favour of phone connections in cars. Gone are the days when we could sit and have friendly chats as we drove around for work. The phone has to be answered. It shrieks 'answer' at us and we do. We are like dancing marionettes that have our strings pulled.

Lauren and I were having an interesting conversation about the merits of Bali against Hawaii, where she's just been for a holiday and where her skin turned a lovely shade of golden brown. It always does that, unlike mine. My skin prefers a colour scheme of white or red. Tan is seldom in the mix. I need a spray-tan at $40 a pop to get the effect Lauren is showing off. It is very annoying. I tell myself it is something to do with having blue eyes. I feel better about it if I think that.

Had we been able to continue with this conversation, I think cheapness is all Lauren has in Bali's favour, but I may be wrong.

Lauren tells The Rev about the black shadowy marks on the wall that the cleaner believes is mould. As I listen I think this is a mistake. We don't know for sure. We only have Wyatt's word. I would have questioned him as to what he actually washed off, if indeed he washed anything off. But then, I always know what to do!

While Lauren is on the phone, I am thinking of a routine inspection I did just around the corner from Ralph's unit a few years back, where I was well and truly on the back foot.

I always think of it as the 'What's with the Fence' inspection

At another company I worked for, I took over the management of a group of villa units.

This takeover showed me that not all property managers record their notes. As property managers our heads are full of stuff that we can access at the mention of a name or an address. This is not a huge help to the person who takes over a portfolio. Most of the information about this portfolio and the villa units stayed in the head of the departing property manager.

The units are more like small houses from the art deco period and built in a horse-shoe shape around a driveway. They are part of a large trust managed by Stan, a professor at a local university. He is the sort of bloke you can imagine out on field trips and under canvas rather than in a lecture hall full of students.

He is an excellent trustee and attends all the routine inspections. He has files on each unit and brings them with him. I checked our files and looked for any previous emails, and there didn't appear to be any issues with the properties. All looked to be in reasonable condition for their age.

Stan was chatty and jokey as we began the inspections. He didn't go in for much upgrading. I learned that there was no point in a tenant asking for a paint job, or to get a couple more shelves in the kitchen. A request for another power point in the lounge in one place was turned down. The tenants had power boards and cords snaking everywhere and this could have been a health and safety issue. When they mentioned this to Stan, he pointed out they could configure the cords differently and they would not have the problem. He showed them how to do this. They watched, silently.

We arrived at the back door of the final place and stepped into the yard.

There was a moment's silence.

'What's with the fence?' Stan asked loudly and looked at me. The tenant and I stared at a new board fence that was erected along the back of the property.

I didn't say anything. I didn't know 'what was with the fence'. I continued to stare at it.

The tenant helped me out. 'That was put up last week. No one told us about it. They just turned up and did it.'

'Why?' Stan continued to look at me. I shuffled around with the few notes I had. There was nothing about a new fence or any fence for that matter.

Stan turned to the tenant, 'What was wrong with the old one?'

'Nothing really. It was old. You know that grey colour.'

'But what was wrong with it?' Stan insisted.

He tenant looked a bit confused, 'The boards were okay. I didn't notice anything wrong with it.'

Stan stared at me again, 'Nobody told me about a new fence. Not a word. It looks as if someone's dropped the ball here. I'm not paying for a new fence I knew nothing about.'

Someone had definitely dropped the ball and while doing so had signed Stan's name to pay his half of the quote that the neighbours at the rear had forwarded to our office.

The problem became who would pay. The property manager who signed the quote had gone. We were left with the paperwork from the fencing company.

In the end Stan paid half of his share. That is, a quarter of the full cost. It was pointed out to him that he now had a new fence and he would not have to replace it for years. I believe he saw that point. He objected to not being consulted. He mentioned how disorganised our office appeared to be. He also said he was never hard to get in touch with and he always returned phone calls, and that no one had called him about the fence.

After a lot of shouting in the office about whose fault it was – real estate directors often shout when money is flowing away from them – the company paid half of Stan's share. There wasn't much else they could do.

I continued to work with Stan and he really was a nice and easy landlord. He liked to chat, and gave me a bottle of red wine occasionally after he found I liked red. But he had this annoying habit of ringing on Monday morning while I was in the middle of Monday Mayhem. There were no preliminaries – he always got straight into the conversation with something like, 'Did you notice my football team had a good win over the weekend?' His team was Hawthorn and at the time it was having a good run.

I got to recognise his voice. It was sort of gravely and warm and sounded happy. He never once mentioned his wife but gossip in the office said he had one.

He ended conversations with, 'Got anything to report?' Then, 'I suppose you're busy. I'd better get on.' He would disappear sometimes for weeks while he was on a field trip, and then suddenly would be back again. I think he rang when he felt bored or lonely, or more likely to let me know he had the ball and I had better keep my eye on it. I think he dug in over the fence to make a point. He made his point very well.

When I left the company I had hoped he would contact me if only for old time's sake. He had my mobile number but he never did.

** * **

Lauren finishes her conversation. 'The Rev wants to inspect the property for himself. We're not to give the bond back until he's done so. He'll call in and get the keys in an hour.'

As Lauren is saying this, we arrive back at the office.

For once there is a park right outside, although only an hour one, which Lauren thinks will be okay as she is heading out to lunch soon.

Day-to-day parking can be a problem. We bring our cars to work because we need them during the day.

Caruthers have a car allowance they build into our salary. That is helpful with petrol and so on, but it doesn't help us to park close to the office. Around our office we have many one-hour parks, a few two-hour parks and then a little further away some all-day parks.

I try to opt for an all-day park even if I have to walk a bit. This is okay in fine weather but not so good in the rain. Parking in a one-hour or two-hour bay is risky. It's too easy to get caught up in something and return to your car to find it has been ticketed. Some people don't seem to care about this. Lauren sticks her tickets along the side of her computer and there is always one or two waiting for payment.

We try to help each other out. If we see a parking inspector hovering, we send an office email – *Parking inspector marking cars* or *Parking Inspector ticketing*.

This triggers a rush from the office and a shuffle around of cars as people try to change spots.

It has become worse of late because a couple of local houses are having extensive renovations and the streets are clogged with tradesmen's vehicles. They park without consideration for others and take up far more room than they need to. As they often start about 7.30 in the morning, they grab the best free spots. It seems to me that they should get a resident parking permit while they work on constructions in these parking-poor streets. There are always spaces in 'Resident Only' parking areas.

I resent paying the council a fine so I can park to do my job. When I do get a ticket (occasionally even I stuff up), it is because I have parked in a one-hour zone as I think I am going out again almost immediately, only to find I am in the office for a couple of hours.

I think of what I could do with money instead of giving it to the council and feel angry. Mostly I think about a stunning meal or a really special bottle of wine.

Lauren takes the keys to leave at reception for The Rev. I can sense trouble brewing with this landlord. Mould is not a good word to have floating about. It can set the imagination racing. Although I'm not sure imagination is a quality that can be found in The Rev.

Chapter 11

I head off down the road to get another $2.50 coffee. As I'm stepping into Café Yellow I remember I have not got any lunch. I always have excellent resolutions about bringing something from home. Now I think about it, I could have brought some of last night's Pad Thai. I was in such a rush this morning I didn't think about lunch. I back out of Café Yellow before Jono sees me and cross the road to the sushi place.

Carmen from a dress shop further down the strip is on a stool at the window bar, eating very delicately with chopsticks.

'Hi. Are you going to eat here?' she asks, as soon as I enter.

'No, I plan to go back to the office.'

'Stay here. Keep me company. Then I can tell you the latest news.'

I tell the girl behind the counter I will eat my shrimp and avocado and a teriyaki chicken sushi with Carmen. Yes, I had the same yesterday. And no, it's not boring, because they are my favourite. I have tried others. These are the winners.

I wriggle onto a stool next to Carmen.

'What's the latest, then?'

'Our shop's closing, I just heard this morning. I'm in shock.'

'I thought you were doing well!'

'Yeah, I think we are. The lease is up apparently. And the owner wants us out.'

'Why?'

'Going to renovate and put apartments on top,' she answers. 'Apartments are popping up everywhere here.'

Renovation means less street car parks and more tradesmen's vehicles taking up the remaining spaces. I listen to Carmen talk about another outlet her company has and whether she wants to work there. She doesn't like the manager.

She's talking to herself – we do that when we're stressed. I don't need to say anything. I think about how many apartments there are around here already. Real estate agents will be pleased – more to sell and more to let. However I'm not happy about these changes. I like things to stay the way they are – with lots of car parks. And I will miss Carmen and our occasional catch-ups for drinks at the Lido. I use my chopsticks to shovel in the sushi. I have not got the same knack with them as Carmen.

* * *

I arrive back at my desk to find two emails from Lauren about people wanting to view Bruno's property. She has added a number of exclamation marks and a couple of question marks to them.

Another email says, *Reception Scissors! Who's got them?* in the subject line. This email has definitely been written by Lisa and not Vicky.

Why would anyone walk away with those, I think as I delete the email? Then I look down and sitting on my desk is a pair of scissors labelled 'Reception'.

I can't remember using them; let alone carting them back to my desk. I do find odd things on my desk. People go out the back to the rubbish or the small shed and leave stuff on my desk on their way in or out. I have a notice saying 'This is NOT a parking spot. Do Not Leave things here.' Most people in this building clearly have as much trouble with their reading as tenants. Stuff is still parked here.

I pick them up and walk down the corridor to the front of the office.

'Scissors!' I say.

'Just as well I labelled them,' says Lisa putting out her hand for them. She turns to Vicky.

'You see why I have everything labelled. Everything walks away from here.' I think walking is a good word. But I don't remember taking them for a walk myself.

Back at my desk I get a call from the plumber about my toilet.

'Hey, I can't do your job today,' he says straight away. 'A couple of my blokes are off sick and I'm really under the pump. If they're back tomorrow, I should be able to fit it in. Funny they're both away sick on the same day.'

'I guess I'll just have to wait until tomorrow,' I say. There is no smile in my voice as I say it.

'It's not blocked or anything like that is it?'

'No, it's just the cistern. It won't flush.'

'That's okay then. Not urgent. You can handle it can't you?'

I want to shout, 'No I can't! You have to come and fix it.' Then I think how obliging he has been to me in the past and how he can't help having staff off sick.

So I say, 'I suppose that will be okay,' but not with any enthusiasm. He doesn't notice my lukewarm voice, or if he does he ignores it.

'Let's leave it until Thursday if you can? I'll book it for then. I'll try and make it the morning. My guys had better be back then. We have so much work on, I'll be working all hours today and I don't see much let up tomorrow. Thursday would be great if you can handle it.'

'Thursday it is then.' I don't smile, but what else can I say? I remember last time I used him he didn't charge me. And I remember that I like him. I also remember that I give him a lot of work on behalf of my landlords so he should see me as top priority. Then I remember he gave me some particularly nice red wine for Christmas.

None of that makes me feel better. I'm annoyed with myself for not standing my ground. Now I have to ring Amy. She is going to be really pissed off and who can blame her? I'll text her. Ringing may be better, but I don't want to discuss it.

I feel guilty. By Thursday it will be almost a week with no flush. I'm wondering if I should suggest a reduction in her rent. She has stayed at her boyfriend Brett's place most of that time. That has been good. One person using the toilet is enough. I'll think about the rent.

I send the text and follow up the two enquiries about Bruno's property in Princess Street. Both groups can make 5.30 this evening, so that is where I will end my working day.

One hopeful tenant chats about coming back from overseas and how she and her partner are living with her dad a couple of streets away, so the position is great for them. I will see how it plays out. I'm not going to mention this to Bruno. There may be a chance of him turning up and I feel we have spent enough time together today, even though it has only been on the phone.

I'm drawing down positive pictures of people loving Bruno's place and loving Bruno when Vince turns up to ask for some advice.

Vince has only been with us a short time. He is very efficient and has a steady long-term partner. He is one of the few people in the office who has. Mandy is the other one. She is getting married about this time next year. Most of us are between partners.

He has given someone a notice to vacate for non-payment of rent. It is now two days after the expiry of the notice and the keys have not come back. His phone calls ring out and there is no voicemail. He wants to discuss what to do next. Usually when we issue a notice to vacate we apply for a hearing at VCAT for a warrant of possession a couple of days later. For some reason this hasn't been done. It takes about two weeks to get a hearing date so doing it before you know what the tenant is up to is a good idea. If your tenant comes good and pays the rent, you can always cancel it.

Vince and I discuss doing this immediately, and then I suggest taking the office keys and going round to check out the place. It is a unit near the back of a block so there is nothing to see from the road.

This is not a legal thing to do and is best done when there are two of you. We could send the tenant a notice of entry. A landlord or agent has the right to enter the property for various reasons; all outlined in the Act. Vince thinks the tenants have probably vacated and disappeared. We plan to open the door and peer inside.

He arranges for the application to VCAT and we head off to the property.

It is a pretty ordinary three-level block, with all the units opening off a walkway. This means that we can be seen by anyone in the car park as we go in. Vince hammers loudly on the door. There's no response. We try looking in the window but the blinds are down. A head pops out from a doorway two down.

'You looking for those arseholes?'

'Yes,' says Vince. 'Know anything about them?'

'I hope they're rotting in hell. Noisiest buggers we've ever had here.'

'Do you think they've moved out?' I ask.

'Bleedin' hope so. It's been quiet for a couple of nights. Didn't see them go, though.'

'Well, thank you very much,' says Vince politely.

'You looking for them?'

'Yes,' I say.

'Well, if you find them, don't bring the buggers back here.'

The face disappears and the door slams.

Vince and I look at each other and he inserts the key. Actually, he inserts four different keys before we find the right one on the ring. He eases the door open. It is immediately clear that the lounge is empty. We walk through to the bedroom. The tenants have vacated. They didn't clean anything and they probably haven't cleaned for some weeks but they have taken their stuff.

We take some photos, lock up and head back to the office.

Vince says, 'I guess I'll have to tell the owner. He's going to blow his stack and he's going to want to get in there straight away. He's that sort of bloke.'

'Has Lisa got any unidentified keys that might belong to it?' I ask.

'I'll check. Then I'll have a chat with Emily and see what she thinks I should do. But I think it'll be okay to let the landlord in there. They've obviously gone and we can get the warrant to cover our tracks.'

'Is Emily in today? She looked dreadful yesterday'.

'Yes, she's here but I understand throwing up half the morning. I told you what I think – pregnant!'

'No! I've thought about that. She hasn't got a partner or even a boyfriend as far as I know, and she's always saying motherhood doesn't appeal to her. And that her mothering instinct has been satisfied by her nieces. She's got two.'

'Mark my words,' says Vince once again as he gets out of the car and we head back to the office. I hope he doesn't keep saying 'mark my words' – it is more than annoying it's smug.

I think about Emily and wonder again if Vince is right, but somehow that is the sort of thing a man would instantly think – throwing up, must be pregnant – although I don't know why I think that. It's unlikely to be the case for Emily. She has been definite on the no-children thing. I start wondering what else could be wrong with her. It's more than simple food poisoning. I knew someone once who got a bug from water they drank from a country stream. They thought the water would be pristine as they were in the country. They would never have drunk from a city stream. They were sick for several months. Does Emily go into the country? I don't know that.

While I am thinking about it, I am reminded of someone I knew who had something called 'cycle vomiting'. She had bouts of feeling well and then suddenly she would be back throwing up. Sometimes she went for weeks feeling okay then she would be leaning over the toilet again. A strange disease.

I don't know if she was ever cured. I lost touch with her. Perhaps Emily has something like that.

I have a message from reception: *Amy rang pls ring her back.*

I do that, reluctantly, and find that she is a bit pissed off about the toilet as I knew she would be.

'I can't understand why you can't get anyone there. Surely there's a plumber that your company uses that can go,' she says.

I try to explain the problem but she cuts me off.

'Brett's got a friend called Lee who should be able to fix it. He's pretty handy. It's only the flush so perhaps a few wires or screws.'

'He knows what he's doing?'

'Yeah. Brett says he does. If you're okay with it, I'll tell Brett to get him to go over there. He can use my keys to get in?'

I'm dubious about the unknown Lee but then I feel bad about it not being fixed so I find myself saying, 'Sure.'

'Great, I'll get Brett on to it.'

Chapter 12

Vince, who is wondering about getting a warrant and fussing about the landlord wanting his property returned from his tenants, reminds me of past tenants Mr and Mrs Boron. They pop into my head on a regular basis, although it is many years since I encountered them. I have mentioned the Boron Effect, so here's the story.

I met the Borons when I worked in one of the outer northern suburbs of Melbourne. A landlord asked me to issue them with a notice to vacate. Mr and Mrs Boron must have been in their late 70s or early 80s at the time. They had been renting the property for about fifteen years. Long enough for them to think the house was theirs and they could live there forever. Mr Boron especially had burdened himself with this thinking.

Forever is a long time and the owners of the property, a retired couple Paul and Jan Young, wanted their house back to renovate for their son and daughter-in-law who were returning from overseas.

It was a small, old and ugly house on a large block of land. 'Ripe for renovation' would be the immediate thought when you saw it. The Youngs paid a gardener to have the lawns mown and some scruffy and dusty bushes trimmed. The place looked fried and exhausted. I thought the gardener cut the lawn too often and too short. He disagreed. He got paid when he attended and I remember seeing him whizzing around with his mower churning up the dust and slicing a few weeds. I could hear the mower hitting stones. This tortured lawn did nothing to improve the look of the place.

Mr and Mrs Boron were migrants from Poland. He spoke good English, but her English was limited. He was hale and hearty, but her health was poor. They were hoarders. The house was chock full of stuff. Stuffed like a festive roast turkey with the stuffing oozing out of it. Every time I was there I thought, we need one of those immaculately groomed declutterers from television, but I think even the most efficient declutterer would have thrown her hands up in horror and beat a hasty retreat. Why are declutterers always women? Why do men never declutter? Neither the man nor the woman in this house decluttered.

I followed the Youngs' instructions and issued a notice to vacate. I rang Mr Boron to let him know I was sending it to him. I wanted to soften the shock.

He said, 'Thank you for ringing.'

Did he get what I said? Did he understand what it meant? He didn't discuss it.

I rang again after he had got the notice and said we would help him to look for a new place. He was polite. He was always polite but he didn't comment other than to say he understood I was telling him he had to move.

As far as I could see, he did nothing about looking for a new home. The office found a couple of places that we thought may work for them. Mr Boron waved them aside. He would not live in those suburbs. He liked where he was.

That was the crux of it. He liked where he was.

Everyone in the office thought it would be good for them to move.

'Give them a new lease on life,' Clare, the senior property manager said. Often, we know what other people need and it is so frustrating when they can't see it themselves. We could see it. Mr Boron didn't get it. Clare pointed it out to him several times but he still couldn't see it.

A few days before they were due to move, Paul Young rang me.

'Have you been in touch with the Borons lately?'

'I rang Mr Boron a week ago to remind him of the vacating date. He told me he knew the date.'

'I've just been there with our architect. They're not packing. Nothing is different. I asked Mr Boron about it and he said it's under control. It didn't look under control to me. What's he doing about moving out?'

Nothing as far as I could see, but I said to Paul, 'We have suggested a couple places to them but Mr Boron isn't keen on the suburbs they're in.'

'The place looks just same – still looks like a tip. Nothing's happening there. And I want them out. I'm not interested in where they don't want to live. They're to get out.'

'I'll book a hearing for a warrant of possession,' I said.

'Yes, do that. Do you think they're taking this seriously?' Paul demanded.

I didn't think so, but I said, 'He says he is. He says he understands.'

'Poor buggers,' said Paul with some feeling. 'I am sorry for them after all these years. But they must've known they'd have to go sometime. They've been bloody lucky they've had it so good for so long. Get the warrant!'

The date for the hearing came and the Borons were still in residence. The hearing was held in the same building as the Magistrates' Court. This is weighty stuff; family violence, traffic violations and intervention orders etc. The car park is always full with a large area sectioned off for police cars. Getting inside takes a while. We lined up for security and the X-ray machine, shuffling along like an airport queue.

I watched Mr Boron and a friend navigate the crowd around the door and the security. Some of these people seemed scary to me, but Mr Boron and his friend wandered along chatting to each other as if it was a seniors' outing.

They were joined inside by a representative from the Tenants' Union who had come to support Mr Boron and see he got a fair deal. Something like that.

'Hi, I'm Dave-from-the-Tenants'-Union,' he said, as he shook my hand with a half-hearted grip. We weren't going to be friends. He came in attacking. 'What's this water bill you want the Borons to pay?'

'It's from way back,' I said. 'It's not in dispute. Mr Boron knows he has to pay.'

Dave-from-the-Tenants'-Union interrupted Mr Boron and his friend's chatter to ask about it. Mr Boron waved him aside and said there was no problem, he would pay. Dave-from-the-Tenants'-Union could have asked when it would be paid. Instead, he deflated a little and moved on.

'You know we are going to ask for an indefinite extension of the vacating date?'

I wondered what he thought indefinite meant. It was like saying the Borons could stay on until death do we part.

VCAT decisions are legally binding and everyone who participates swears themselves in. For some reason Mr Boron's friend tried to swear himself in. The Judge in this court who is conducting the hearing is for some unfathomable reason called the Member, wondered if he needed to do this. Was he going to participate in the proceedings? Mr Boron and his friend chatted about it. The friend, with Mr Boron's help, swore himself in and we moved on.

I had only three copies of all the papers. I didn't know such a crowd would turn up. I passed one set to Mr Boron and the friend tried to take them. Mr Boron pulled them towards himself. Then Dave-from-the-Tenants'-Union made a grab for them and placed his hand heavily on top, securing their place in front of him.

'Are we ready? Can we begin?' asked the member tersely. We got under way.

I started to explain why we wanted the warrant and to bring the member up to speed on the procedures we followed. I had only just got under way when Dave-from-the-Tenants'-Union interrupted. The Member ignored him. It was as if he hadn't spoken. She turned to Mr Boron who was still chattering to his friend. It was as if they were waiting for a movie to start rather than deciding his living accommodation.

'Mr Boron, do you understand English?'

Mr Boron turned from his friend who was still talking and said rather haughtily, 'Of course I do.'

'What plans have you got to vacate?'

'We're looking.' I am sure he lied because I was sure he had not looked at any properties. Perhaps he looked at the local free paper which at that time had rentals listed on the back.

Dave-from-the-Tenant's-Union jumped to his feet. He wanted to be noticed. 'We think it is unreasonable to ask them to vacate after such a long tenancy. Mrs Boron has poor health you know.'

The member turned to me. 'Has your office been helping them secure another property?'

'We have suggested a couple of properties to Mr Boron but he hasn't liked the areas,' I said this smugly. I could not be criticised. I had done the right thing.

During all this Mr Boron's friend chattered away. I was sure he didn't understand English, because as he had sworn himself in he could have put his five cents worth into the mix.

Dave managed to get the vacate date extended for another four weeks. So I guess he did a better job than I did. Paul and Jan Young thought three weeks at the outside.

As we left I said to Mr Boron, 'You will have to start seriously looking for somewhere because the Youngs do want their property back. Why don't you go to the council and see if they can help you?'

'My wife's carer has done that.' I gaped at him.

'What did he say?' asked Dave-from-the-Tenants'-Union.

'His wife's carer has contacted the council about it.'

'It would have helped if he told me that. We could have got a longer extension.' He took off after the two old men who were wandering towards the exit. They walked through the crowd and the heavy police presence as if it were a stroll in the park.

I got the warrant but held off executing it. I was hoping for a miracle. In our office everyone was hoping for that miracle and I am sure Paul and Jan were hoping for the same miracle. I tried to avoid them.

I wondered how the Borons could sleep at night knowing we had a warrant to get them out.

The vacating date came and went. There was no miracle. The Youngs were angry. They blamed our office. Why couldn't we do something? They rang regularly to ask what we were doing. Their dream was to never hear the name Boron again. They said several times that they wished they had never clapped eyes on them in the first place.

We were angry and Clare was in a dilemma. I'm sure she didn't sleep at night. She couldn't bring herself to issue the warrant and get the police involved. She was angry with herself because she felt responsible for their welfare and she didn't see why she should. Every time Paul or Jan rang she said to us, 'This isn't my problem. Why can't I issue the warrant and leave it to the police to get rid of them? I am not responsible for these people!'

One day Mr Boron came into the office to pay some rent. When he saw me he said in his polite voice, 'We are looking for somewhere else. I understand we have to move.'

I wanted to hit him and shout that he was lying, that he was a difficult and cranky old man and he was driving us all to a nervous breakdown. I rushed away. Instead of punching Mr Boron, I punched the wall in the toilet. Fortunately, it was a brick wall or I would have punched a hole through it. For several days my hand hurt. I never spoke to Mr Boron again. If he came into the office, I left.

One day Mrs Boron's social worker rang to say she had found housing for them. Mrs Boron was obviously the one staying awake at night.

It felt too good to be true – even when I saw it in writing I was afraid to hope. And there was almost a death knell – Mr Boron did not like the property. It was in the wrong location.

That is, it was about 2km from where they were. But the machinery had got into gear and his objections were overruled.

They were moved with the help of wonderful volunteers.

The question I asked over and over again during this trauma was, 'Why hadn't they bought their own place during their lifetime?' I asked the question so often people in the office got sick of me asking it. That was the Boron Effect. Seeing someone turfed out of what they saw as their until-death-do-us-part home. I had visions of it being me.

Did it change me? It brought out something that had been lurking below the surface. The Boron effect said to me 'Really? Is this what you want drifting from one rental to the next?'

I told myself I would take control of my life. I put a savings plan into action. When I felt like going out and splurging on good red wine I thought of the Borons. When I thought of buying a beautiful Italian leather jacket, I thought of the Borons and went to Target. I brought a coffee plunger to work and saved the cost of a couple of coffees a day. You'll notice that now have a place I no longer make my own coffee. It is so much easier to buy it from Jono.

Of course nothing is completely perfect. I am the one responsible for getting the toilet fixed and paying for it. Mr Boron never had that problem – he rang us, we organised it and Paul and Jan Young paid.

Chapter 13

Vince comes to lean in the doorway and tell me he has checked Lisa's unidentified box. The keys he wants are not there. He has tried again to ring the tenants, but they are still not answering and an email has bounced back. This means he will have to attend the hearings for a warrant of possession and the bond for the property. He goes off reluctantly to ring the landlord who is likely to be out of pocket what with the rent owed, the cleaning and the locksmith. I am hoping he has landlord insurance.

I get a text from Amy. *Lee can't come until Wednesday. I'll stay another night at Brett's.*

I am getting more and more pissed off about this. I don't really want Lee there, whoever he is, but it looks as if I haven't much choice. I want to text back and say forget it. I'll wait for my plumber. Somehow that doesn't sound friendly or obliging when Amy, who is paying me rent, is inconvenienced.

I text and say, *That's fine. I hope he can fix it.*

Then from Amy, *I'm sure he can. I'll see you tomorrow when we can flush away.*

I don't text back.

***

I need to update Emily on Bruno's key problem and tell her that Lauren is over dealing with him. I will volunteer to take him on. A chance to show off as a good team leader. I trot upstairs to see if Emily's free.

I could have buzzed her but in my effort to keep my weight under control, I tell myself I need to climb the stairs not buzz or send an email. Emily greets me with, 'I was coming to see you. I've got a big favour to ask. Are you busy this afternoon?'

I never want to say I am not busy. It gives the wrong impression but I do want to be helpful, so I say, 'No more than usual.'

'Have you got time to do a routine inspection for me?'

Have I? I don't want to do a routine inspection. I want the afternoon to drift uneventfully to a conclusion.

'Of course,' I say. 'I have an appointment at Bruno's place to show a couple of groups through at 5.30. I've got time before that.'

'I would be grateful. I forgot an appointment I'd made, and booked this routine with a landlord.' The little voice in my head says 'pregnancy brain'. I push it down.

Emily is looking pale and stressed. I hope this is a doctor's appointment. I think she should tell me what it is. Why keep it a secret? I don't ask because she is bit closed up – sort of shut down.

'That's fine. There's plenty of time before I head to Princess Street.'

'It's not far. The landlord may be a bit difficult but I'm sure you'll handle him. I'll let him know you'll be there. I'm grateful. Thanks.'

She hands me some notes and the keys as she starts to collect her things. Obviously this is not the time to discuss Bruno's lock and Lauren.

I read the file and the notes Emily has given me and I am off to meet the landlord. I brace myself for the encounter. There has to be a reason why Emily didn't pass the management of his property on to one of us after she signed him up. I place my beautiful boots, with the magic marker repair, firmly on the footpath and feel the power they give me as I march off to my car. I am well psyched up. I can deal with anything.

* * *

This is the first time Goran has seen his property. He's working overseas and wanted to invest some of the proceeds from his ex-pat lifestyle. Instead of coming back here and looking around himself he asked a buyers advocate to find a property for him. He had a virtual-reality tour and a spiel from the advocate on why this was the place to buy. He thought this was enough and he didn't bother to fly home to take a look himself. That would have been a small cost considering what he spent.

It's no wonder he's anxious. Has he bought a pig in a poke, or has the buyers advocate excelled and present him with a diamond?

If it is a diamond, it is a diamond in the rough. It is a large un-renovated two-bedroom ground floor unit in an Art Deco block. Before the sale the place was given a quick paint job in my favourite shade of white – Dulux's Antique White USA. It was splashed around everywhere. Emily mentioned the colour in her notes. The crisp-white look apparently showed to advantage in the virtual-reality views Goran got. Real reality can be different.

Goran is outside the property pacing up and down giving the impression that I'm late. I check my watch. No. Right on time. We shake hands and as I lead the way into this rather rambling block, he says, 'I hope you've got good tenants for me. I value this property and I don't want to find they aren't treating it properly.'

I see a head in the window.

'They appear to be home.' I say and knock on the door without following up on his comments.

Emily's notes tell me the tenants are Annemarie and Jake Yeo.

It is Annemarie who answers the door, and after the usual introductions and greetings she steps back to let us enter.

Goran is about to head into the living room on the right of the hall when Annemarie says, 'There are a few things I want to point out to you.' She has a list in her hand.

Goran seems taken aback.

Annemarie goes on. 'We're finding we're having trouble with some of the kitchen drawers not shutting property. I'll show you.' She leads us away from the living room and down the hall to the kitchen.

The kitchen is un-renovated so the drawers are old, wooden and painted blue on the outside with raw wood inside. I wonder why they didn't get the Dulux Antique White USA treatment. In my opinion the blue looks tacky. Annemarie pulls out a drawer and the only way to get it back in is to sort of jerk it along.

'All the drawers are like that. We would like a tradesman to come and fix them.'

Nothing like getting straight to the point. I make a note of this on my clipboard. A clipboard makes me feel 'I am on the job'. I see a tap is dripping and reach forward to turn it off.

'Yes,' says Annemarie, 'that needs fixing too. I was going to email you. Then when I knew you were coming I thought I'd leave it so you could see for yourself.' I make a note of the tap.

Goran goes back to the drawers. 'They're old drawers. This is the way they're made. There's nothing we can do about it.'

'We have a friend,' say Annemarie with great authority, 'who says they need to be planed. It is something a handyman could do.' I am suddenly sorry for Goran. He is on the back foot. His unit is not up to scratch. He was prepared to find fault with the tenants and now the tables are turned.

I say, 'I can ask our handyman about making them run smoothly. What do you think Goran?' I can see how irritating it would be living with the drawers working like this. I'm not sure that Goran gets the irritation bit.

'That'd be a good idea,' says Annemarie.

As Goran has not said anything. I say, 'Goran, you and I can discuss this. I'll make notes and we can chat, later.' I don't want an argument about it now.

Before Goran gets a chance to add anything, Annemarie says, 'There a problem in the bathroom, too.'

We follow meekly into the bathroom where there is a quantity of mould around the bath and above the shower area. The tiles that have been painted in Dulux Antique White USA are peeling.

Annemarie sweeps her hand around, 'We didn't realise when we moved in that the tiles were painted. I think the painter painted over the mould. You can see how the mould's coming through the paint.' Annemarie points to where some of the paint is lifting. 'When I started to clean, the paint just came off.'

Goran stares at this.

I bet Annemarie is right. The bathroom had a previous mould problem and all it got was a quick paint job before the sale. The quality of the job would not show up on virtual reality.

The room is stuffy. There is no fan. The ventilation is three louvre windows near the ceiling that are fixed open. There is a piece of mesh to stop insects.

Goran clears his throat. 'What are you using to clean it with? You shouldn't use something that makes the paint peel.'

'We use bathroom cleaner and we've used Jiff. Everyone uses that. And of course we've used Exit Mould to try to get rid of the mould.'

Goran is getting off the back foot, 'Whatever you've used has ruined my paint work. You must be using the wrong products. This shouldn't happen.' He is not going to win. Annemarie had the big guns on her side.

'We've been reading up on mould and this is a health hazard. We can't live with this mould.'

I'm over the word mould and I want to say, 'Well, push off then. Find somewhere else to go'. I can't say that so I ignore the health angle.

'I wonder if there's enough ventilation. You have those louvres at the top of the window. That doesn't seem much to me. I think we want a fan here.' I make a note on my clipboard then turn to Annemarie. 'Do you keep the door open after you've showered to help ventilate it?'

'Why would we do that? I like the bathroom door shut.'

'It helps ventilation. You have to keep the place dry so the mould doesn't get a chance to grow.' I may be able to push some blame onto them.

I go on, 'If you leave the door open you get a cross draught from the louvres and it will help to dry up the moisture.' She doesn't say anything, so I say, 'Let's have a look at the rest of the apartment.' She has deflated a little and we walk through the bedrooms and the lounge where there are no problems.

As we prepare to leave I say to Annemarie, 'Remember to keep the bathroom door open for ventilation. We'll discuss getting a fan and someone to look at the kitchen drawers. I'll confirm what we are going to do in an email.'

She waves her list at me, 'Can I give you my list or would you like me to email the problems.' I take the list. I want her to be happy and feel positive so I say, 'Thank you for looking after the place so well. You've made it look lovely.' And she has, if you like pink.

As soon as the front door shuts Goran says, 'I don't think they are looking after my property. They have damaged the bathroom. It wasn't like that when I bought it.'

I can see Annemarie sneaking a look at us from the window. I would be doing that too just to see what we're up to. I move Goran on so we are out of sight in case she pops out. Then I say firmly, 'We can't blame the tenants for the paint.' I believe this to be true so I go on. 'Do you know who painted it? We should get them back to have a look.' Goran does not know who that was and he's not going to pursue it. He makes noises about renovating the bathroom. That is one way to get rid of the crap paint job and the mould.

He agrees, reluctantly, to get a quote for the kitchen drawers and for the handyman to fix the tap, which, as he points out, is not dripping badly.

'It's not as if the water is pouring out. Just the occasional drip.' I don't comment.

Overall, Goran is happy. He believes he has bought a diamond in the raw. He's keen for these tenants to leave so he can begin polishing his diamond. I'm to get quotes to renovate the bathroom including a separate quote for a fan. He is into quotes.

The tenants are to be given notice to vacate at the end of their fixed term tenancy. He has taken a dislike to Annemarie. 'She's someone who complains,' is the way he put it. I promise him I will discuss all this with Emily.

***

I'm interested to see Goran's place is covered in Dulux Antique White USA. My place is the same. Dulux Antique White USA everywhere except in the kitchen where the drawers are a light coloured wood, with an easy wipe finish. No blue.

I have Emily to thank for my unit, although I selected the paint colour. It's the perfect white to live with. I always recommend it if a landlord asks my advice.

People think that if you work in real estate it is easier to buy a property than it is for anyone else. It doesn't work that way. You still have to get your money over the line and there are all sorts of rules about buying through the company you work for. Then there is the hardest part, finding what you like and you can afford.

When I started looking I was excited and upbeat. But after trailing through numerous opens and not seeing my dream unit, I got to the stage where I thought I would never find what I wanted. I whinged about it and after a while became despondent, which is not like me. Well, I thought it was unlike me, so I talked about that, too. I even wondered if I would end up like the Borons because nothing was right. I understood Mr Boron a bit better then.

Emily, who I'm sure got sick of me going on about how difficult it all was, told me I should just get out there and buy something. It was good advice, but it didn't work for me.

One day she said, 'There's a unit you should see. I drove past today and there's a for-sale sign on the block. It's a good block. I've managed a couple in there.'

'Where is it?'

She told me.

I said, 'Oh, I saw that advertised. It looked rather dreary.'

'There's nothing remarkable about it. It's just a red brick block. The units have two reasonably sized bedrooms and there's a balcony. But then you aren't looking for the Taj Mahal are you?' She looked questioningly at me and I knew she was thinking, 'I'm sick of this. She is looking for a Taj Mahal and she just needs to wake up to herself.'

I think everyone got sick of me talking about how expensive everything was and how dreadful everything was in my price range.

There was one ground floor place I was keen on. It had been tarted up for the auction and the courtyard was full of pot plants, giving a Balinese look rather like the courtyard of my favourite house. A huge mirror hung on the back wall of the living room that reflected the garden so the space looked enormous. It felt glamorous. The auction took off and in no time it had soared past my meagre budget.

At the end of the auction, a guy standing next to me said, 'A ridiculous price. All smoke and mirrors. Take that mirror away and you'd see there is no space in the lounge. The garden only gets sun at midday that's why the auction is now. Good thing you didn't get it.'

'I'm a bit disappointed. I thought I would like it. It's so hard to find anything.' I was feeling dispirited.

He laughed. 'I live round the corner and I wouldn't live here. The bins for all the apartments are on the other side of the courtyard fence. A good smell to have wafting in on a forty-degree day. You'd have to wear a gas mask if you were out there.' He wandered off.

I just stood there. I hadn't noticed the bins. I had been too busy looking at the garden reflected in the mirror. I did need help. I needed a shot of reality injected into my veins.

Emily injected the reality. She arranged an appointment to view her find.

The unit was on the first floor. My preferred floor. I feel safer there. The agent swept open the door and we went in.

'This is a deceased estate and it hasn't been on the market long. We're hoping to sell it quickly. There's already been a lot of interest in it.'

Emily and I ignored the bit about the interest. We work in the industry. We know all about that. What I could not ignore was the wallpaper and the worn floral carpet. It was dreary. The place had an all over brown tone. Emily pointed out the rooms were spacious and the balcony a good size. It was like Goran's diamond in the rough. For me the diamond was well buried.

I expressed my thoughts on the drabness and the brown to Emily. She ignored me and discussed the price with the agent.

Then she said to him, 'It'll take a bit of work. Not ready to move into, yet.'

He agreed that it wasn't quite ready to move into. Emily took his card and we left.

In the car, she said, 'It's great. Just what you want. You can afford it but let's see if we can get him down a bit. He wants a quick sale.'

'I couldn't live there with it like that. It's brown and floral.'

'All it needs is a coat of paint, the carpet lifted and the floor polished. A piece of cake.'

Why couldn't I see that? I have been around real estate for a while now but I imagined I would find a property I loved and just walk in and it would be perfect. With my money I was dreaming. Emily cut through that dream and made me see reality. It took me a couple of days but I did see it. I will be grateful to her forever.

Sometimes when I am feeling extra pleased with my purchase I think I would crawl over broken glass for her, but that would be the red wine talking. Once I thought I would ring and tell her but I managed to stop myself. Emily doesn't like over the top.

The moment I signed the papers I was elated. Just like Ralph. I had done it. There was no auction so I had a three-day cooling-off period. I didn't need it. I felt released. I had secured my own place. The hunt was over. My goal had been achieved. I don't think any of my colleagues said congratulations to me. They may have congratulated Emily. I think there were a couple of 'well dones' and I could see everyone was relieved. The guy that sold it to me said congratulations, and for a moment it made me wonder if I had paid too much for it. I brushed that thought away. I bought it – that's what mattered. And the Boron curse was behind me.

I had the dreary walls hidden behind a few coats of Dulux Antique White USA and the floors lime washed.

When I suggested lime washed floors the advice flowed freely.

'Oh, you don't want to do that. It'll be too white.'

'Oh no! You don't want white floors. They'll get dirty. You'll never keep them clean.'

'It will be glary. You want timber coloured floors. Something neutral.'

I'd got my mojo back. I was no longer despondent. Buying my own place was empowering. I went with the lime wash and I love it. The brown and the drab are a faint memory.

Why couldn't I see what Emily could? I was struggling like a non-swimmer at the deep end of the pool. I couldn't see how to get out of the deep water I had thought myself into. I can't believe now how hard I made it for myself.

* * *

Back at the office I leave my notes and the keys I didn't need on Emily's desk, with a note saying 'Talk to me about it.'

It is nearly time to leave for the inspection at Bruno's property.

Before I do, I ring Lauren to see if she has heard back from The Rev about Ralph's bond. She hasn't and will wait until tomorrow to check it out. That doesn't seem a good sign. If the Rev didn't have any issues he would have come back to her this afternoon. I bet he is fixated on the M word. Mould has reared its ugly head today. I feel protective towards Ralph. I see him as a friend and I want it to go well for him. She asks me if I have told Bruno about the inspection. The answer is a firm 'No'.

* * *

I pull up at Princess Street to a small group of people and a dog. I look at the brown and white terrier and I wish I had not likened myself to a terrier after a rat. I have spooked up this animal and brought him to life.

I grab the keys, trot over to the front door and open up. No lock problems here. Before I can say anything about the dog, one couple pushes in. It is not their dog. There is always someone who pushes to the front. You see them at airports and on trains and you see them at open for inspections.

As I begin my dog speech, the couple are out again. It is not for them. Not modern enough.

It is dad's dog, and they have all walked round from his house, two streets away, to see the place. The dog is introduced to me as Cody. He goes in with them. I want to say, 'No. No. I'll hold Cody. It's no dogs.' But that sounds silly. I am just glad I didn't tell Bruno about the inspection. If he turned up and saw they had a dog, even if it was dad's, there is no way he would have them for tenants.

I leave them to it and stay outside. That way, I can't see Cody wandering around and sniffing everything.

They take a long time but finally they leave and ask for applications, then decide to apply on line.

Dad says it is a bit run down, but okay, and his daughter Joanne is positive about it because the back courtyard is completely private. Her partner, Rod, doesn't say anything to me.

I explain that if their references check out Bruno will need to meet them before he will accept them. I think it is good for them to know this in advance.

'Fair enough,' said dad. 'We'd be okay with that wouldn't we?' The other two nod.

If we get that far I will tell them on the phone not to bring Cody. I lock up and head off to a local pub to meet a group of friends from my college days that I catch up with most Tuesdays.

Tuesday is locals' night with all the meals costing $15. If I am lucky, it will still be happy hour when I get there.

I try not to think further about these tenants. I may jinx it. They still have to discuss it at home, and I remember dad's remark about it being a bit run down and Rod still has to express his opinion. I won't even keep my fingers crossed. I will put it right out of my mind. It is easy to do that with a glass of wine and a lady parmigiana and everyone talking about their day. I should order something else. I always order parmigiana. The parmigiana, even a lady size, is not exactly light on calories. I love them and they are the best at this place.

I listen to everyone talking about their day and I shut up about mine. I'm not giving the jinx a chance.

Wednesday

Chapter 14

Eight-thirty, time for the weekly property managers' meeting. We drift into Caruthers' boardroom. This is in our sales office at the other end of the retail strip, giving us an excuse to be late.

'Boardroom' is a very grand name for this cream painted office. In the centre is an oval table made from laminate in a pale-wood colour with uncomfortable grey chairs dotted around it. A screen for presentations covers one wall; a couple of large display trestles like those used by portrait painters are on the other side. A high, oblong window runs along the fourth wall. At the moment, this window is giving a view of a large construction site that will eventually become an apartment complex. I have wondered if, when it's finished, we'll be lucky enough to peer into someone's apartment. That would give extra spice to spending an hour or so in this drab room. There is so much construction going on around here that this sort of thing is bound to happen; look out one window and straight into another.

We usually sit in the same place, like people who regularly go to a church service. I like the right-hand side of the table about half-way down. Emily sits at the top near the doorway.

We invite Lisa, as she deals with the never-ending flood of over-the-counter and phone enquiries. She needs to be up to speed if she is to retain her place as The Pivot in the company. She likes to sit on Emily's left. Today she has brought Vicky who is sitting next to her.

The property managers from our two smaller offices are in attendance, as well our administrative assistant. All these people turning up give the meeting an air of importance.

Mandy clicks her newly French polished and gelled nails along the desk. She got the extensions last week and is rather proud of them. Running them along the shiny laminate appears to give her pleasure. I find it irritating, but I can see why she's doing it. Last week she had nails bitten as far back as the first knuckle. These new nails have done wonders for her short stubby fingers. It is hard to nibble away at all that acrylic or whatever the gel is. Last week she couldn't make the irritating clicking noise, though.

Emily arrives and puts an apple down beside her. She brings the meeting to a start with her usual words, 'Are we all here?'

We're not, because at that minute Skye arrives, panting as if she has run up stairs.

'Sorry! Sorry! Trouble parking,' she says as she flops into a chair.

We begin.

Emily is a good chair. She stays calm. As I listen to her welcoming us, I look around and see that everyone is sipping a coffee from Jono's takeaway cups. This is not a bad haul for Café Yellow at $2.50 a pop. If Jono was charging full price, they could have come from any one of the numerous cafés around here. Even time-pressed Skye managed to stop off there to get one. Other cafés take note, if you treat your local fellow workers right, they stick by you.

Emily hasn't got one. Her pale green apple appears to be her crutch this morning. What's with the apple? Has she brought it as a visual aid for some point she is going to make? Or is she going to sink her white teeth into the green skin in a moment of boredom?

The main reason for the Wednesday meeting is to discuss any general business, check any arrears and compile a list of all the properties that we want open for inspection on Saturday.

We start with the Saturday opens.

Our administrative assistant, Hayley, has the list on her laptop and Emily has a printed one in her hand. Hayley used to be a property manager but prefers this job. She prefers dealing with paper rather than people. She can go for days without speaking to a tenant or a landlord. She says this make the job worth doing.

She arranges the order for Saturday's opens and looks after the rental listings on the website. This has the advantage of giving our website uniformity. It can become a big mess when every property manager is fiddling around with their own properties, loading things up any-old-how and often making mistakes. The motto in our office is, 'Leave it to Hayley, she'll sort it'. It is a different story when she goes on holiday. We panic. It is not a job I want. I prefer people to paper.

As we go through the opens' list, we come to Bruno's place in Princess Street, with Skye's name beside it.

'That's ridiculous!' she says immediately. 'No one should have to open that place again. I have personally opened it at least six times. It's not as if we don't get people through and give out applications. It's a joke.'

We are all silent and her voice hangs there. She comes from Caruthers Bayside, and doesn't hold back.

Emily clears her throat. 'I know it's frustrating, far more so for Lauren than anyone else, as it's in her portfolio. Remember, we are working for the landlord and we have to follow his instructions.'

'Well, I think it's stupid. We should get rid of him. Ask him to come and get his file,' Skye's voice is softer this time, more conversational. No one else says anything. Most of us think the same as Skye. Management are always reluctant to ask a landlord to take their file somewhere else. The landlord represents money. We put up with a lot from landlords.

I bring everyone up to speed.

'I showed a couple of groups through yesterday, after work. One couple seems keen. Said they would apply online.' I turn to Lauren. 'If their application comes in, could you flick it through to me and I'll get onto it?'

'In your dreams,' Skye grins at me.

'Well, let's think positively,' says Emily and we begin to go through the arrears.

Here, we are concerned with tenants who are ten days late on their rent, and we add their names to the list. At this time of the year there are more defaulters than usual. That's because it's at the end of the holiday season. Some tenants put their fun before a roof over their head. This amazes me. It is hard to have much fun if you are living on the street.

Emily is checking who has paid since last week and if we have issued vacate notices to those who haven't.

Hayley puts any new defaulters into her laptop.

Mandy, who is usually quiet and laid back at these meetings, says apologetically, 'I've got one who is more than ten days in arrears. I sort of forgot about them.' Then she adds in a rush, 'Actually they are now about twenty days overdue.'

We all stare at her. Discussing arrears at these meeting is supposed to mean no one slips through the net. Emily prides herself that her department always has the arrears under control. It is something she plugs when she's pitching for new business. 'We come down hard on rent defaulters! We don't have arrears.'

Mandy clicks her new nails on the table. She gives the address of the property. 'They always pay on time and I thought they'd pay. I rang and left a voice message but they haven't got back to me and then I sort of forgot about them.' Only Mandy would 'sort of forget' people who weren't paying their rent. Her mind is more on what her bridesmaids will wear. Should they match or colour coordinate? She has been discussing that.

'Have you spoken to the landlord?' asks Emily

'No.'

'Do that as soon as you get back to your desk. It's a wonder he hasn't been in touch complaining about his lack of money. Perhaps he's on holiday.'

'He has to be on holiday. He doesn't like these tenants. He thinks they should mow the lawn more often.'

Skye says, 'I bet it's pretty long if they've done a runner. His next drive-by should be interesting.' We all laugh and it eases the tension.

Emily says, 'Even if you can't get hold of him, issue the tenants with a notice to vacate today and keep trying to contact them.'

I can see Emily is a bit tetchy about this. It's hard to know how it will play out. A very angry landlord would seem to be the result. He probably over-spent on Christmas, too.

'Let me know later today where you're at with it,' adds Emily. She turns to Hayley, 'Make sure it's on the list to follow up next week. But I hope we have it sorted by then. We can't have tenants getting behind like this.'

Mandy nods, but doesn't comment and I notice she doesn't click her nails this time.

Emily flaps her list of properties scheduled to be opened. 'Let's see if we can lease some of these and get everyone to sign up before Friday. We've got too many on the list and it's going to be hot on Saturday.'

Everyone groans, even those who aren't working, and I am one of those lucky ones.

Emily is looking strained. I think she wants to have a real go at Mandy and she is keeping herself in check. It is not her style to bawl someone out while we are all together.

'Now, to general business,' she continues. 'We have arranged for an in-service course on time and desk management for next month.' She goes on quickly before anyone can say anything. 'This is for everyone. If you think you know it all, it will be a refresher for you. There are two dates. I'll send an email around and you can let me know which date you prefer.' A few of us look at Lauren; perhaps the state of her desk has prompted this. I wonder if Emily got one of the promotional emails on Monday that sold the idea to her.

I'm happy. Courses are fun. We get to meet other property managers and usually there's great food for lunch or morning tea. Sometimes both. Why am I focusing on the food? I need to eat less and drop some weight. Warm muffins at an in-service course are not going to help. Of course the food is there so it would be silly not to eat it. It is like a breakfast buffet. I'm not one of those people who say, 'Oh, I only eat a little muesli for breakfast,' then to prove it serve themselves a small quantity and go back to their seat, looking smug while everyone else is diving right in. I am of the dive in variety. Where else are you going to get such a choice? Not at my home; you can eat a little muesli there.

Emily turns to Vicky. 'I hope you've all met Vicky by now. Let's try to make her job an easy one while Lisa's away. If you can help her out, please do so and be a bit patient until she's up to speed. It's a busy reception and it's easy to get flustered.'

That's kind of Emily. She's right – it is easy to panic when the phone is ringing and people are waiting. Not that Lisa ever gets flustered, and she doesn't care if people are hanging around waiting. She lets them wait.

'Unless anyone has anything urgent to bring up we'll finish now,' says Emily, as if she is keen to get rid of us. There is hardly time to draw breath before she says, 'Okay, off you go and have a good day.' I'm waiting for her to sink her teeth into the apple. She doesn't do that, instead she picks it up and carts it off with her. Just a bit of stylish decor? It is a very pretty green colour.

We troop out behind her and I can see Lauren is hoping to have a second coffee with a friend from Caruthers Dennison. I grab her arm. 'What?' she says, then 'Oh, you want to know if there is an app on Princess Street.'

'Yeah. I have a good feeling about these people.'

She raises her eyebrows. 'I'll bet you a glass of wine it all comes to nothing. In fact, I'm so sure I'll make it two glasses.'

'Okay,' I laugh. 'I'll hold you to that!'

I head to my desk thinking about Emily. She used to live with one of the electricians we use. He is an older guy who runs his dad's company. I know they 'consciously uncoupled' about the time Tim and I broke up. We discussed our break-ups. We talked a lot, but I'm not quite sure what went wrong for her. It may be that I did all the talking and she didn't get a chance to say much. I was not happy with the 30s mid-life crisis thing – drifting into the wild-blue beyond. I thought it was mad, and I was angry. I let my feelings be known. I couldn't shut up about it. I think Emily let me talk while she said very little. She's a private person. She's friendly with us but only to a certain extent. She believes that as the boss, she should keep her distance. She needs to be the same with everyone – no besties in the office. It seems to work. Every-one respects her.

She has never mentioned she's dating anyone else and there is no gossip around the office. I think, like me, she's giving the whole couple thing a bit of a rest. I am doing that while I regroup and experience living in my own place. It would be living on my own if I had not felt lonely and invited Amy to share. My mind moves to Amy's friend Lee. I hope he's there fixing the toilet at this very moment. I have no idea when he planned to do this. Now would be the time, is my thinking.

There's an email from Emily: *Thanks for doing the routine with Goran yesterday. I'll take it from here.* I'm pleased. I think getting quotes and working with Goran could be stress-ful. He is the type who is always going to want to pay less than the job's worth and then he will criticise the end product. I have seen people like him before. I will be interested to know if he finally agrees to have the kitchen drawers fixed. I had thought of volunteering to follow it all through as a chance to show just how helpful and ready I am to take on more respon-sibility. I think Emily's email was quite clear and not open for discussion. No need to do any volunteering.

* * *

Small miracles do happen. Last night's tenants have applied for Bruno's property. I was anxious that Rod, who was so quiet, didn't like it. Sometimes it is the quiet ones who later give something the thumbs down.

I keep calm. I'm not getting too excited as I check them out. They both have jobs which they have been in for two months since returning from overseas and I get positive reports on them. Their rental history is in England and I can check that by email if Bruno needs it. He's not too worried about a lack of rental history. Meeting them is the cruncher for him.

I ring Bruno to give him a rundown.

The first thing he says when he answers is, 'What's happened to my lock. I've been thinking about it all night.'

Somehow Bruno has taken possession of his daughter's property. It has become his. Do dads do this? I wouldn't know. My dad died many years ago and Mum's Clive is more like a friend. He is a lot younger than Mum – nearer my age.

I don't answer Bruno's question, instead I say, 'I've got an application on Princess Street. I showed a group through after work yesterday. Can we talk about them first?'

'An application! I talked to you yesterday and you didn't tell me you were having an open.'

'Well, it wasn't really an open – I just took these people through because they were interested.'

'You could've told me. I was free yesterday. I could've come along.' I thought of Cody and was glad all over again that I didn't do that.

'It was a last minute thing.'

'So, what do you think? They'll be okay?'

'I liked them. I think they could be good tenants.'

'Well, fax me over their applications and arrange a meeting. I can be there anytime this afternoon. When you come back to me, I want to talk about the key.'

***

I fax the applications and set up a meeting for the end of the day. I ring Bruno to tell him the time.

'Now, about that lock,' he says, and I find myself wanting to run away. I give a little shudder as I answer. 'There's no email from the tenants. I think we should give it another day before we worry about it. Let's concentrate on these tenants and what you think of them.' He makes some noise that I take as agreement. I say goodbye and hang up.

I confirm the time with Joanne and explain about Bruno's aversion to dogs and if they like the place it would be better to leave Cody at home. They seemed to get it. I hope they have. Taking your dog for a walk when you are just going around the corner is the normal thing to do.

Chapter 15

Many landlords have strong prejudices and often hostilities when it comes to selecting tenants. Their dislikes can be just as strong as Bruno's. This is one that struck me as odd. I encountered it when I signed up a new landlord.

He owned a charming three-bedroom villa unit that had just been painted throughout, with new carpet and curtains in the lounge. It was in one of those semi-circles with the drive down the middle and the villas built on each side of it. This one was right at the end. It is an ideal place to be because no one drives past it. The owners corporation maintained the front gardens and the tenants had to look after their own private back area. A good rental property.

We chatted and I went through my usual spiel about percentages and the advantages of signing up with us. He seemed okay with it all, and then he said very firmly, 'You said I could make choice of tenant.'

'Yes,' I replied.

'I don't want Asian. No Asians in my unit.'

I looked at him and I must have looked surprised because he was obviously Asian.

'No Asian. No Asians cooking in my unit.'

I got a picture in my head of a stove covered in tin foil. Some Asians are very careful cooks.

As if he was reading my thoughts he said, 'I know how Asians cook. They not cook in my unit.'

'Okay,' I say.

'Yes. Not in my unit. In my family, I cook. I cook in garage.'

'What about your car?'

'In drive. Very secure. Garage for cooking.' I got a picture of him stooped over some burner in his garage with the overhead light blazing but perhaps he keeps the door open. I hoped it had a door straight into the house. Without that, it would be a bit grim in the winter.

'Yes,' he went on firmly. 'No Asian. I had old man who was here before. Not cleaning. The toilet…very bad. Not flushing. I had to replace. Very angry. His bond, not enough for cleaning and painting. No more Asians. You write that down.'

This friendly Asian man signed up with our company, and we followed his instructions.

I think landlords have a right to feel angry when their property is damaged. They let off steam by shouting and threatening us. They call our professionalism into question and suggest they could get our licence to operate revoked. If we get the tenants to pay for the damage, they usually calm down. This man obviously decided to move agents. He became our client and we followed his instructions. He did not mention smoking. Smoking can cause problems.

We have a clause in our lease saying tenants must smoke outside. At the first routine inspection if it is obvious that the tenant misread this clause I point out that smoking must be outside. Tenants always agree to this and I confirm the conversation in writing.

They might smoke outside for a couple of weeks then the weather turns or they wake in the middle of the night and need a ciggie and fall back into their old habits. I can tell this when I go next time and the place still reeks of smoke.

Smoking on the balcony, which is essentially outside, can also cause trouble. Flick a glowing butt over the edge and you don't know where it will land. Too often it lands on a balcony below where it can do all sorts of damage before it finally goes out. Fortunately, most outdoor tables and chairs don't burst in flames.

I'm always pleased to see a squalid tin of butts on the balcony during an inspection. Usually the tin is half full of rain water and revolting but it tells me that smoking is outside and the butts are not flicked.

It is not only cigarette butts that can cause a problem on balconies. There is an owner-occupier in a large complex who caused problems for one of our tenants.

My tenant, who lived on the first floor, complained about straw appearing on her balcony. The balconies are a good size and the photos she sent showed pieces of straw near the edge of hers. It looked like pea straw. I thought the upstairs resident was using it as mulch on the pot plants. If you stood in the common area, this balcony looked lush with plants and bamboo – rather tropical and obviously a lot of pots to keep nurtured. Pea straw helps stops water evaporation.

There was not much I could do, and I told her that. In the photos there were only a few pieces of straw. Not really enough to make a fuss about, but I suggested she go and talk to the people in the unit where the straw was coming from. She didn't do this.

A few months went by then I got another email with a photo showing considerably more straw. Straw that according to my tenant smelt vile.

I contacted the owners corporation to see who managed the apartment. That's when I discovered it was owner-occupier so no property manager for me to get onto. My tenant invited me to have a look at the straw. She kept it in a supermarket bag until I found time to come and view it. The bag was about half full. She was right – it did smell bad. It nearly knocked me over.

The obvious answer was for my tenant to go upstairs and talk to the people above her. She was't going to do this.

'Talking to them is your job. You're my property manager.'

I trotted upstairs expecting them to be out at work.

I was wrong. A smiling young woman with long dark hair and a toddler clinging to her leg came to the door. I explained the problem.

'Oh.' she said, 'that would be straw from our guinea pig.'

She took me out onto the balcony and there amongst the foliage was a cage housing two sweet, long haired and rather beautiful guinea pigs.

'I didn't know the straw floated downstairs. They do like to scratch about and kick it all up. Why didn't she tell me?'

I mentioned the recent smelly stuff. She was puzzled then she said, 'Oh! Of course! I know what that would be. We were away and friends came to feed them but didn't clean out the cage.' She smiled. 'I don't suppose we could expect them to. It isn't the nicest job. My husband did it when we got back and I guess he wasn't very careful. Tell her I'm sorry.'

'Could you try to be more careful?' I said. 'It does upset her to have straw floating around.'

'Of course,' said the guinea pig owner. 'She should have come and told us if it bothered her.'

That was my thinking too.

A few weeks later, more strands of straw landed on my tenant's balcony. She took another photograph and emailed it to me. What else could I do? Sneak up at night like a cat burglar swinging from balcony to balcony and dispatch the guinea pigs? But then they would be replaced. If you like guinea pigs, you like having them. The straw would still float and my tenant would still send me photos.

In the end she left without ever having spoken to the guinea pig owners. I think that was her loss. By insisting that I deal with the issue she may have missed a friendship. I liked the guinea pig lady.

It is ridiculous the way some tenants think their property manager is there to deal with the smallest thing that upsets them. We have enough to do and sometimes, just sometimes, common sense could prevail. Common sense should send a tenant off to discuss a problem with an offending neighbour. The neighbour may not know there is a problem and be happy to fix it. Common sense is a quality we should value and it is rarely found by property managers.

A ping from my computer announces incoming email.

Who belongs to the toilet seat stored beside the reception desk? It appeared earlier in the week. There is no room for it here. If it is yours, please remove it asap. Only email if it is yours. Do not email with all sorts of funny comments. Vicky and I are very busy today.

I laugh. The seat is nothing to do with me, and I curb my urge to send a funny email.

My guess is that a landlord has bought a really cheap toilet seat, one that was on special and left it for the handyman to pick up and install.

Our handyman will get a replacement seat himself but he's going to charge to do this and he won't bother to find the cheapest. The first that comes to hand will do for him.

* * *

Landlords are on my mind, and I remember another one who was very clear about a nationality he didn't want.

Carlos would not allow English tenants in his property. If they were English, he turned them down. He didn't want to know anything about them. The fact they were English was enough. If you valued your job, you would not put an English person in his property. You could bet your life he would find out and the proverbial would hit the fan.

He believed he had a good reason. He owned a smart town house in a complex in a desirable area of the city with a very large tree nearby. We signed up an English lawyer John and his wife. John instructed us to put the lease in his name. He had a three-year contract with a company here, and it looked like an excellent choice of tenant and everyone was happy at the beginning but it quickly went downhill.

John hated the leaves from the tree. These leaves fell on the property and onto the balcony outside the bedroom. They fell onto the couple's car too, which they parked in the street, but that didn't seem to bother them. It was the balcony. If they had the door open, the leaves blew inside. John wrote emails about this. He rang up. He said their cleaner (who came weekly) should not have to sweep them up. It was the landlord's responsibility to get rid of them. The landlord should arrange for this to be done.

Carlos didn't see it as his responsibility.

After one heavy downpour, the drain on the balcony was so blocked with the leaves no one had bothered to clean up, that the water flowed into the bedroom, soaking the carpet and damaging a brief case. According to John's email it was an extremely expensive brief case he had bought from some exclusive place in London. He didn't accompany the email with a copy of the receipt. This had disappeared in the move, and apparently could not be duplicated.

John – and it was always John, I never heard from or met his wife – disturbed my sleep, his name appearing in my in-box ruined my whole day. I would wonder how long I could wait before replying and before he emailed again demanding attention. He wrote long, involved emails. Perhaps that was the lawyer in him. He made Carlos so angry he could hardly speak about him.

John demanded a rent reduction because since the flood they couldn't sleep in the bedroom, therefore as they were one room short they should only have to pay rent for two bedrooms not three. The wet carpet was professionally dried, steam cleaned and deodorised, then dry-cleaned. John said that they could still smell damp and would not sleep with the damp smell.

Various people from our office took their noses along to sniff. They could smell cleaning products, but definitely no damp. John had recorded his nose registering a damp smell in various emails. His nose was more sensitive than all of our combined noses.

'Bloody English,' said Carlos when he visited. He could not smell anything not even the cleaning products when he applied the nose test.

John caused Carlos to get into trouble with the owners corporation. They rang Carlos to say another resident in the complex had reported that there were household items and rubbish stored in his parking space. This was against the owners corporation rules. He needed to get everything removed.

If Carlos had bothered to tell the owners corporation that we managed the property, he would not have got caught up in this problem.

He rang me.

'What stuff? What are they talking about?' he spluttered. Words were failing him. I could hear his heavy breathing. 'Get them to get rid of everything at once, like immediately. I don't care if you have to carry it out yourselves. I'm not having the owners corporation on my back.'

I went to have a look. Our Englishman had a few pieces of furniture, a fan, a drying rack, a stack of boxes and a pile of flattened cartons dumped there. They spilt over into the next door parking spot. It made his end of the otherwise neat undercover area look like a tip.

I could see why John's car was on the street. There was no room for it here.

We sent John a breach of duty notice giving him fourteen days to move the stuff.

After fourteen days I went back to see what had happened. Nothing. Everything was just as it was.

I emailed him with a copy of the breach notice attached and pointed out that fourteen days had passed. He immediately fired back his answer. His point was that he rented the parking space. There was nothing in his lease to say he had to put his car in it. He could use it how he liked. He also went on about how he was already paying for a room he couldn't use. His emails included everything he had brought up in the past, even if was not relevant to the current issue.

I got caught up in this and stupidly said that his belongings were creeping into the next door space which he did not rent. Thereby giving credence to his statement about renting it and doing what he liked with it. John noted this in an email.

He maintained that all the items were not his. Other people dumped stuff in his space. He may have been right. If you have something you want to get rid of, you sneak out at night and add it to a pile of items that look exactly like rubbish waiting to be removed.

Some of the things he claimed other people had dumped there and were creeping out of his spot had his name on them - photos showed this clearly.

We sent another breach notice. The only thing that happened was that he re-stacked the items, including those he said were not his. The adjoining park was now free of them.

Issues like these make landlords aware that it is not easy to get a tenant out of their property if they are paying their rent. The landlord wants them gone, but there is no legal way to do it.

Carlos told me that finding John in a dark alley and taking a baseball bat to his legs would be one way. I am sure he was serious. He sounded it. I didn't warn John of the impending danger to his limbs. It was hard to visualise him strolling along a dark and undesirable alley. He was more likely to be at an upper-class restaurant waiting for a chauffeur to take him home.

I took heed of the threat. I stayed away from dark alleys in case Carlos felt the same way about me.

There is a window of opportunity where you can give your tenant 90 days' notice to vacate that coincides with the end of their fixed-term lease. I was so busy dealing with all the

issues I forgot to do this until it was too late. I felt inefficient, apologetic and more concerned for my limbs. Strangely,
Carlos accepted my mistake without too much fuss which
made me like him immensely and dislike John more but I still
watched my legs.

John's fixed-term lease expired and he moved to a month-
to-month tenancy. I carefully followed the legislation and
gave him a '120 days notice to vacate with no particular reason'. He did not dispute this and they left before the 120 days
were up.

They took most of their stuff with them and we used the
bond to get rid of the leftovers. Oddly, John didn't complain.
He signed the bond claim with the deductions without disput-
ing it. Perhaps he was sick of it all, too.

The mystery was John's wife? We never saw her. She never
emailed or rang the office. If we had not seen women's clothes
and toiletries in the townhouse, we would have believed her to
be a phantom. We supposed she had a hidey-hole somewhere.
Or were John and his wife the same person? A cranky lawyer
in the daytime and a glamorous woman in the evening? It did
seem odd that there was never a sighting of her and she never
answered the landline. He left a mystery behind.

As I said, Carlos would never have an English tenant again
but any other race was fine. After John we found a German
couple who we never heard from. Carlos would have Ger-
mans again in a heartbeat.

I believe it was the lawyer in John, not the English, that
caused the problems but Carlos was having none of that. He
had a lot to say about the 'Bloody English'.

Chapter 16

On Wednesday, we contact all the landlords whose properties will be open on Saturday to discuss the advertised rent and whether we think it should be dropped to get more action. I begin that process.

We often think the rent needs an adjustment but the landlords can have a different take on it. Some think if you lower the rent you are somehow lowering the value of the actual property.

There are some landlords who know exactly what the rent should be and it is our job to get it. Often a friend has told them what the place is worth and they believe the friend over us. What would we know?

Sometimes landlords explain how a friend or relative has told them that the rent they are advertising is a bit low, so the tenant is actually getting a bargain. A landlord who has an empty property without much action can express this view.

Other landlords think because they have done some work, painting, replacing an old stove, putting in a dishwasher or replacing the old flooring, the rent should go up to cover this outlay. Usually this work means the property is keeping up with the market. Without the work, it would be going backwards.

An empty property can cost the landlord. It can be hard to explain to an owner that the empty property is losing more money than it would lose overall if the rent was lowered and we got a tenant.

Have a look at this example.

A property is advertised at $420 per week, but the market price is more like $400. If this property sits vacant for four weeks, it will cost the landlord $1680 in lost rent. If the property is advertised at the market price, that is $400 per week, and let in the first week, the landlord will actually be $640 better off over one year even though the rent is lower. You may want to check my maths.

There is also the old adage, 'property is only worth what someone will pay for it'. That applies to rentals too. Rents can fluctuate depending on the time of the year. In January and February, you can get a better rent than say June and July when there is not so much demand. It makes sense. Who wants to move in the middle of winter unless they have to?

At the moment, newspapers and news broadcasts are making the job harder when advertising with the right rent. They are full of articles about the state of the rental market. According to an article written last week, properties are in such demand, prospective tenants are making offers well above the asking price and people are becoming homeless because they cannot find somewhere to rent.

This may be so in another city or another suburb. It's not like that in the market where we operate. The cheapest place on my list last Saturday was a large one-bedroom unit in a rather dodgy block for $310 per week. There were four groups through it on Saturday and only one group applied. These applicants checked out and will move in. The rent was right, but three people thought they could get a better deal somewhere else.

Journalists would do us a favour if they were more specific and identify exactly where this demand for rentals is happening. They could list the places where there is not a huge demand and where a bargain may be possible, but I guess that is not a headline story. 'Priced Out of the Rental Market' is attention grabbing.

* * *

I ring the man who wants more sausages through his property with the idea of getting him to lower the rent.

He's ahead of me.

'I know what you're going to say to me. That I should drop the rent by $10. Well, I'm not going to – not yet anyway.'

I say, 'I think a rent drop would help you get more people through on Saturday. And you're right, I was going to suggest $10 a week.'

'Yeah, I do want more people but what I really want is one person that wants it. I've been looking at the ad, and the photos don't do it justice. Did you take them?'

'Yes,' I admit. 'Don't you remember I suggested we get a professional photographer and you didn't think it was necessary?'

'I still don't think it's necessary. I'll send you through some that I've taken. They're better than yours. See if they make a difference this Saturday. We'll leave the rent the same for this week. Saturday's going to be hot. That should be good for business.' Where did that thought come from? His take on the heat is different from mine.

I agree to use his photos and accept my photographic skills are not up to his standard. I don't take offence at this. What's the point? There's not much scope for creative and artistic photos in an empty cream-painted apartment. When his photos come through, Hayley can change them in the advertising.

Sometimes different photos do help. He may be lucky or he may have to bite the bullet and lower the rent.

The sausage man and I know each other well. We are not chatty, but over the years we have developed a good professional relationship. I managed another apartment of his before I came to Caruthers. After I had been here for a while he brought it over for me to manage. The place had spooked me, so I wasn't pleased to see it again but it did make me look good to have landlords following me from place to place. He is the opposite of Bruno who happily has his property empty for weeks on end. The sausage man gets agitated if he has more than a week's gap between tenants.

The property that followed me here is now occupied by one of his family members, but I remember it well. In particular, I remember an open I did there in the winter. Remember this happened in winter. Winter changes the dynamics.

It was a damp and foggy day when I arrived at his three-bedroom unit in a quiet tree-lined street.

I found three young men lounging around outside, waiting for me. I had the usual bunch of keys and, as always, it was the last key that opened the door into the block. This block shows individuality by having the unit numbers hidden behind heavy screen doors so they are only visible when the screen door is open. I ploughed up the stairs with the boys behind me. We studied the doors.

'Excuse me,' said one in a polite voice. 'I think seven is on the ground floor at the back.'

We ploughed down the stairs. He was right, and I went through all the keys again to find the unit key.

The boys spent a while looking around, then took application forms and headed out. One popped back. 'Excuse me. Are you here for much longer?'

'A few more minutes.'

'Would you like us to wait with you, so you're not on your own? We're not in a hurry. We could do that.'

I thanked him and said I was fine.

'Are you sure? It's no trouble for us.'

When I left, he and his mates were leaning on a fence at the corner of the street – proving they were not in a hurry. The street was empty. No one was around. It occurred to me that I had been in the unit for some time with just the three of them. What had been going through their heads? Why did they think I needed their company? We hadn't chatted – they had chatted amongst themselves. Was it just any company or theirs in particular I needed to stop being alone? I felt spooked.

It is interesting to think about the risk. Was it risky to be in there with them? Was it risky to be there on my own or was there no risk?

I headed to the next place and as I arrived the sun came out. A cat sat on a balcony bathed in a warm glow and watched me park the car and struggle with yet another bunch of keys and an armful of applications and rental lists. If I could look into the cat's head what would it be thinking? I would like to know that and I would like to know what the boys were thinking. It unsettled me.

I treated my unease like falling off a horse – get back on again immediately. I felt very brave when I thought this. The young men didn't apply for the place so I 'got back on the horse' and with lots of deep breaths and brave affirmations, I opened it the next weekend. Nothing unusual happened and I let it to a couple with a baby. When I think of the property now, it still feels a little sinister.

As I sit here at my desk with the back door open, breathing in the cheerful scent of the hot day, it is hard believe how spooked I was back then.

I can't remember being spooked in summer but I remember another time in winter when I let the spook get me.

* * *

It was early evening on a cold July day. I was collecting a key from a property we were about to manage. I had the address, the code for the gate and instructions that the key was under the door mat.

Again, it was a quiet tree-lined street with large, old and interestingly designed blocks that showed no uniformity or pattern. Some had gates at the footpath, others winding and tree-shadowed paths to the doors.

The one I was looking for had disappeared. There was no number 27. The street lights came on, the trees cast more shadows and the street numbers became harder to see. I searched through the gloom.

Number 27 was definitely missing. There was no number 27. The spook found me and edged in.

I watched workers head home. Dogs and their owners came back from the park. I walked up and down and crept into dark gateways. No 27.

Apartment lights flickered on and bright television screens beamed out from uncovered windows. In one room, a large glass of white wine waited on a pale wood table. In another a couple leaned on a kitchen bench, talking. Usually, I enjoy these glimpses of other people's lives. But that day I had let the spook get hold of me. It walked all over me.

I gave up and drove to one of the main thoroughfares where the shop lights lit up squares on the pavement and people surged up and down. It was an oasis of relief.

At home, I checked the lock on the door twice. I put on all my lights and pulled my blinds. I didn't want anyone looking in on my life. I put the heater on high and was secure and cosseted. I got rid of the spook.

As I said, on this bright Melbourne summer's day it is hard to believe I felt like that. It makes me feel rather silly when I remember how anxious I was to get home. I never managed that property, and I still avoid the street if I can.

***

Lauren has heard from The Rev and the news is not good. She walks down to my desk to talk about it and let off steam. She stands in the open doorway for the air and sun. She needs the air. She had mentioned the word mould to The Rev, so when he looked at the shadowy marks he knew immediately what it was. Mould.

The word is out there and we can't reel it in, however much we'd like to. It's unlikely The Rev, without Lauren's help, would have noticed the shadow or if he had, not given it a second thought.

'Don't put out too much unnecessary information' is a motto I try to stick to. I believe I am doing everyone a service with this motto. Too much information can only lead to confusion and worry. Perhaps it is a bit sneaky of me and I should praise Lauren for being so honest. It's a sun-less unit and being on the south-east corner of the building it's cold and therefore liable to mould, regardless of whether it was Ralph living there or the landlord himself. Not that I think The Rev ever envisaged residing there himself. Not The Rev's style.

He asked Lauren to get a quote to have the rooms painted and take the cost out of Ralph's bond. Lauren has spoken to Ralph. He has refused to have anything taken from his bond and hung up abruptly. Lauren, in something of a dilemma, goes back to her desk to ring the painters we use to arrange for a quote.

Ralph rings me. His charm is threaded with steel.

'Lauren tells me the landlord wants me to pay to have the place painted. I'm not having it,' he says very firmly. 'The walls needed painting when I moved in. I've got the condition report and I've checked it. 'Some wear marks' is written for all the paint work. What you really mean is 'marks on the walls'. I've been there for three years and there is no way I'm paying to have it painted because there is a dark shadow near the ceiling that could be mould. That's nonsense. It is perfectly reasonable to expect more wear marks after three years. I could have told him it needed painting when I moved in, but I didn't really care at the time.'

'I understand that you would feel like that. But Lauren is only following the landlord's instructions. That's what he has asked us to do,' I say. This is not helpful and I want to say, 'You're right to be angry,' but of course I don't. I represent the landlord, however much I disagree with him.

'You or Lauren can tell this landlord I want my full bond refunded. If he's not happy with that he can take me to VCAT.' Ralph rings off. No friendly chat.

Experience tells me that VCAT will not judge in The Rev's favour. They believe that after five years or so the owners should expect to repaint or recarpet.

Lauren rings The Rev to say she will get the quote, but Ralph is refusing to pay and did he want us to follow through and book a hearing at VCAT?

'Ring him again,' says The Rev. 'He'll be bluffing.'

Ralph rings me to make himself clearer. He will attend any hearing at VCAT that is demanding money from his bond and he will fight it. He can't believe that we are doing this after he has been such a good tenant.

'Three years and no problems for you or your landlord. He's been lucky. There's a lot I could've complained about. So what's his problem? Tell him to get a life.' I have never heard Ralph like this. I could have told him 'greed' was the problem. It is a common problem. We see it all the time.

I can see Ralph with his charm, likable manner and friendly smile winning the VCAT member over and getting us tossed out with the suggestion we are wasting everyone's time. The Rev may try to harness some charm from God, but God's charm, after it has come through the medium of The Rev, will not be a match for Ralph's.

In my head I can see Ralph's charm and likability getting him awarded a large rent refund, because the landlord has been lucky to have him. That never happens of course, but however fanciful a scenario, that would give some sort of justice. It would be fun to see it playing out. Some landlords don't know when they have had a good deal.

Lauren, after several stressful phone calls, is able to persuade The Rev not to continue with his demands for a paint job. Finding out he would be up for a fee for someone from our office to attend the VCAT hearing and learning he may not get anything from the bond, made him less keen to go ahead.

'He's not going to pay to have it painted himself,' says Lauren when she, once again, turns up at my desk. 'We're not to bother with the quote. He's decided it doesn't look too bad. He also said,' and she puts on a sort of pompous voice that captures The Rev, "the new tenant won't notice. It's a guy isn't? There you go. Guys don't notice that sort of thing"'.

I wonder if he was referring to himself and I think again that telling him about the supposed mould was a mistake. How is it I'm always right?

The new tenant will be Lauren's problem and I am interested to know whether he will notice anything. He won't have his attention drawn to it!

My last conversation with Ralph suggests I will never know how his 'cave' moved and settled into 'Further East'. That makes me sad. I will always wonder and I will miss him.

Chapter 17

These negotiations take us to lunch time. I try to bring my lunch most days. It is a bit of a chore sorting it out in the morning, but now I have a mortgage, these little economies still need to be part of my life. I tell myself it is worth it. I don't practise the economy on Monday. Monday doesn't need the extra stress of thinking about lunch at breakfast time. Yesterday I didn't get my act together, but this morning I was organised.

I'm in the kitchen fishing my boring chicken salad out of the fridge. I need to keep the carbs down, especially after last night's parma. Vince wanders in to toast his sandwich. We trek back to my desk and sit by the open door so we can pretend we are outside and not shut in an office. Vince's toasted cheese and ham smells delicious.

He is asking about Bruno and Princess Street, and I am trying to pull down positive images of Joanne, Rod and her father all chatting happily with Bruno. The pictures I work on do not have Cody in them. I hope I am sending the right vibes skywards.

Vince leans back in his chair with his feet on the edge of my desk. We are not saying much. Just sitting.

Emily appears clutching a bowl of instant noodles. 'Can I join you?'

Vince drops his feet to the floor and finds her a chair. 'Instant noodles!' I think. 'Is she trying to settle her stomach? Or is she on a low carbs kick?'

'How's it going?' asks Vince.

'Fine! I just need to get something in my stomach.'

'You don't look great!' says Vince. 'Are you sure you're okay?'

Emily shovels up some noodles and doesn't comment. I look at her and wonder about various diseases again. I wonder if she has an ulcer. That can make you pretty sick. I wonder what she has done with the pretty, pale green apple. It has not come to lunch. Was it something she did get into her stomach? Or did she just like the colour?

Vince used to work at a real estate company on the other side of the city. In the silence that follows his remark to Emily, he starts telling us about a problem he had when he was there.

'I had this landlord. A real nightmare. You'd never get one quite like him again – he's one out of the box. He owned a pleasant but unremarkable two-bedroom place. I put in an older couple who had their main house in the country and stayed a couple of nights a week in the city. Nightmare thought he was on to a winner – little wear and tear and they looked stable. After about nine months their circumstances changed and they wanted to break their lease. I explained about the penalties and they were fine about that, and when they moved their furniture out they paid another month's rent on the understanding that we would refund whatever they were owed when we got new tenants. All good. No issues and it sounded like a piece of cake. Nightmare was furious when he heard they were breaking their lease.'

'What was the problem?' Emily asked as she continued to fork up noodles.

'Hard to tell. He seemed to feel he was being cheated. He insisted on knowing as soon as the place was empty. I rang him to say the tenants had paid the rent and still had keys but they had essentially moved out. They had hired cleaners in so could I do a final bond inspection. Would Nightmare like to join me?'

Apparently Nightmare was eager to do this, but when Vince turned up there was no sign of him. He found out later that Nightmare had keys and had gone in the day before. Vince said he made it very clear that the tenants still had keys and were paying rent and he couldn't just walk in when he liked. I would say that in light of future events, Vince couldn't have been as clear as he thought he was.

'There's no way I could have been clearer. It was crystal.'

A couple of weeks later, Vince had the police on the phone checking out the legality of the tenancy.

'Do you know that the bloody Nightmare had gone in on a Sunday and snooped around the place? Just used his keys and barged in. He found a couple of sleeping bags and some clothes and removed them.'

These belonged to the daughter of the tenants breaking their lease and her friend. They came to Melbourne for the weekend and decided to spend a couple of nights in the property.

Vince went on. 'They were still paying rent so why would they book into a hotel? Apparently they arrived on Friday. Went to some big bash on Saturday where they stayed until Monday morning. Then they went back to collect their gear. Of course they found everything had gone. They rang the police. They were nervous about the break-in and sat outside in the cold while they waited for them.'

Vince said the police were puzzled as to how the thief had got in. There was no sign of forced entry and all the windows were intact. Not a broken one in sight. The police dusted for prints and told the girls to make a list of everything that was missing and explained how to get a police report for the insurance.

When the police were leaving, a locksmith turned up with instructions to change the locks. The locksmith had come with instructions from Nightmare. That is when Vince became involved. The police rang to check the status of the tenancy.

Nightmare had decided on Sunday, when he illegally entered, that squatters had moved in. He removed the girls' things and dumped them outside an op shop.

'I suppose you have to give it to the guy,' said Vince. 'He didn't just trash the stuff. He thought of the needy. Of course, when he dumped it in the op shop doorway it was Sunday and available for any passer-by to rat around in and they did. By late Monday it was impossible to recover anything.'

'What on earth was he thinking?' asks Emily.

'There's some frigging low life in my place. That's what he was thinking. He didn't ask himself any questions about how they got in. Or whether they should be there, or who they might be. Just got all agro, collected their stuff and dumped it.'

'Unreal,' says Lauren, who is now propped against my desk. She arrived with her sushi in time to hear most of the story.

'It was pretty unreal. I'd have liked to have seen his face when the police rang him. He found himself paying pretty heavy compensation for the stuff he disposed of. The sleeping bags turned out to be the type the girls would take on a Mt

Everest climb and they never bought anything from Target or K Mart. Everything came from trendy designer boutiques. The police warned Nightmare about entering a tenanted property without proper notice. He became quite subdued for a while. He even asked my opinion about things. He had never done that before. He always knew best.'

We all laugh.

Emily has finished her noodles.

'Is that all you are going to eat?' I ask.

'I'll get something later if I feel hungry.'

'I'm off to get another sushi,' Lauren says. 'I think they're making them smaller. I used to think two were enough but I'm still hungry. Perhaps dealing with The Rev has given me this appetite. Do you want me to get you one Emily?'

'No, I'm right. I've got some apples upstairs. I haven't eaten a Granny Smith apple for years. I saw them in the super-market and I had this urge to eat one, I've been eating them ever since.'

'I always thought they were for cooking.'

'No, you can eat them raw,' adds Mandy, who has turned up and seems to have a problem. She's looking anxious.

Emily turns to Lauren, 'Do you want to try one? I can't stop eating them now I've started. I sort of crave them. All that slightly tangy juice. Delicious. Better than chocolate. I've got some at my desk if you want one.'

'No, thanks. But they're a beautiful colour. I was looking at the one you had in the meeting. I'd love some shoes that colour.'

'It's a sort of summer green,' I say. 'Pale and beautiful.'

Kylie, who wanders along to put something in the outside recycling bin, nods, 'Yes. Wouldn't some strappy sandals in that colour look good?'

'You wouldn't want to call them Granny Smith.'

Kylie laughs and moves away, saying, 'I'm not seeing anything that suggests Granny. I'm looking at stylish and sophisticated.'

We all laugh and I get a picture of green strappy sandals with thin stiletto heels – perhaps silver heels.

'It's time for me to get back to work,' says Emily as she gets up. We all take the hint, if it was meant to be a hint.

'Well, anyone for sushi?' asks Lauren. 'I bet it's The Rev – I wanted something to eat the moment it was all sorted out. I just needed something. Sushi's better than cake, I suppose.' She is convincing herself rather than us.

Mandy says, 'Emily, before you go I want to let you know about the arrears.'

Emily turns to her, her face forming into a question.

'Hayley's doing a notice to vacate for me and I've tried to ring the tenants again but they're not answering.'

'Have you tried their next of kin? They may know where they are.'

'There's nothing on the system about them.'

All the information about our tenants and landlords is supposed to be loaded into our property management program. There can be failures with this – a busy day, someone in a hurry and a bit slack.

'Have you checked the paper files to see if there is anything there?' asks Emily. Her voice suggests she is still tetchy about this.

Our paper files are kept in a sort of large storage cupboard upstairs. It is rather like a pantry with shelves all around the wall. It is stuffy and hot and a place to avoid if possible.

'No. I didn't think about that.' What Mandy is thinking about is her wedding and the thousand and one details that need to be covered before she can marry her long-term boy-friend. 'I'll do that now.'

She and Emily head for the stairs.

***

I settle back at my desk and begin to type up some routine in-spection reports that I did last week and that are in my diary for action this afternoon. I am half-way through them when Vince shows up.

'Hey are you busy?'

'Well, I'm…

'You wouldn't believe it. The new tenants for Axminster Street want to move in on Friday. They can't get their re-movalist on Saturday. I'd planned to do the condition report on Friday…nice quiet day and I have it booked in for just be-fore lunch. I can't do it tomorrow because the builder is going in to fix a couple of things. You know how unreliable he is about times. I want to miss him and his long-winded conver-sations.'

'What's he fixing?'

'Nothing much. A couple of hinges, a window that's stick-ing and some drawer handles that are loose. Have you got time to come with me? We'd knock it off in less than half an hour if there are two of us.'

One of the things I like about this job is the chance to get out of the office. So I say yes, and put the inspection reports on hold. We head off with an iPad and the office camera.

The property is a modern three-level town house in ex-cellent condition. There are two bedrooms on the entry level with a family bathroom. On the second level there is a large living room, stunning kitchen, a powder room and a balcony.

Above these is the top floor with a large master bedroom, walk in robe and en suite. The bedroom opens onto a wide terrace that gives great views across the suburb to the city.

Vince uses the iPad and I take the photos. He's right – everything is spotless, and except for the minor maintenance, perfect. It takes me longer to take the photos than Vince to write it up. He leans on the terrace upstairs in the sun preening himself and looking at the view while he waits for me. He is so handsome and graceful; all he needs is a glass of bubbly to complete the picture. We resist that temptation and head back to the office where Vince prepares the condition report. Three copies, one for the office and two for the tenants. They make amendments, return the agent's copy to us and keep their copy.

I am back at my desk gazing at the printouts of the vacant properties I have on the pin board behind me. I am putting off getting back to the inspection reports. The mood has passed. I am admiring the pin board and wondering if I move some of the property printouts around I will get a better effect.

I like having the available properties in my portfolio displayed like this. I make comments on them so I can glance around and know exactly what is happening to each one. I have put them up artistically, not in straight, even rows. People who like symmetry could say they are all over the place, but I call it artistically arranged, like pictures on a living room wall.

While I am admiring this arrangement, Lisa puts a call from Bruno through to me.

'I rang you before but you were out. I want to talk about the lock.'

'I still haven't heard anything.'

'You said to wait but I've been thinking about it. Supposing the lock is broken, how are they going to get in when they come back?'

I find myself sighing. I try never to sigh, but this needs a sigh.

'What was that?' Bruno doesn't recognise it as a sigh.

'We should wait,' I say again.

'No, I want you to take your office keys and check if they work. I can meet you there in half an hour.'

'Bruno you can't go in even if our keys do work. You can't go in without their permission. We don't have their permission.' I say this very firmly and I'm sure my exasperation is in my voice.

'Okay, we won't go in, but I want to know if your keys work or not. I can be there in thirty minutes and it's not far from you.'

I'm silent while I process this. Bruno breaks the silence.

'You've got keys. I gave you a set. You haven't lost them have you?

'No.' I say

This is nuts I think. It's ridiculous. What on earth are we going to achieve?

'I'll see you there in half an hour. Bring your keys,' he hangs up.

I've been outmanoeuvred. How did that happen? I don't want to think Bruno's too smart for me but this is one up to him.

I trot upstairs to see Emily. I need to let her know what is happening here. This is not like a game. It is like some mad maze.

'That man can be a menace,' says Emily, with uncharacteristic condemnation of a landlord. 'I'll come with you. There needs to be two of us if we're opening their door. When are we going?'

'Well, more or less now. I'll meet you out the front in ten. I'll get our keys.'

'My car,' says Emily, as I head for the stairs.

I scramble into Emily's SUV. She has a company car park which means her car is right here. None of this hiking off to get it. She pulls into the traffic and says, 'Tell me again why we're doing this? Why does it matter if our key fits or not?'

I start to answer and she says, 'No, no, don't tell me. It'll be far too complicated. I wonder if Bruno's got nothing to do. A busy person isn't going to get involved in a Mickey Mouse performance like this.'

'We're busy and we're involved,' I say with a laugh.

'Well, what does that say about us?' She laughs again and she is starting to look a bit better. A bit more colour. Then she asks, 'What are the tenants like?'

'Bruno doesn't like them. His daughter wouldn't let him choose them.'

Emily laughs again. 'Good on her. I wonder how she managed it?'

We pull up and Bruno is waiting for us. He's holding the block's security entrance door open and moving from foot to foot, sort of hopping about as if his thin body was involved in a few dance moves. We get out and head for the door.

'Ah, there you are,' he says with his bony face creased into a frown. 'I've been here a while.' That can't possibly be true, unless he was here when he rang me.

Emily says, 'Hello Bruno. We haven't met for a while. How's it going?' Why did she ask that? He's going to tell us. He begins the saga of the keys in case she didn't know why she was here.

He bounds up the stairs leading the way to the unit while he's talking. Emily's not too good with the stairs. She's panting.

I try our keys in the door. All three of them. None work. Bruno, who is hopping about behind me, insists on having a go. They don't work for him either, even though he tries each key twice and spends time wriggling them around. Emily decides not to try. She accepts the results of our efforts and says, 'I'm heading back to the car – there's nothing we can do here.' She goes back down the stairs with Bruno and me following. I can feel Bruno's reluctance to leave. He's saying, 'I am wondering if the lock is broken and I should replace the lock.' Emily half turns and snaps, 'Don't even think of doing that. We'll wait until we hear from the tenants.'

Her long legs cover a lot ground. She slips into the high driver's seat of her SUV as Bruno and I exit the building. I turn to see if the security door of the block is shut properly. When I turn back, Emily is leaning out of her car and throwing up into the gutter.

Bruno stares at her. He is struck dumb for a moment. Then he says to me, 'That lady is sick, you should take her home.' Bruno is spot on. Emily is leaving the instant noodles and the delicious, tangy Granny Smith apples that she got into her stomach in the gutter.

'You're right Bruno,' I say. 'We'll go. When I hear from the tenants I'll let you know.'

This is a one-way street and Emily has parked with the driver's door next to the kerb.

'Shall I drive?' I ask.

'No, I'll be okay in a minute.' With that she leans out and is very noisily sick for a second time.

This gives Bruno a chance to come up to me and say, 'If they haven't changed the lock then it is broken and I'll have to fix it.'

I stare at him. For a moment I have lost the thread of the lock saga. I wonder if I am going to laugh. A scream seems more likely. I do neither. I look into his small brown eyes and say, 'I have to go.' After the suppressed scream it is like an anti-climax.

'Yes, the lady is very sick.' Has he forgotten Emily's name?

I get in the car with Emily.

'Do you want me to drive?' I ask again.

'No. There's a bottle of water in the back. Can you find it?'

I have to get out to do this, and I see Bruno changing direction when he sees me opening the back door. Could he be coming to offer help? He is a kind man and that could be part of the problem with the door. He doesn't want the tenants locked out.

'Just finding some water,' I call out. 'We'll be right'.

Emily gulps down mouthfuls of water and we leave taking the aroma of 'sick' with us.

'You should go home,' I say.

'I'll be okay.'

'Are you sure?'

'You think I'm going to be sick again, don't you? Well, I'm not, so you can relax.' Had I thought that?

'Are you sure?' I say this again for some reason.

But I guess she is sure. If Vince heard her being sick this morning and now she has spewed up her lunch, there is not much to be sick with.

'Yes, I'm sure. I'll tell you about it sometime, but not now.' She is a bit snappy.

We sit in silence while I wonder what is wrong with her. I want to ask this, but Emily has closed down. When she closes down, she is unapproachable as far as the personal goes. I don't know how she does it but it prevents intrusive questions. I wonder if a question about heaving your lunch into the gutter is intrusive. I guess it would be personal, but it is normal to ask, 'What's wrong with you? Why the hell did you just puke your lunch into the gutter?' While I'm thinking of the right words to say we drive into Emily's car park.

* * *

As she goes slowly up the stairs to her desk, Emily turns and calls back to me, 'Make sure you note this Mickey Mouse excursion in the computer notes. We don't want to forget we were conned into making this ridiculous journey.' I can hear laughter in her voice.

'Right,' I call as she disappears.

'We'? That is nice but I have to accept that I was the one conned. I will have to watch it with Bruno in future.

Bruno didn't mention his meeting with the tenants at Princess Street. I hope he hasn't forgotten, but I have no intention of ringing him.

Vince's thinking is mathematical; sick equals pregnant. He may be right. I want it to be true because I don't want Emily to be really sick and of course there is her job. Now I have formulated the possibility of acting in her job, the thought floats about in my mind. Not settling just floating. I hope I can catch it and nail it into place. That depends on Emily.

Chapter 18

I wonder half-heartedly if I should get back to my inspection reports when Lisa puts a call through to me from Anna, who now wants a property that I have given to someone else. She was undecided from the moment she saw it, but it seems now she likes it better than anything else she has seen. One of the reasons she couldn't make up her mind was the electricity.

She asked some strange questions. Well, questions that I think are strange and that I would not ask. Like, 'Can you tell me how much the electricity will cost per quarter?'

I didn't know. She asked me if I could I contact the last tenants and ask what their electricity bills were.

It's one of those silly questions, like how long is a piece of string? There is no right answer. For the electricity, the only answer is 'it depends how much you use'.

The previous tenants moved out of this property a couple of weeks before these tenants saw it. I have their forwarding address, but it's not the sort of question I think I should ring them about or send an email. They have their bond back and everything is finalised.

It's an expensive town house, $1000 per week which works out at $4345 per calendar month.

Anna and her partner who now want it have recently returned from overseas, so perhaps there is some point to their question and their worry about the electricity. Well, Anna's worry really. As we talked, her partner kept wandering around the place.

'There's no ducted heating,' she said.

'No,' I said. That doesn't make sense to me either. Why would you build a three-bedroom, two-bathroom, two-level townhouse with no ducted or hydronic heating? I didn't say that. Instead I said, 'You have a reverse cycle unit in the lounge and the dining room and all the bedrooms.'

'Isn't that expensive?' she asked me.

I have no idea what she considers expensive, so I say, 'They are reverse cycle so you get the advantage of cooling for summer. You're going to want that. It can get pretty hot upstairs.'

She can't leave it alone.

'But how much is it going to cost?'

'I can't tell you that. It would depend on how much you use them. They're supposed to be an economical way to heat and cool.'

'Compared with what?' She is like me – I would have asked that question. But that does not make it any easier to answer.

'I guess I'm thinking of other forms of electric heating, like the wall panels along the skirting boards.' I don't know how helpful that was. Not very, it seemed.

'Can't you give me some idea of how much we could expect to pay per quarter?' As she asks it again it begins to seem a reasonable request, but I don't have the answer.

'I'm sorry, I don't know. After a couple of months of living here, you'd get an idea and if you thought it was too much you could cut back. You know, not have the units on so often.'

I can see she is very irritated with me and I decide at that point that I do not want them for tenants. She is sounding as if she could be difficult.

'You also need to remember that you'll use them in the summer for cooling, so the cost may be much the same all year.'

She is silent for a moment. We can hear her partner opening and shutting doors upstairs. He didn't seem worried about the electricity.

She brings it up again. 'I'm worried about the cost. Before we apply can you get hold of the previous tenants and ask them what they paid, so we can get an idea?'

'They've gone overseas,' I lied. I hate lying, but sometimes I think it is the only way. Even if I did ask them I wouldn't know how often they used them. I don't want Anna coming back to me with, 'You told me that it would cost X amount for the heating and it is twice that. What are you going to do about it?'

'If you're worried about the cost of heating,' I say, 'perhaps you need something smaller. The spaces are really big here. It is an extra-large town house so I can see how you could be worried about the heating bills.'

My thoughts are that if you can pay $1000 per week in rent, you should not have to worry about the cost of making yourself comfortable. That is a lot of rent when you think you may have to wrap yourself in your winter woollies and puffer jacket to save on the heating bills.

They came back for a second look and then applied, but by then I had some business people who were here on a two-year contract and the landlord went with them. I need to tell her.

It did make me wonder about the cost of using my reverse cycle unit, but just for a minute. I didn't let the thought hang around. I'm not prepared to put on a thick jumper and mittens to keep myself warm while I fuss about my electricity bills. I suppose they are quite high, but nothing seems to be cheap these days.

* * *

In real estate, we are always looking for an excuse to celebrate or, failing a celebration, just to have a few drinks after work. Today, Lisa is leaving to head off on a three-week cruise. She sends an email around.

Drinks to farewell me and welcome Vicky, my temp. After work at the Lido. All welcome.

The Lido is a favourite watering place. It has a large outdoor area where the tables can be pushed together allowing us to take over most of the space. It also works in the winter when the gas heaters are on.

Some of our staff, who talk constantly about giving up smoking, need a place to pretend that they are just having one with their first drink. Then finding an excuse to have a second. The Lido is a difficult place to give up the habit of drawing nicotine into your lungs. The outdoor area attracts people who are caught up with the habit.

I have not done a survey about this, but I think real estate people have a higher percentage of smokers in their ranks than other professions. It takes a strong person to give up and sustain it with the fog of smoke their colleagues create while puffing around them.

Those of us who don't smoke can get caught up in the second-hand smoke issue. We can make a big fuss about sitting downwind from the smoke. I'm not sure it is worth the fuss at the end of a tiring day, so I try not to complain, but I do try to sit away from the smokers. It sort of divides us into two camps.

We settle into the Lido and Lisa behaves as if she was already on the cruise with the $400 on-board spending money she has been talking about. She begins knocking them back and tries to persuade Vicky to do the same.

'Come on Vic. My treat! What are you having?' Vicky is reluctant and I don't blame her. You don't want to get drunk with the mob before you have your feet securely under the desk. She has one drink then goes home, leaving the rest of us there.

'Come on everyone. Have a cocktail on me. I have to get into training for the ship. That's all we'll be drinking on board.'

That would be why I haven't been on a cruise. I'm not into cocktails. Lisa knows about cruising. She has been before. It is her preferred way to holiday.

I can see Mandy leaning on the bar with Lisa while the barman shakes away at a cocktail mix. Mandy loves these social occasions. She always is ready to match anyone in the drinking stakes. She grabs her cocktail and heads outside.

'Has anyone got a spare ciggie? I haven't had one for at least two weeks.'

'I thought you'd given up,' says Lauren who offers her one.

'Yeah, well, I have. But I just need a taste sometimes.'

'Have you given up on that fancy wedding dress then?' Vince grins at her.

'Not exactly. Sometimes I go and look at it, and I still love it but it would blow the budget. The funny thing is I was going to save my ciggie money towards it but I don't seem to have the ciggie money sitting around in my wallet. I'm not sure where the cash goes.'

Lauren tells her. 'You spent more than I do on fags but then I only smoke in the evening, That's a good habit to get into Mandy. But I give up in the evening when I have dinner at home. Mum makes such a fuss if I say I am just going out for fag. You'd think I was going out to poison myself. Dad doesn't say much but mum goes on and on. I don't smoke when I'm there now.' She gives a laugh. 'Of course, it is the first thing I do when I get in the car to go home. Light up.'

Mandy ignores all that. 'I do want that dress but it's expensive. When I asked mum about it she said, 'I'm sure you could find something just as good at half the price'. So I've been looking. But there's nothing.'

Vince is studying her. 'I think you could save your ciggie money. You know how much you frittered away on them every week. Put that money in a separate bank account. That's what I would do.'

Mandy gulped down the remains of her cocktail.

'Another?' says Lisa and Mandy agrees then says, 'I'll finish this first,' and she flutters her cigarette about.

'I'll get them,' says Lisa

'Thanks,' says Mandy. Then to us, 'I wonder if the extra money does go on cocktails? That's all I drink now.'

'More wine?' I ask anyone who's listening.

'No,' says Vince. 'I'm off to pick up Tom. He's working late.'

'I'll go too. I don't need another glass of wine.' I am getting caught up in the hype Lisa is generating so it's good Vince is breaking up the party. I'm always a bit anxious driving home when I've had two. So I don't need a third. I turn to Vince. 'I thought Tom took his car to work.'

'Not in the summer. He's been catching the tram.'

'You two aren't going are you?' yells Lisa. 'It's far too early. I've only just got started. I need to get some practice in.'

I look at Lisa. She's grinning. How relaxed she is. Perhaps she is more stressed on reception than she lets on.

'Have a good trip!' I call. 'Drinks when you get back.'

'Do everything I wouldn't do,' yells Vince and with these banalities we leave and head for our cars.

I'm sure three drinks would take me over the limit. I have never had to put this to the test and I am not keen to. There is no public transport from where I live to Caruthers. A taxi home and then back again in the morning is an unnecessary expense.

I drive under my building and into the parking area and creep between the white lines into my space. The car in the next park has not made it easy. The park belongs to an old man with an old Volvo. It's a large old Volvo, and he often has trouble getting it between the lines. He swings a bit to the left and encroaches on my spot. He is always very apologetic when we discuss it and promises to take more care. This evening is one of the nights when he found strength in his left arm and the arm has pulled his power-tank to the edge of my spot. I open my door and slither out into the tiny space that is left. It is good to be home. I feel affection towards this old man. He's part of being home. I float up the stairs and into my unit.

The bathroom is a mess. I had forgotten about the toilet. How could I forget a non-flushing toilet? I gaze at the mess. The lid is off the tank and the tank's innards are decorating the white floor tiles. Bits of black gunk are spotted about.

My first thought is, the toilet's not fixed. My next is, did Amy know about this? I fish in my bag for my phone and find a text message from her. 'Lee couldn't fix the toilet. Sorry. See you tomorrow.' I notice it was sent at 6.05 while I was in the Lido. With all the noise that goes on there, I didn't hear it.

I ring Amy. When she answers she says, 'Hey, Lee's really sorry about the toilet. He just couldn't fix it. You got my text? Right?'

'Yeah,' I say. 'Did he tell you why he left all the bits lying about on the bathroom floor?'

'Did he? I suppose he thought there wasn't much sense putting it all back together again. He's not going to charge or anything like that.'

'What?' Did I hear her correctly?

'I said he wasn't going to charge for going out.'

I'm proud of myself for not responding to that. I am getting more self-control. All I say is, 'Okay.' Then Amy says, 'You didn't cancel your plumber did you?'

'No! I'll be in touch tomorrow.'

I disconnect and get a supermarket bag to put all the bits in. Then I wash the bathroom floor. The moment I finish I think how stupid that was. The plumber will be walking all over the tiles tomorrow. But I feel better having done it. I removed all traces of Lee and some of the knowledge that he thinks he is being generous and not charging me! I hope I never meet him.

I wander onto my balcony. I do this every evening even when it is late. I breathe in gulps of calming air and unwind. The view is blurred by the night lights. It is never really dark in this city. If you want dark, you have to get block-out blinds. No block-out blinds for me. I like the night lights. There is magic and mystery in them.

Thursday

Chapter 19

My alarm goes off and I know the decision to leave the Lido
when I did was the right one. As it is, my head feels heavy and
my mouth is dry. Second-hand smoke?

I shower as I think about this. I try to remember who was
sitting near me. I was so busy being part of the group, the cigarette smoke was all around me. My heavy head has to be the
second-hand smoke and not the crappy happy-hour house red.
I only had two glasses. Definitely not the wine, even though I
know the house red is very ordinary wine.

I start my day by heading over to Caruthers Bayside to collect some keys. Thank god I hadn't let Lisa persuade me to
have some cocktails at her expense. Not that I mind drinking
at other peoples' expense but it is nice to know that 'free' does
not mean I have to drink to excess, that I am able to show
some self-restraint.

Now I own the four walls I live between, I don't stay for
these long drinking sessions half as much as I used to. Is it the
cost? Partly that, but it is nice to come home and wallow in
the fact that this is my place. Mine! My name is on the title.

The bank's name is there too, but I give little thought to that. Believe me, there is an enormous sense of achievement and relief in getting the pre-approved finances. In my view, it is no good looking for a place unless you have some guarantee that you can come up with the money – only then can you move forward with the dream. I'm pretty smug about all this but I do see the downside.

This week it's the toilet. I heave several buckets of water down it to make sure it is well flushed for the plumber.

If I was a tenant I would not have waited until today to get something done. I would have badgered my property manager. I would have talked about health and safety. Not that I think it is a health issue but it is a fashionable flag to wave about. It's amazing how many issues can be seen as a health or a safety issue or both.

Take a cracked tile in the bathroom. Unless it's actually broken with sharp edges, it is not a safety issue. It may be ugly and you may not like it, but it is not a threat to your safety. I often find myself explaining this to someone.

I think I've been meek about the toilet. That is not a word I like, so I ring the plumber to confirm he will be doing the job today and to let him know I will have my keys at reception for him. I also let him know that I think I have been very patient. I do this in a sort of joking way, but I want him to get the message. Not meek today.

He says, 'I've got it booked in for late morning. I'll pick up your keys before I head over there.'

The supermarket bag with the innards of the cistern is on the bathroom floor in case he needs them. I will only tell him about Lee if he asks.

* * *

I'm looking corporate this morning. Charcoal tailored pants and a crisp white shirt. As it is warm, I have a black jerkin that serves as a jacket. I've dressed this way because I want to feel in control if I have an issue with the plumber. Corporate is confidence, even if I'm on the phone. I'm not going to be manipulated today. I focus my mind on a picture of the plumber in my bathroom pushing the flush button. I was so busy pulling down positive views of Bruno and his tenants, I forgot about myself.

I ease my car out of the parking space. The old Volvo still lurches to the left. I head to our Bayside office.

It's always hard to gauge the traffic in this city. A male traffic reporter's voice flows from my radio – why is it always men who give this information – where are the women?

'Traffic is quiet this morning with about the usual number of minor mishaps. There's been a crash on the corner of the Nepean Highway and King Street. More a bingle than a crash. There are no ambulances in attendance and the traffic's starting to move again. So no real problems there. Take care if you're heading towards Lyndhurst – a truck's lost a load of mandarins. The boxes split on impact. Mandarins everywhere – they do roll about,' and he chuckles. *'Traffic's driving over them, so take care…'*

Driving over mandarins. I laugh thinking about it – the colour of sunshine and vitamin C under the wheels of the cars.

There are no problems on my route. No bingles. No mandarins.

There is a parking spot outside Caruthers Bayside in the one-hour zone that I can zip into. It is my lucky morning; confirmation from the plumber and a park just where I want it. Corporate dressing?

No one at this office was at Lisa's drinks last night. They got the email inviting them, but they didn't turn up.

I swing through the doors and find Skye standing in the centre of the property management department. She is in a state of heightened sexual excitement or perhaps it is frustration. She is giving the office a detailed description of it. She believes in opening up, letting everyone in. The desks are around the wall in this big room and everyone's chair is swivelled towards Skye.

'There was a male in my bed last night,' she announces turning to me as I come in. She is getting me up to speed.

'Did you sleep with that pooch of yours?' asks Jeremy with a laugh. He is a quiet, amusing guy who sits in the far corner. 'I can understand that. The temperature dropped a bit. Whiskey's warmth would keep you comfortable!'

'No, no! I shut Whiskey in the living room and he wasn't pleased. Kept howling and scratching the door. It was a real man. You know, Adam.'

'Is that your friend who suggested you were wasted in a bank and that real estate would be the right fit for you?' I ask.

Skye was working as a teller when a customer suggested real estate after she whined to him about being bored and wanting something more stimulating and exciting. She was sick of sitting behind a glass window.

'Yes, him. But we didn't do anything.'

'I thought you were starting to fancy him?'

'Yeah! Well, we just cuddled. We talked a bit and then he went to sleep.'

'No sex?' said Jeremy.

'No, not then. In the morning I woke him to get him out of my bed for work and he mentioned it then but there wasn't time. I had to shower and get to work.'

'So, what are you worried about? He would have done it but you had to go to work.' Jeremy has engaged with this.

'I'm sure he knew that, and I bet that's why he mentioned it. If he really wanted to do it, why not last night? Why not during the night? I was awake most of the night. And I feel like shit this morning. I'm hung-over. I know I am. We were all at some sort of life saving fundraiser and he came home in the taxi with me.'

One of our salesmen, whose desk is in the room behind this one, was roused by Skye's voice. It is like her personality fills every space. He comes in and asks why she didn't take the initiative in bed if she wanted him.

'He's the guy. He should take charge in the bedroom.' She says this with great certainty. There is no doubt in her mind that this is how it should be.

'Don't you believe it,' says the salesman, whose name I am trying to remember. 'You have to let them know what you want. I lived with this woman a few years ago, and she always took the initiative and showed me what she wanted. I'd be woken up because she wanted it. I was able to go then, but it was her not me that started it. I could've taken it or left it.'

'What was wrong with her?' asks Skye.

'Nothing. I liked her. You know sometimes we guys are sitting on the fence and we need a sort of push. You should show him what you want next time.'

'It's over to him, not me.'

No one else says anything. A silence fills the room and hangs there until the phone rings and we can turn our attention to it. Then I remember who *he* is. He has recently come out as gay. So his experience may not be an ideal one to follow. It seems he was sitting on the fence in more ways than one. Odd he didn't see that. Maybe he's bisexual.

I still can't remember his name, but I am clear the gossip was about him. He wanders off believing he has contributed some useful advice and Jeremy agrees.

'He's right of course, Skye. This isn't last century. Take control. Show him what you want.'

'Last century or not, he's the guy and he should take charge in the bedroom,' Skye says with even more firmness. We all stare at her. She is the last person I would suspect of having such ideas. She turns to Jeremy.

'What do I do now? Should I ring him and ask how he is? I can't sit around and not contact him.'

'I don't see why not. But you could text him and ask if he got to work okay.'

'Should I tell him I enjoyed him staying?'

'No! Why say that? You're a mess. Why say you enjoyed it?'

Skye takes her phone and starts on the text when Jeremy says, 'No. Don't do that, now I think on it. Don't text him now. Wait until about 8.30 tonight then text and say you hope he's fine and had a good day and you're exhausted and you're off to bed. It suggests you aren't available. Or that you are only available in bed if he wants to see you. Why you should be exhausted beats me. You didn't do anything.' Jeremy is now in control. I wonder if he takes control in the bedroom. I would have said no. He is too quiet and non-aggressive. I'm tempted to ask but Skye interrupts my thoughts with, 'I couldn't sleep with him there,' so I leave that question for another time

'Go and get some breakfast,' Jeremy says firmly.

Skye points out to us, as she heads out, that tonight her bed would smell of man. Not of Adam; just a man smell.

I am glad I arrived in time to catch all that.

No one has got the keys ready for me. There is a block of apartments that has been managed from the Bayside office but now Emily is going to take the block on because the owner wants it managed from the main office. It is a company which owns the apartment block, and the accountant liaises with us regarding tenancies and maintenance. I guess he is a good person to do it because he deals with the money. He also has the job of approving the tenants and that is why he wants the properties moved. There have been a couple of unsatisfactory tenants that he sees as our fault. As he puts it, 'I approved them on your company's advice.'

It was always going to happen – there are sixteen units in the block and the occasional stuff-up is inevitable. It's a pity there were two stuff-ups in a matter of weeks. I suppose he has to report to his CEO and I suppose the CEO thinks he is not doing his job when there is a problem, and a subsequent shortfall in the rent.

Emily thinks by managing them herself she will appease the accountant and the CEO. The files were sent over a week ago, and I said I would collect the keys.

The receptionist at Bayside is a very pale, silent girl who looks as if she is going to disappear into a cloud of vapour and who didn't get involved in the previous conversation. She says she knows nothing about the keys and no one asked her to get them ready. I asked her yesterday.

'I don't remember that. Did you ask me?'

I assure her I did. Perhaps at that moment she was a ghost. She looks like one now.

She reads out the key codes from the computer in her soft ghost like voice and I scurry around finding them in the key safe. A ghost can be very irritating, and we do this without talking except for key numbers.

Sixteen bunches of keys are bulky and heavy. We find a box that once held A4 printing paper to put them in and I head off. As I go out the door I say, 'Thanks for your help.' I say it in what I imagine is a sarcastic way.

'That's okay. Anytime,' she responds and I feel I didn't get my point across.

Chapter 20

Back at my office I find people suffering from last night. Not Vicky. She's on reception and is very bright and perky but Mandy is not too good.

It seems Lisa managed to get some people to stay with her and get plastered. If she was paying I can see why they would. Wednesday is cheap cocktail night, so more for your money!

I ring Lisa to wish her a good trip.

'Hi,' I say when she answers. 'I thought I'd just ring and see how you were. And wish you well.'

'You're the fourth person to ring this morning,' she snaps.

'Sorry,' I say feebly. I thought I was doing something nice – being a friend.

'Yes, well, I'm not leaving until six this evening. I just wanted a bit of a sleep-in.'

'I'll go then, I wanted to say have a good trip. If it makes you feel any better, you're not the only person suffering. Mandy is definitely struggling.'

I can hear a grin in Lisa's voice. 'Yeah, we did drink a few. It was a good night. Nothing like getting them for half price.'

'Enjoy the trip. You can go back to sleep now.'

'As if. With all these phone calls, I may as well get up.'

'See you when you get back,' I hang up. She would not have liked it if no one had rung her.

A yellow sticky-note on the side of my computer says 'Bruno's tenants'. I don't know why I left a reminder. There is no way I could forget.

I'm anxious. I want this to be over. I want these tenants in the property. I can't see Bruno not liking them unless they didn't listen to me and walked around with Cody. Would they like Bruno? That is the real question. I am so anxious I want to delay the phone call. Better to be in limbo for a while and not have to deal with a 'No'.

Then, there it is in an email!

We looked over the property again yesterday with the land-lord and we are still interested. If the landlord liked us, we are happy to go ahead.

'Wow!' I shout and clap my hands, applauding my success. Then I leap to my feet and punch the air. It is unreal.

I fire the email on to Lauren with added exclamation marks.

I ring Bruno. I'm holding my breath. Was there some little thing that didn't suit him or got him out of sorts? Or was he introduced to Cody?

He answers immediately. Phone in his hand perhaps? I some-time wonder if he wears it around his neck.

'Their dad seems a nice guy. They had another look through and I had a bit of a chat with the dad. They want to go ahead do they?'

'Yes,' I say, trying to keep it low key. I want to scream 'Yes! Yes! Isn't it wonderful?!'

Instead I say, 'I'll give them the go ahead shall I, and get them in to sign up and pay the first month's rent?'

'Yes, do that. Let me know when they come in.' Bruno is very calm, as if months have not gone by with the place sitting empty and gathering dust. I still think there is something dodgy about him being happy to keep it empty for so long. I wonder if he saw the dad as his next best friend. The chat obviously went well. The ball is almost in goal. I just need the rent and the bond!

Before I can draw breath he says, 'Now, about that key?' I become a mouse running in a maze. No goals to score. 'Have you heard anything? I want to know what's going on. You haven't told me yet what 'this and that' means. I asked you several times but you haven't told me anything. I'm going to email my daughter about the key and I'll ask her about 'this and that'. I'm sure she would know but I think you should tell me. You're managing the property. She's paying you to do this.' He stops for a moment and I feel sorry for his daughter getting caught up in all this. I feel sorry for myself. I was so pleased about letting Princess Street, and now he has dampened that with a jug of lukewarm water.

'No. I haven't got an email from her tenants, yet. Emily says we are to wait until we hear from them before we do anything.' Push it on to Emily, I think, although she did say something like that.

'Yes. I remember, but that lady's sick. Is she sick today?'

I haven't seen her today but I say, 'Fine! Fine! It was just a passing thing.' I wonder why Bruno has not got the mathematical thinking of Vince. Sick equals pregnancy. I wonder what sick does equal in his mind. Not that I am going to ask.

He's still on the ball. He doesn't lose the thread. He says again, 'I want to know what 'this and that' is?'

'I'll find out,' I say. 'And I'll let you know when your new tenants sign up.'

I see that as the end of the conversation, so I hang up. Four months and we finally get a tenant for his property, and Bruno is still fusing about the keys and 'this and that'. Do I really want him for one of my landlords? Does anyone want him?

I take a couple of slow deep breaths and I can't keep my excitement and relief down. Princess Street has tenants. The ball is not in the goal yet, but I am seeing it falling through the hoop.

I email the whole company to let them know. I add to the email that Lauren owes me two wines and Friday seems a good time for her to pay the debt.

Skye emails back, *Thank god. I won't have to open it on Saturday. Hallelujah!!*

Emily in her usual lovely way says, *Well done. I'll join you for that drink.* Then she adds, *I'll shout everyone a drink who can make it to the Lido on Friday after work.*

I'm amazed. There must be another reason for this. Letting Princess Street hardly warrants free drinks for everyone.

I ring Joanne, and we arrange a time for them to come in to sign up. They can only make it at five on Friday. We finish at five as it is our early closing, but I would stay back until midnight to get this deal signed and sealed. I can wait for my drinks. I think of trying to get Lauren to do the sign up as she is still the property manager and they can meet her. But somehow, I need to know the ball is securely in the goal. I have to do it myself. There's many a slip between the cup and lip as they say. I want to be sure if there is a slip, I am there to put it back into the cup or onto the lip – secure it in place.

I fill in the right forms for Hayley to prepare the paperwork. I can't keep the exclamation marks off this either. Then I walk up the street. I'm so excited. It is as if I have won some amazing prize. In a sense, I have. I won't have to speak to

Bruno about tenants or set up times for him to meet any likely renters and then find it's a fizzer. I will not have to concern myself with his property on Mondays. That is a prize and a big one. Although it is not quite the prize it would have been last week because now we have this madness about the key and 'this and that'.

***

'How did those arrears go?' I ask Mandy when I get back to the office.

'Oh, everything's okay,' she says sounding rather pleased with herself. 'I found her mother's number and I gave her a ring. She was so nice. She thinks they must've forgotten. She's going to pay it for them.'

'Forgotten to pay their rent?' I raise my eyebrows. Forgotten is an excuse I have heard often but it still surprises me.

'Yes. They're overseas. They've gone climbing in Chile. I think she said Chile. Anyway, it's their trip of a lifetime, she says, and she can understand the date the rent was due could have slipped their mind. I gave her the DEFT number and their reference and she'll pay.'

'Did she wonder how long we'd wait before we evicted them?'

'No, I don't think she understood about that. When I told her how many days overdue it was, she did ask if the landlord was a bit cross.'

'What did you say?'

'Just that he was on holiday too. Not that I know that for sure, but it seems likely. I've emailed him to tell him they're paying. I don't know how I let them get so late. I was so upset in the meeting yesterday when I had to tell Emily. I always follow the procedure. If I don't hear from them I issue a notice to vacate and then book a VCAT hearing.'

'You did email them didn't you?'

'Yes but their mother said they're not getting emails. She is contacting them on Viber or something.'

'Why do you think you forgot to follow up?' For some reason I need to know this. It's not as if it is really important. So she forgot. Big deal. I should let it go, but she answers, 'I think it was because they always pay on time. I just thought they'd pay. When I looked at the arrears list I didn't see their name. It was there but I just didn't see it.'

'Was your mind on your wedding?' I couldn't resist.

She just looked at me and said, 'Anyway it all worked out which is just as well. I'm really hung-over. I don't need any stress. It was a good night, wasn't it? I wonder how Lisa's feeling.'

'Snappy,' I say and I wish I had not made the comment about the wedding. It feels mean. 'I rang to wish her a good trip and she bit my head off.'

Mandy laughs. 'She wanted to get into training for the ship. I guess she still has a bit of training to do.'

I laugh too and head for my desk.

Mandy saying she rang the tenant's mother gives Bruno the opportunity to swim to the top of my mind. There should be some trick we can play on our brain where we say to it 'don't bring that name up again until 4pm'. Here's Bruno, and it is not even lunchtime. It occurs to me that I could ring his daughter's tenant's next-of-kin.

Some wonderful person has entered a next-of-kin with a mobile into the computer. I don't need to spend time in the heat and dust of the filing pantry.

I ring the number. It's answered and I smile.

'Hi, I'm Juliette from Caruthers Real Estate. I understand your daughter's renting a property we manage in King Street?'

'Yes. What's happened? Is there a problem?' I can hear panic in her voice.

'No. No. It's okay,' I say quickly. 'There's no problem. It's about the heater.'

'Oh,' she says. 'They're overseas and I thought…well, I don't know what I thought. It's about the heater you say?'

'Yes,' and I wonder if the whole country, other than the hard working team at Caruthers, is overseas. 'The landlord has a new part that he wants to install and he is having trouble with his key.' The moment I mentioned they key I wished I had swallowed my words. Why on earth mention the key.

Her voice is cold, 'Why would he go when they're not there?' Why indeed. It is a question I've asked myself.

'He left a message to say he would be there and as no one was home he tried his key. There seemed to be a problem with the lock.' I smile widely as I say this. I can sense a certain tension.

'What do you mean he tried his key? Why would he go in when they're not there? I have a new key. They've changed the lock and a good thing too. They don't want him walking in whenever it takes his fancy.'

'Of course,' I say. 'It's just that he wants to get the heater up and running.'

'No, it's not. He's been inside before. My daughter says they're sure he has but they can't prove it, so they changed the lock. He'll have to wait until they're home. I told my daughter we could report him to the police but there was no proof. He didn't take anything.'

'Right,' I say. I feel a need to protect Bruno although I don't know why. 'He was concerned that the lock had jammed. He wanted to make sure the tenants could get in when they came home. It was a kind gesture on his part.'

'Well, that's as maybe. But he's a nosy parker. He wants to know everything about them. Keeps asking personal questions. You tell him from me that he can wait with his heater part until they can let him in and stay with him while he fixes it.' She hangs up.

That didn't go so well. I was definitely on the back foot. My corporate look didn't save me there. This is a moment for 'right'. It is definitely not a moment to tell her of the absurd visit Emily and I made. The least said about that the better. I'm going to ring Bruno and impart this knowledge when I remember 'this and that'.

It occurs to me if I want to find out about 'this and that' I will have to go and fossick in the hot and dusty pantry and find their original applications.

* * *

'This and that' means project manager for a bank. Could you have guessed? I have no idea what a project manager does but perhaps when he described it as 'this and that' he was accurate.

I decide to keep this information to myself for a while. There's no need to share it with Bruno, yet. Let him stew if that's what he is doing. He has nothing to complain about. They didn't tell us or him they were leaving the country. So what! He would have something to complain about if they hadn't paid the rent. I imagine he has access to his daughter's bank account, so he would have jumped onto that.

* * *

For those tenants who fail to pay their rent and don't have lovely mothers to pay it for them, eviction is the next step. This usually means a loss for landlords.

I would like to see Caruthers put in a policy that says all landlords must take out insurance. It would save a lot of agro. Emily feels differently. She thinks it is their choice. Without insurance, it can be a lot of hassle and stress for the landlord if a tenant takes them down the path to arrears and eviction. A lot of stress for us too.

I do remember one case where the landlord didn't have insurance and came out okay financially in a rather unexpected and drawn out way.

The property, a two-bedroom ordinary 1970s unit, was owned by an elderly couple and we dealt with their son, George. He had made a sort of friend of his tenant, Jimmy, or thought he had. George lived with his parents a few houses down the road and if he saw Jimmy, he stopped to talk and occasionally, so I was told by Jimmy, arrived at the door with some weak excuse to chat and be friendly, or as Jimmy put it, snoop.

'He pretends he's my friend. Chats on about sport which he knows nothing about. He's not my friend, he just wants to snoop. That's what he's about.'

'Oh,' I said. 'I think he does want to be friends.'

'Why would he want to be my friend? They're all snooping. His mother comes round. This bent over old lady in black. If I don't have the curtains pulled she peers in the windows. Snooping. That's what they're all doing.'

George insisted that his uncle do any maintenance that was needed. His uncle's skills or lack of them brought him back to the property often.

When uncle was on site, George would turn up too and sort of hover around and chat while the repairs were happening.

Sometimes George's mother, the old lady in black with little English came and watched uncle and chatted away to him.

'They're all snooping.' Jimmy pointed out, 'Their uncle goes into the bedroom even though he's fixing a tap in the kitchen. Do they think I've got drugs or something?'

Jimmy had a job in the construction industry when he moved into the apartment. Rent was paid on time more-or-less, and the only complaint George had was that his car was noisy. He would roar up the drive of the units and come to a screeching halt when he got to his parking spot. George and I both spoke to Jimmy about this. Neither of us had any effect on his driving habits.

In the early days Jimmy reported any maintenance to us. Uncle got to do it and George got to work on his friendship with Jimmy. Uncle's handyman skills meant he regularly had to make several visits to fix whatever it was. He and George were at the unit on a regular basis.

Jimmy got tired of this.

'I want you to send out a proper tradesman. I'm sick of things never getting fixed.'

I said to George, 'Your uncle appears to have problems with some of the plumbing – would you like me send our plumber out?'

'What makes you think that? Uncle does all our maintenance. He knows what he's doing.'

Jimmy ceased to report any maintenance. It was as if uncle had solved all the problems.

Half-way through Jimmy's tenancy, his rent began to fall behind. He had always paid in dribs and drabs and it got so it was over fourteen days late. George tried to see him but he was never around. He thought he knew Jimmy's schedule but he couldn't link up with him. He was never at home when

George knocked on the door. We couldn't rouse him either. He didn't answer his phone.

We gave Jimmy a notice to vacate and booked a date for a VCAT hearing. George's mother said she saw someone in the apartment but it didn't look like Jimmy. When she knocked there was no answer. It's hard to know what she would have learned if they had answered. Her English was so limited. No one had seen Jimmy or heard his car roaring up the drive.

Jimmy didn't vacate but turned up at the hearing. He explained, 'That construction job I was working on finished. I've got another job lined up and I've got someone to share with. Everything'll work out.' He sounded positive and optimistic. So that was the person George's mother saw. His new roommate.

'Why didn't you ring your agent and discuss this?' theVCAT court member asked.

'I thought I had it under control.'

The member was to the point, 'You obviously didn't have it under control. You're almost a month in arrears now. You would have saved us all a lot of trouble and time if you'd taken some responsibility and stepped up and discussed it.'

Jimmy mumbled something, inaudible. Stepping up and taking responsibility was not something Jimmy appeared familiar with.

'I'm going to put you on a payment plan and let's see if you can stick to it.'

He outlined a payment plan whereby Jimmy paid the weekly rent and a little extra for the shortfall. He asked Jimmy if he thought he would be able to stick to it.

'It should be okay when I get this new job. I'll do my best.'

'If your best turns out not to be good enough, ring the agent and let her know what's happening. The rent's your responsibility. Get your roommate to fill in an application form. Step up and be responsible.' The member repeated this and I wanted to clap and cheer him.

Jimmy muttered something and we left.

I gave Jimmy a rental application form to be filled in by his roommate.

We didn't get to check out this person. The application was never returned. George and his parents put up with the situation.

Jimmy stuck to his payment plan for a few months and then we were back to where we had started. Fourteen days late with the rent. This time Jimmy didn't turn up to the hearing. We got a warrant of possession but we knew that Jimmy had gone because George had used his key to check out the place. It was not in a great state. Jimmy had painted one bedroom wall a shade of battleship grey making the room dark. It was a streaky and uneven paint job. There was large hole in the living room wall where a piece of furniture had obviously charged across the room and smashed into it leaving a hole at waist height that you could put two fists through. The place was filthy, especially the kitchen. There was unreported maintenance; a trickle of water under the sink that had ruined the shelf underneath and drips from a bath tap that had left a green stain. The robe door had broken off its hinges. Uncle got busy again.

We claimed the bond but repairs, rent and cleaning were about twice as much. It was a low rent place and four weeks rent didn't cover much. George and his family didn't have landlord insurance so they had to fork out the cost to get it up to standard. They decided, reluctantly, to take out landlord insurance when they rented it to the next tenant. They thought the cost high.

A couple of years later there was a happy outcome. I had made an application to a debt collection agency to recover the money owed by Jimmy. Time passed then the agency came back to me. Jimmy had applied for a loan for a new car and a search had brought up this debt. He started to pay it back in small fortnightly payments. We told George who grinned and said, 'I don't suppose he was such a bad guy, really,' and pocketed the payments. By then he had an Irish couple who paid their rent on time. The tenancy was going so well he wondered why he had landlord insurance. I said by taking it out he was insuring that things continued go well. He didn't get it. When it came up for renewal, he didn't renew.

Chapter 21

I have a call from Michael, a landlord I like. He is very easy, chatty and friendly and usually everything in his world ticks over smoothly. It is the owners' corporation that has upset him.

'Did you read that document you sent me from the owners corp?' he asks. He's referring to a letter they sent about an owner in the complex wanting to put his split-system condenser on the front of the building. For that owner it probably makes sense. His unit is in the front left hand corner and I assume he wants to attach the outside condenser as close as he can to the inside reverse cycle unit. This means on the front of the building.

Michael went on. 'They are writing asking if anyone objects. Do you remember when I put my reverse cycle in a couple of years ago I got clear instructions on where the condenser could be sited?'

I try to think.

Michael goes on. 'I remember clearly. The front and entrance side of the building were no-go areas for condensers.'

I vaguely remember. 'Yes, I think so. I remember there was a bit of cabling.'

'Are you able to find that email they sent to me and forward it to this new person they've got? What's his name?' He pauses, 'Well that doesn't matter. I can't understand why they're asking for objections when it is quite clear in the rules what should happen. What's the matter with them?'

What is wrong with them in my opinion is that they are one of the worst owners corporations around. This building is managed by them by default. It was managed by a smaller company which was bought out by this lot. In these business transactions, the owners of the units in the building have no say in the matter. They are simply shoved on somewhere else. Inefficiency appears to be the mission statement of this company.

I would take a bet that the new guy, Sebastian, has not looked in the file before he sent out the letter. I have got the feeling since I have dealt with him over a couple of issues that he is not interested. He is there to draw his salary. He needs to take on board that the owners of the units pay his salary.

Michael's unit is in a lovely old Art Deco building. It is fairly plain outside, but each unit has some beautiful features, including double doors from the hall to the lounge featuring stained glass from the period. There is a fireplace with an Art Deco surround showing off all those jagged and repeated lines that are like a sunburst.

I love the charm of Art Deco. There is an elegance in the pretty plaster ceilings, the leadlight windows and the uneven lines on the fireplaces like the one in Michael's property. It gives a style not found in new blocks of apartments. These old places are usually roomy with big bedrooms and living rooms. A king-size bed fits comfortably into the main bedroom of an

Art Deco place. You can't always say that about a new apartment in the same rental price range.

Although Michael's building is plain outside, a condenser sitting on the front of it is going to look like a boil on a beautiful face.

It takes me a while to hunt out the email Michael is talking about and email it to Sebastian. I copy Michael in and make a note in my diary to check that Sebastian replies. He is unlikely to reply in a hurry. There are a couple of efficient owners corporations that I can name, and some like this one that are just inefficient and lazy. Occasionally, a landlord will ask me to recommend one when the committee is thinking of sacking their current one. I delight in naming the ones I hate dealing with as places to steer well clear of. Not that that is going to make any real difference, but I get a little glow of pleasure when I do it; getting some of my own back. It is in the back of my mind when I deal with them next time, and I want to tell them that if they don't pick up their game I will bad mouth them. One day...

A few years ago, a landlord I had at another company bought a rundown first-floor apartment in a well maintained Art Deco block, with an eye to giving herself a project. She was excited about renovating and putting her stamp on the property. No expense was spared and she ended up owning a stylish and elegant place with beautifully polished floors. Like some Art Deco places, it was a little dark. It had a shared and covered balcony in the front and this helped keep the light out but also kept it cooler in the summer. The back door led to a wooden landing with stairs down to the parking area.

We always showed the place with the lights on. The polished floors glowed a warm gold and the landlord loved them. She added some standard lamps to enhance the glow.

I let it to a professional man, Nigel, who travelled a bit. His rental reference was from an agent in another state. I rang them to check it.

'Oh, you would ask me about him,' said the property manager I got on the phone.

'Why, what's the problem?'

'It's just that our records are gone.'

'Gone?'

'Yes, gone! We got a new program and upgraded everything and some of our records didn't come across. They got lost somewhere. It's been a nightmare, especially with the ledger and things.'

'It must be,' I say hoping I sound sympathetic. 'What about this guy – can you remember anything about him?'

'I managed the properly when he was in it, but I don't really remember him. The name's familiar but that's all. I'm sure I would've remembered if there'd been any problems. He must have paid on time, that sort of thing. I'd say he's okay.'

'Would you rent to him again?'

'Yeah. I can't see a problem.' She laughs. 'I always remember the problems. There are some people I'd never recommend but I'd say he'd be okay.'

'Thanks,' I say. 'I'll tell the landlord.'

We gave the property to Nigel, but we did not find ourselves in such a comfortable position at the end of his tenancy as the previous real estate company. I would not say 'he'd be okay'.

He moved in and immediately complained about the next door tenant – a slim glamorous woman who smoked on the shared balcony, and whose smoke drifted into his apartment, so he said. We came to a compromise with her and she agreed to smoke on her back landing when she knew Nigel was home. There is room for a chair on the landing with views of the city skyline so it was not quite the compromise it sounds. We also wondered if Nigel had started making a move on her, as she was so easily persuaded to shift to a location that was not shared by him. Later events showed we were probably wrong there.

A couple of months went by. The rent was paid on time, otherwise Nigel was invisible. This is the way I like it, because usually no news is good news.

I went with my boss to the first routine inspection. Nigel was on site and showed us around. We couldn't see any problems and he said he didn't have any maintenance issues. He had a few stylish pieces of furniture and lots of candles, especially in the bathroom. Minimalistic would describe the kitchen. The bench had a jug and an expensive coffee maker. I sent off a positive report to the landlord.

A couple of months later, the downstairs resident, Barry, who had been overseas, complained that our tenant disturbed his sleep and he was not happy.

He wrote a graphic description about heavy ladies who arrived at night and thumped up the stairs past his door. He accosted one and asked what she was up to and where she was going. Apparently she was happy to chat and gave him the details and her card. She may have thought he could be a prospective customer. If that was the case her antennae were switched off. Barry's puritan side came out and this side of him seethed with righteous indignation. After a while he heard them in bed.

This was part of his complaint: *I'm kept awake by the bed banging and bashing about. I can hear it bouncing around and every time it hits the wall my bed shakes. I can hear them panting and huffing and puffing and then the bed hits the wall again. I can't sleep and I shouldn't have to put up with this sort of thing in my own property. You have to do something about it. Get it stopped. I can't sleep and I can't live like this.*

Obviously the insulation between the floors was not very good which was strange because sound proofing is usually one of the good things about Art Deco buildings.

Barry, when questioned, did not hear verbal activity but what really annoyed him was the thump, thump, thumping as the bed rocked around and hit the wall. He may have exaggerated the panting and huffing and puffing as he couldn't hear actual voices.

His graphic letter went the rounds of the office and everyone enjoyed it. Our minds and imaginations ranged freely, especially as our tenant was a small, slight man. It had been clearly spelt out to us by Barry that the ladies of the night were all of whale-like proportions.

It was hard to know how to address the problem.

I rang Nigel.

'I just want to let you know that your neighbour who lives underneath you has come back from overseas. Have you met him?'

'No. Why should I?'

'Oh, no particular reason, but he's asked us to let you know that there isn't much sound proofing between the floors and he's a light sleeper. You know his bedroom is right underneath yours. I thought he may have mentioned this to you.' Of course, I knew he hadn't.

'No. Why would he do that? Is he complaining?'

'Well, not exactly,' I said, as I made a complete hash of getting across what I wanted to say. 'He just wanted you to know so you would consider him. He's a light sleeper and easily disturbed.'

'I'm always considerate. If he has anything to complain about he can come and see me.'

'Right,' I said, knowing full well that was not going to happen. 'You could always have a word with him, yourself.'

'Why? I've got nothing to complain about.'

'Right.' 'Right' was my word in those days, too. 'I just thought I'd mention it to you.'

'Thanks,' he said. 'Is there anything else?'

'No,' I admitted and got off the phone knowing I had not achieved anything and I was sure Nigel was laughing at me.

Barry then addressed his concerns to the owners corporation and they contacted our landlord and suggested she carpet the floor again.

She decided to visit the property. She had no desire to carpet over her beautiful floors. The visit was delayed because Nigel went to China on a business trip and wanted to be there during our inspection.

There was a lull while we waited for his return.

Before he was back our impatient landlord decided she wanted him out. I was to give him notice to vacate at the end of his fixed term tenancy. Fortunately, this time I was inside the time frame to do this.

The final inspection for the bond is what led us to VCAT.

The moment we walked into the empty bedroom we could see what all that huffing, puffing, heaving and banging had done to the glowing, golden floor. Four areas had been deeply gouged. My gaze was fixed on them. It was hard to look anywhere else. The floor was ruined. It would never be the same again. I was struck into silence, but not so the owner. It had the opposite effect on her. She said it all loudly and repetitively.

She was right. It was ruined and it was hideous. She got her floor sander to quote for reinstating it. He said it was impossible to completely reinstate. The damage was too deep. He would never be able to get it out.

Nigel refused to pay to have it re-sanded and re-polished.

'It isn't my fault the floor is so soft it can't stand up to usual wear and tear,' he said.

'Usual wear and tear?' I wanted to laugh in his face. The owner was stunned. Then we realised he was serious. For him his activities were usual wear and tear and to give him the benefit of the doubt he may not have noticed he was damaging the floors.

The senior property manager and I trooped into VCAT. I thought we had prepared well. We had photos of an unmarked, beautiful, golden floor and photos of it now with deep gouges. The condition report that said 'new floors'. We had the letter from Barry although we were not sure we wanted to present it. Every time we thought of it we saw our slim tenant enveloped in a luxurious pillow of flesh. It was hard to look at him and not get that vision.

Would the VCAT member have sexual fantasies or kinks? Would the letter help our cause? We could not decide.

The condition report let us down.

'I want to dispute the condition report,' Nigel said.

'I see you've signed it,' said the member, bringing her photocopied condition report to the top of her pile of papers.

'Yes, I did,' said Nigel. 'But I signed it under a misapprehension.'

The senior property manager and I looked at each other. Misapprehension? Condition reports are pretty straight forward.

'Go on,' said the member.

'It says here,' and Nigel jabbed his finger at the relevant line, 'it says here that the floors are new. New floorboards.

It says that quite clearly and I know for a fact that that isn't true.'

'What do you know?' The member was oozing patience. Perhaps she fancied him. Of course, we could see that she was not his type; far too trim and toned.

'I heard from someone in the block that when the renovation was done the old carpet was taken up and the floor polished. So no! Not new flooring.'

'Is this true?' The member directed her gaze at us and I had to admit it was. Of course we all knew what I meant when I wrote it, so I did not spell that out. Instead I had to agree that they were newly polished but they were the original boards.

My boss added her bit. 'As they were newly polished and beautiful when he went in, it should've occurred to him to put pads under the legs of the bed to stop it marking the floor.' This wasn't particularly helpful.

'There's nothing in the lease about that,' Nigel replied. 'It says that high heels aren't to be worn on the floors. Nobody's done that. If I'd been told to put pads under the legs of the furniture I would have put them there. I've done everything that was requested of me.'

He went on. 'No one mentioned the floor during the routine inspection. If it was such a problem, why didn't someone mention it then?' There was no answer to that question. Well, I suppose there was an answer but as neither my boss nor I had looked at the floor under the bed we didn't have it.

'When they left after the inspection,' he continued, 'they thanked me and said everything was fine. I'm sure they used the word 'fine' which indicates to me that they didn't really look, if it wasn't fine.'

He said several times that if I had written the need for pads under the furniture, he would have gone out and bought them and put them there. He also said that if we had wanted him to protect the floor we could have supplied them to him. He mentioned a number of times that it said new floorboards on the condition report and it was clear they were not, and therefore his signature on it meant nothing.

I wanted to hit him. He was so smug about it. I had always found him a little creepy, especially once I heard about the well-upholstered ladies of the night. Now I saw him as not only creepy, but sly and far too clever. Why didn't he want to slink under a log and disappear? We were all sure he knew we knew what had caused the gouges. It was as if he was proud of it. And I am sure he knew we would never be able to explain or prove it was not what he was doing but the weight that he was doing it with, that had caused the damage.

I hated the way he turned it around to be my fault. Although I couldn't help but admire the way he fought to have his bond returned in full. He had prepared well.

Strangely and I say strangely because sometimes you can see someone trying a con – I don' think he was trying it on, I think he really believed he was in the right.

The result was, as it often is at VCAT, a compromise. The member thought the damage to the floor was more than you would expect after twelve months in a property but the landlord had to expect some damage, especially as we had not given him protector pads for the furniture. The tenant was to pay half of the sanding bill and the owner the other half.

The landlord blamed us, and in particular me. My condition report was wrong and I had not told her to supply pads for the legs of the furniture. She could not understand why I hadn't seen the damage at the routine inspection. Neither could I, but I didn't look closely at the floor by the bed and neither did my boss. Now I do. Now I always study the floor under the beds when I do a routine but these low-down modern beds don't make it easy. I'm not keen to get on my tummy and squirm around.

The landlord made such a fuss about us managing her beautifully renovated property and letting it become damaged that the company paid her half of the flooring cost. They did this because she had other properties managed by us and the director wanted these to stay with the company so if she sold them they would get the sale. The commission from a sale would be much greater than the few hundred bucks they coughed up to satisfy her for the flooring. She did not get the floor repaired. She pocketed the money and put down a wall-to-wall carpet for the next tenants.

Several years later, when I was at Caruthers, I noticed the unit for sale with a different agent from the one who paid her flooring bill. I wished I had known the road the owner travelled to make the decision to sell with someone else. What else had happened to displease her? I never found out, but I could imagine the anger in the sales department of that company. It was an office where there was a lot of shouting from the director when things did not go his way. Shouting appeared to make him feel better. The staff did not feel the same way. They didn't find this style of letting off steam conducive to their wellbeing and they usually found things to do that took them out of the office. They would have needed to absent themselves a good deal before that disaster blew over.

Chapter 22

Vicky puts a call through to me.

'This guy's getting angry. He's already left a message.'

'Right,' I say, 'I'll take it.'

I smile in preparation.

'What's the problem?' I say, sounding perky and friendly. He is not sounding the same way.

'Are you in charge here? I said I wanted to speak to someone in charge.'

Why me? Where's Emily?

'I'm Juliette, the senior property manager.'

'Well, you'll have to do.' He can't see me raise my eyebrows.

'I rang Mandy this morning and left a message about the cracked tiles that have been replaced in my property. I want them checked. Do I have to do that myself? I thought that's what I'm paying you for.'

'Mandy's been out at an appointment this morning.' As I say this I wonder where she has gone with her hangover and her arrears-problem relief. 'Give me the address and I'll see that they're checked. One of us will get back to you.'

'I want that to happen today. I agreed on a cash job with the tiler and I'm not paying until I know they're okay. Take some photos to send to me.' A cash job? It must be his own tiler. We don't do cash jobs through our office.

'I'll sort it out for you.' I say still smiling as I take down the address.

I'm not smiling as I ring Mandy. No reply. Vicky has no idea where she has gone. I check her desk, find some keys to the property and head to reception.

As I leave I wonder if I should update Emily about Bruno.

'Where's Emily?' I ask Vicky. 'Is she here today?'

'Yes, but she went out. She said she had an appointment. That was a while ago.'

'Did she say when she'd be back?'

'No. I didn't ask. She told me about the appointment as she went out the door. Do you want me to tell her you're looking for her?'

'No. No, it's not important.' I open the door and go out into the sun. There is no hurry to update her on Bruno. She's probably happy not to be updated.

* * *

This is a chance to get out of the office. At the moment I feel frazzled. I'm not sure why. I put it down to the Bruno Effect and I still have to ring him again. Out of the office and into the sunshine is good. There is a light cooling breeze and I relax. What could go wrong on a beautiful day like today? I remember the mandarins. I like the thought of driving over mandarins. It's the sort of day to do that. It would feel even better if they had fallen off the trees. Driving along a country road and driving over mandarins. For some reason it sounds romantic.

This apartment is on the top floor and has views over roof tops and a glimpse of the sea from the second bedroom. I slog up the stairs panting and wishing there was a lift. There are a lot of stairs in this job.

I have no puff. Perhaps it is last night's second-hand smoke. Yes, I decide. It's the second-hand smoke. Not the red wine or my lack of gym attendance. It is the second-hand smoke. I saw an article recently on how good red wine was for us. It mentioned some doctors advising heart patients to drink it on a daily basis. A glass full of deep-ruby coloured medicine. I like the idea. I like to know when I'm enjoying a glass of red I am caring for my health. Usually it is the other way around. Some health professional is telling me something I enjoy is damaging my health.

I unlock the door, flounder in and head for the bathroom to look at the tiles. I thought I would take a rest on the loo.

'What?' calls a voice from somewhere in the interior. I step back out the door and onto the landing above the stairs.

'Is anyone there?' I call. That is the most stupid question when obviously there is somebody. Why do we always say it? What's wrong with, 'Who's there?'

A bleary eyed Mandy stumbles out of the bedroom. 'What are you doing here?'

'Why are you here? You didn't answer your phone.'

'I was having a nap until you barged in.'

'Here?'

'On the carpet. I'm whacked. I've no idea what you are doing here, but I'm going to lie down again.' She retreats to the bedroom. I follow her.

She says. 'You could do with a rest too. You look a bit done in. It must be the stairs.'

'I wonder if it's the second-hand smoke.'

'Have you noticed,' says Mandy, 'that non-smokers are always going on about second-hand smoke?'

She lies down again.

'Have a rest. Then we can worry about the tiles. I'm sure that's why you're here. I'm sure he's getting his knickers in a knot about them. He's always fussing. He should take a pill.' She is somewhat snappy.

I stand still for a minute. It's tempting.

'Are you going to make me feel bad? Don't be such a goody-good. I'll feel guilty if you leave now. I'll have to leave too. Why don't you just kick back and take some time out?'

It's tempting. The carpet looks inviting. Steam cleaned with a nice pile. Mandy adjusts her bag to make a pillow and closes her eyes. I don't want to make her feel bad.

It is just a bit of time out and I have still got Bruno to deal with, so I need some strength. It is quiet and peaceful up here.

I have a set of keys. Mandy has the other set. No one can barge in as I did. We are safe in this world of our own that is above everything.

I lie down and play around with my bag to make a comfortable pillow. It feels good to lie down. There is no noise just a bird tweeting somewhere outside. I relax and shut my eyes. I wonder if I am a goody-good always doing the right thing. Is it annoying? While I'm thinking this I drift off to sleep.

I'm the one who forgets to turn off my phone. I don't answer it but it draws us back to reality.

Mandy takes photos of the new tiles. The tiler has done an excellent job. She heads off to Nando's for lunch. Our office considers Nando's hamburgers are pretty good for a hangover. I have my boring and almost calorie-free lettuce and tuna salad back at the office.

* * *

There's an email from Vince, marked urgent, saying he needs to talk to me.

'Yes?' I say when he answers his phone.

'I've just had a ring from the owner of the Axminster Street property. You photographed everything didn't you?'

'Yes - all saved to file.'

'The owner says she found a stool in one of the toilets.'

It takes me a few moments to get it.

The word 'stool' has several meanings in the English language. Vince means a dump.

Caruthers prides itself on photographically recording the condition of the property before our tenants move in. Vince and I had done the condition report before the builder went there to attend to the few maintenance items.

I had saved photos of three pristine toilets into our files. Photos with the lid shut and then with the lid open. The owner of this stylish, town house rang Vince after she went there to give it a final check and to leave flowers and wine to welcome her new tenants.

'What exactly did she say?' I ask Vince when I get the meaning.

'She said, 'I am embarrassed to have to tell you this and as well as being embarrassed I'm upset. There was a stool floating in the powder room toilet'.'

I prefer the word 'turd'. Stool sounds too medical. Vince thought 'shit' would cover it.

'She went on, 'I thought you checked the property fully and it is not as if it could have swum through the pipes'.'

Vince and I address ourselves to the problem of who had owned the object. Obviously it had not swum though the sewerage system. Knowing that was a comfort. I don't want to blunder into the bathroom in the small hours and find some weird and wonderful matter swirling up in the bowl. I want to think there are no returns from the sewerage.

No one is pleased about the turd. The owner wants answers from Vince. We need some explanation to give her.

Slightly embarrassed, Vince confronts the builder who was, as far as we know, the last person in the property. He said, 'Not me. Could have been the young lad helping me. I'll look into it. Have a chat with him.'

By this time the owner had flushed the offending matter away so there was not much to look into.

'I bet it was the builder,' I said when Vince told me. This builder can be annoying. He never turns up when he says he will and walks away leaving a job half-finished and has to be called back. I bet he walks away from the toilet without flushing.

Vince says, 'I'd go for the young lad. It will have been him.'

'You'd know more about young lads than I do Vince, but I don't think he was there. It has to be the builder.'

'That's just because you don't like him.'

'We'll never know. If you ask the builder again, he'll say the young lad and I won't believe him.'

'No good putting money on it, then.'

I say, 'I wonder if the builder did it as a sort of fingers to you with your fancy town house and all your money. He can be quite odd about the work he does and doesn't do.'

Vince looked at me in a startled way. 'That's nuts. I don't believe that for a minute.'

'Are you going to wait for him to finish looking into it before you ring the owner?'

'No I'm going to tell her that the builder thinks it is his young assistant and he's going to talk to him. I'll point out that young lads often forget to flush. They think someone is going to do it for them. If you've been around school bogs you'll know what I mean. Schools could employ someone as a full-time flusher – there'd be enough work.' We both start laughing.

'From my hazy memory of the school toilets I think girls flush – no need for a flusher there. What a job that would be.' I say.

Then right on cue my plumber rings.

'Hi, how's it going?' I say.

'Well, I'm at your place now. Did you have a go at fixing it yourself?' He's laughing as he says this and I remember the plastic bag of bits.

'No. Not me.'

'That bag of the innards on the floor. Looks as if someone tried their hand at the job.'

'That was someone Amy knows. But he couldn't do it.'

'No wonder he didn't have any luck. The system needs to be replaced. It's old and it's history. I thought I'd better tell you before I put a new one in. Do you want me to go ahead?'

Of course I want him to go ahead. I'm over the bucket.

'Yes, go ahead.'

'That's fine. I'll have your keys back to you in about an hour. You'll like the new one. It's more streamlined.'

I decide not to ask the price. 'Thanks. Can you leave my keys at reception and get Vicky to let me know when they're there?'

'Will do.' He hangs up.

Vince has moved off and the phone goes again. Sometimes there is no rest in this job. This is a landlord checking that his property will be open on Saturday. I'm not sure why I have got the call. It's a property Mandy manages. Perhaps Nando's was too much for her and she is out for the count again.

She should be dealing with this. I am about to transfer it back to reception when I remember what Emily said about helping Vicky, so I find out what he wants. I know the landlord and the property. I used to manage it so perhaps he asked for me. It was the first lock-out I did when I joined Caruthers.

The tenant was being evicted for non-payment of rent. He had been notified by the police of the date and the time they would be there for the locks to be changed. Caruthers had booked the locksmith to attend at the same time.

The tenant, Dale, had been given a chance to pay but as he was over two months in arrears it was a lot to come up with when one month seemed beyond him. No kind mother here who paid up.

I took someone from our office with me and the office keys.

We all assembled around the door. The police woman knocked a couple of times. No response. Thinking Dale must have vacated we opened up with our office keys. The place was still furnished.

As we considered this, a Chihuahua rushed out of the bedroom yapping. It was followed by a dishevelled, bleary-eyed young man wearing nothing but a pair of jocks.

The ball was in the police's hands. They run a lockout. Dale pleaded ignorance to the event happening.

'Knew nothing about it,' he said.

The police had a record of their phone call to him and his responses. He still maintained he knew nothing about it.

All this was unsettling and it was very unsettling for the young locksmith who had never attended a lockout before. We got him to change the locks, which he was reluctant to do seeing Dale was still there with all his stuff, and let him go off to his next appointment.

'Come on,' said the police woman. 'We haven't got all day. Grab some things and let's see the back of you. You can get dressed outside.'

He stared at her then he slowly put on some clothes. We waited patiently.

'You'll need shoes,' I said a bit like a mum. I was like the locksmith. I began to feel sorry for him.

He looked blankly at me.

'No I won't, it's a nice day.'

'We've changed the lock. So you won't be able to get back in to get them. Why don't you put them in a bag and take them with you?'

The police woman chimed in, 'If I was you, I'd scoop up those clothes on the floor so you have more than that Tee you're wearing. Come on. Make it snappy.' She shoved stuff in a bag for him and pushed him out the door. I grabbed some shoes as she pulled the door shut. We heard the lock fall into place.

'Well, fuck you all,' he said when he realised what had happened.

'Here's my card,' I said. 'I'll open up for you when you want to get your stuff out.'

'Fuck you,' he said again, but he took the card, put it in his pocket, scooped up his little dog and settled it under his arm. He slung the bag over his shoulder, picked up his shoes in the other hand, and walked away.

* * *

When I got back to the office I filled out the form for Consumer Affairs to come and value the items left. If they have no commercial value, we can dispose of them. I did it then so I could get the ball rolling – I could always cancel if everything was removed.

Dale, the Chihuahua man, did come back and I opened up for him but he took away only his electronic goods, some DVDs and a few clothes.

'You can fucking well do what you like with the rest,' he said in a rather ungracious manner.

Consumer Affairs came and wrote off everything left as of no commercial value and said we could dispose of it.

My colleagues saw this as a chance for some free stuff. They kept asking me what was there and could I take photos. In the end I gave a time I would open the property up again.

It's amazing the attraction of something free. Everyone in the office pitched up. It was like a Myer's Boxing Day sale. People pushing and shoving and grabbing stuff before anyone else could get their hands on it. Not a sight that enhanced the image of Caruthers' property managers.

A few people claimed large items like the couch by attaching their name to it while they worked out how they were going to remove it. There was an argument between two property managers who have since left about a pair of bedside tables. In the end they took one each and felt disgruntled about the compromise. A pair always looks so much better than one.

The CDs and DVDs that he left were sifted through time and time again. I have a couple of Nora Jones that I still play and my bedside reading light reminds me of that sunny morning when a shoeless young man left his home carrying his Chihuahua. It is a poignant memory that I don't always want to have in my mind, but I still hang onto the light. It's a good light.

What was left (and there wasn't much) was collected by the Salvation Army.

The property is vacant again and the owner wants to confirm it will be open for inspection on Saturday and at what time. I confirm this and the time because Hayley has now posted them on the internet. He could have checked there.

* * *

I have just hung up when Lauren appears at my desk. 'Bruno's in reception for you.'

'What?'

'I was at The Monster and I heard his voice. He asked for you.'

'Are you sure?'

'Of course I'm sure! I'm going to hide down here until he's gone away.'

Should I wait until Vicky rings to tell me? No, take the bull by the horns and just go and see him.

'Make yourself at home at my desk but don't touch anything,' I say to Lauren. 'I have everything organised. I don't want it messed up.'

My phone rings. 'Tell Vicky I'm on my way.'

Bruno is hopping about – moving from foot to foot in his usual way and standing back from the reception desk. No wonder he's thin. He's never still. I wonder if I hopped about like that whether I would burn up the calories. Then Bruno spots me.

'I was passing. You haven't rung me. I thought I'd come in see how you got on with the key.'

I bet he wasn't just passing, and even though I know that's why he's here I want to scream. I'm back in the maze and nowhere near the exit. Instead of screaming, I put a smile on my face and say, 'Good news. The tenants have changed the lock so no need for you to worry about it being broken. They're on holiday.'

'How is that good news? I don't like it that they've done that. What if there's an emergency?'

I don't ask what sort of emergency, I don't want to know what sort of emergency would require Bruno to use his key.

'Well, I think it's good news.' I say again. 'We'll wait for them to come back and then we'll arrange a time for you to work on the heater.'

'I'm not happy with this. You can tell the tenants that. I need the key to my daughter's property. I want to be able to get in if there's an emergency.'

I'm not sure what to say about an emergency that would require Bruno to get in when the tenants were not there. They are not going to want to give me a key either. I remember about 'this and that'.

'I found out what 'this and that' means. He's a project manager at a bank.'

'A project manager? What sort of job is that? What does he do?' I want to say 'this and that' but humour is not something Bruno gets. Maybe it's not funny. Probably just feeble, but I would laugh.

'I don't know exactly what he does but the bank confirmed that was his job.' That's true. I never know what people do when I read Project Manager on their application. Now I see that it can be 'this and that'.

I'm starting to edge Bruno towards the door. 'Your new tenants will be in tomorrow to sign up.'

As I am about to open the door he says, 'Why not today?'

'Busy today. Can't make it.' I manage to open the door. 'I'll confirm it with you when they've signed. Thanks for popping in.' Why am I thanking him? But I have got him out the door.

'Goodbye,' I say and manage to close it with him on the other side.

I miss Lisa on reception. She would have appreciated that manoeuvre.

I don't hang around. I rush back to my desk where Lauren is checking her Facebook page and ring Vicky.

'If Bruno comes back, I'm not in. I've had to rush out. An emergency's come up.'

I don't think she quite gets it. She thinks I am really rushing off. Instead I say to Lauren, 'Off my chair. I have to sit down.'

'So he has that effect on you too?'

'He's exhausting. Well, he has been these last few days.'

'I always need time out when I deal with Bruno!' Laruen moves off to the front of the office.

I need time out, too. I can see the issue of the key coming up again. But perhaps it won't. I am going to send positive thoughts his way. One is that he will never think to ask about it again.

It is 5.20 pm and I'm heading home. I turn onto the highway and there in front of me is the cityscape. It's not as dramatic as Ralph's picture but the sun is glistening on the gold of the Eureka tower and a few puffy white clouds play around in the blue sky. It is very still and none of the leaves on the beautiful plane trees alongside the highway are moving.

I picture myself on my balcony, relaxed in the last rays of sun, not that I can see the Eureka Tower from there. I am going to eat the Pad Thai that was left over from Monday. I froze it so it should be okay. But the first thing I am going to do when I get home is check out the toilet to make sure it flushes and continues to flush every time I push the button.

I am getting near my turn when my phone rings. I press the symbol on the steering column.

'Hi.' I don't recognise the mumble so I answer again, 'Hi, it's Juliette.'

'Have you got the keys for 6/75 Charles Road? I can't find them.' I see why the mumble. There is panic in this voice. The voice in my head says of course I don't have them. I glance down and there are a set of keys with a red tag sitting in the cup holder.

'Right,' says my head-voice, 'These will be the keys.' I'd forgotten to put them back on their coded hook.

'Yes!' I say. 'Sorry. They're in my car. I'll come back.' I start to prepare to turn off the highway.

'No, don't do that.' The voice is a little clearer now and I realise it is Kylie. 'You'll have to meet me at the property. I've got an open there at five-thirty.'

'Okay. Will do.'

I continue to drive on, past my usual turn and through St Kilda junction and turn into High Street.

I arrive, find a legal park and glance at a couple of groups lounging around the gate. When they see me they get up from the fence, stand up straight and prepare themselves for action. As I have the keys I head into the block, climb the stairs and open up. More stairs! I should be fitter. I should be able to take them at a run or at least a trot.

It is an oddly shaped apartment. The door opens into the middle of the hall. To the right are two bedrooms and a bathroom. To the left the hall carries on to the lounge and the kitchen. I enter first with the tenants behind me and head to the lounge. I know this unit and know how having the entry door in the middle of the hall causes congestion. It opens inwards, thereby blocking off half of the hall. To get down the hall you need to close the front door and inconvenience anyone coming in. It's like slamming it in their face. When you open the door again you block off people coming from the bedrooms. At an open there is a lot of confusion and a lot of people saying 'I'm sorry'. If you lived there, there would still be confusion. When I was looking for my place, there was a unit for sale in this block and sort of in my price range but I could never have coped with the door.

I like the lounge. It faces north and has a full length balcony. Outside is one of the street's plane trees. The leaves cast shadows on the balcony. In winter it is nice to have the bare branches. The problem in the kitchen is the space built for the fridge. It was designed by someone who obviously never ate at home. Two bar fridges on top of each other would be about right.

Someone likes the place and takes an application from Kylie as she arrives.

We lock up and I ask her if Nic is coming for drinks at the Lido tomorrow.

'I've asked him. I told him Emily said drinks were on her and he should turn up. Is she celebrating Princess Street?'

'I don't know. It seems a bit over the top.'

'Well, I told Nic he should come. Emily buying a full round isn't likely to happen again. He'd better take advantage.'

'Have you seen him since the weekend?'

'A couple of texts. He's been really busy.'

'Oh, well I guess you'll see him tomorrow. He won't be one to turn down a free drink.'

'No, none of us are going to do that. I'm sure there will be a big turnout, even if it's only to find out why Emily's shouting.'

'It could just be my success with Princess Street. You never know,' I say.

'Yeah! Right! As you said it's not that big a deal.'

We move to our cars, Kylie with the keys firmly in her hand.

I head for home again. This has been one of those days. One of those days when I wonder whether I'm over this job. And whether there is not a better way to earn a living.

Friday

Chapter 23

The alarm goes off. It's 5.45 am. That's more dramatic than a quarter to six. The five makes it early. The way something that costs $5.99 sounds cheaper than $6. I'm focusing on the five as I get up. I have a routine inspection at seven. I have slept yesterday's negative feelings away, but I have the need to make a point. I need to acknowledge the sacrifice I am making – playing the martyr feels good and I admit I am smug.

Even so, this is a ridiculous hour. The time is at the tenant, Susan's, request. She has her own business and needs to be there to open up. I understand that, and I understand her need to be on site while I do the inspection. It's her home and her pets' home and I do get it that she doesn't want anyone poking around when she is not there. It is not just me. If she needs a tradesman, she takes time off work. Still, early is early, and I'm not loving 5.45.

I 'm on time and Susan is dressed to kill in a cream suit, a white shirt and strappy white high-heeled sandals. Two fat cats greet me at the door and rub around my legs and I regret wearing my black trousers. I have teamed them with a loose rose coloured shirt and my favourite black vest.

This is a charming unit. It had a makeover a few years ago and the owner took out some walls to make it open plan. It gets maximum light and sun in the winter; ideal for the cats that live inside.

We walk through the place together and I jot down the minute problems Susan points out to me.

'If you look down there,' she says, 'you'll notice that the socket has a hairline crack.' She doesn't get down there in her beautiful cream suit to show me. I crouch and take a photo of the almost invisible crack and note it on my clipboard; yes, I've got that with me. One of the cats pushes his nose down to have a look too, so we are nose to nose.

'I thought I should point it out to you as it may get worse. But I don't think it is a problem yet.' I agree. I can't see it ever being a problem.

We move to the bathroom.

'Another thing I think we should record is the hinge on this door. It has moved a little. You can see the mark where it was originally.' I note this down and take a photo.

It's surprising during a routine inspection how many tiny things some tenants find to complain about. It's as if they feel the visit is a waste of time unless the property manager trots off with a list of problems. I watch their minds working, searching over the last few months, trying to find something I can write down. When they do, it is as if we have both achieved something; justified our time.

'Yes,' says Susan in her immaculate suit, 'I think it's good to keep up with these little problems. We don't want them to become big problems.' My view is that there won't be any problems, big or small. Out loud I agree with her.

We finish and she says, 'Now that's done would you like some coffee? I'm going to have one before I head for work.'

'Thanks, but no. I need to get on.' I head out feeling peeved. Who thinks about their property manager's comfort? Why did I get up so early? Why didn't she make our appointment for after she'd her coffee? I head to a café I like nearby. I can read their paper and have one of their delicious savoury muffins and I won't be tempted to mention how early it is.

I don't need a savoury muffin, if I'm thinking of calories. Savoury muffin sounds healthier than a blueberry muffin but I'm sure they both have the same amount of sugar. This one is feta, spinach and leek; a healthy vegetarian combination. I plan to enjoy my time sipping, eating and reading until it is time to head to the office. But instead of concentrating on *The Herald Sun*'s current take on the world, I find myself thinking about cats.

Cats don't cause the same problems in rental properties as dogs. There are owners like Bruno who won't have a pet of any kind, but more landlords will take a cat although they refuse a dog.

When I first joined Caruthers an email was sent around with a request for a home for a cat. The photos showed a lovely, healthy, tortoiseshell cat.

The owner moved out of one our properties and she couldn't take the cat or didn't want to take the cat with her. The cat was up for grabs. A day or so later another email came round with another photo of the cat attached that said, *This lovely cat now has a new home. She'll be living near the beach. Thanks for your help.*

Lucky cat, I thought, and I felt relieved it had found a home.

* * *

Before I joined Caruthers, I worked for a small real estate company where I was one of three property managers. We had a receptionist and a couple of sales guys, and one Christmas we had an abandoned cat that caused great distress in our pet loving office.

I managed a 100-year-old, one-bedroom house. It was one of a few homes that remained in the industrial area. The bedroom was by the front door, and a short narrow hall led to the living room and a kitchen area with a small bathroom leading off it. The back door opened to a tiny yard, the outside toilet and to what we described in the advertising as a second bedroom. It was really a converted shed. The tenant used it as an office. He was a good tenant, kept the place clean and paid on time. He worked from home and had a cat that was always with him.

Once I visited to check some damage caused by a leak in the front. We – that is the tenant, the cat and me – all looked at the large mark on the ceiling and the swelling floorboards beneath.

If I knew the cat's name I have forgotten it now but I am sure it was referred to as 'He' by the tenant. Perhaps his name was just Cat. Cat was a good friend for someone who lived alone and worked from home. He followed us around during a routine inspection and always answered the door with the tenant. I do remember the tenant's name but I don't want to dignify him by using it.

He moved out a week before Christmas. When I did the final bond inspection on the property the cat was there. He greeted me at the front door and rubbed around my legs. I opened the door and he rushed inside and down to the kitchen. Then he was back rubbing around me and getting in the way. When I left I picked him up and put him outside and closed the door quickly. I was afraid I would shut him in. But there was no danger of that. He was trying to stick himself to me and came to the car with me. There was a chance of running him over him.

I rang the tenant

'Oh!' he said, 'that's not my cat.'

'What do you mean?'

'It just turned up one day and I let it stay.'

'That makes it your cat! How long ago was that?'

'Probably about a year. No. More than that…about eighteen months ago. It's been around for a while.'

'Well, you can't just leave it there. How's it going to look after itself?'

'The same way it did before it attached itself to me.' For some reason we were both calling the cat 'It'.

'You can't walk away and leave it. It's your cat now.' I was so angry I wanted to shout at him.

'What am I supposed to do?' he asked. 'Poison it?' I gasped. I was shocked. I stuttered but nothing really came out.

In the gap he said, 'If you're so concerned, why don't you do something about it?'

I hung up.

I was so furious I couldn't stop talking about it in the office. I got everyone else upset. Evelyn, an animal lover, asked, 'Who's feeding him?'

'As far as I can see no one, and the tenant doesn't care.'

She and I took a plate from our office kitchen, bought some cat food and went back to the house.

He gulped down the food. It disappeared so quickly we thought he may throw it all up again. We knocked on the only neighbour's door but no one was there. It was almost Christmas and the holiday season had begun.

I went past on my way home to leave him some more food. It was easy to drive away while he was scoffing the food. Had he thrown the first lot up? He was certainly hungry.

We tried to find a home for him but we weren't successful. Evelyn's partner was allergic to cats. At the time I lived in a tiny apartment on the second floor with no balcony. Not a place for a cat. I needed permission from my landlord via my property manager to have a pet, and considering the type of accommodation that didn't seem likely. Am I trying to excuse myself for contributing to the final outcome? I think I am.

The receptionist lived at home with two dogs and a cat. Her parents thought that was enough. The other property manager was leaving in a couple of months for an extended overseas trip. There was a flat 'No' from one of the sales staff and the other one, after consulting his wife, declined. They were off on their Christmas holidays. It was not a good time to take on a new pet.

The next day Evelyn and I went round to feed him and he was waiting by the gate. He knew my car; he was a cat that learned quickly, a cat that is a friend, a people cat. We fussed over him, talked to him and felt depressed about it all.

Evelyn picked up a carry cage from the RSPCA on her way to work the next day. We left the receptionist in charge and the three of us went around to give him a small meal and to collect him.

He was so friendly and trusting and we got him into the cage easily but he was not pleased. He howled and shuffled around and fidgeted. We tried to talk to him but he was not having any of it. We felt we had betrayed him.

Evelyn took the rest of the morning off and drove back to the RSPCA where she gave him a great reference.

When she got back she said, 'I felt so bad. Here I was saying what a wonderful cat he was and talking him up and I could see them wanting to ask me if that was so, why I wasn't taking him. I blundered on a bit about Bill and his allergies. They seemed to understand, but I hated walking away and leaving him.'

We all agreed that we would not ring to enquire as to whether he was re-homed. I kept my thoughts positive and drew down pictures of him living in comfort with a family of friends, somewhere away from factories, warehouses and offices that would be closed for the long Christmas holidays.

I wanted to take money from the tenant's bond as a sort of punishment but I couldn't find a reason. He had left the property in excellent order and his rent had always been on time and was now paid up to his vacating date. I posted his bond claim form and never spoke to him again but I do remember his name. It is filed away for the future.

At Christmas, a couple of days later, I had a quick silent drink to the cat's prosperity and luck. I did this silently because I didn't want to discuss it with anyone. I didn't want anyone to ask me why I hadn't taken him. I still don't know why I didn't move him into my place and flout the rules? Perhaps Mandy is right about me being a goody-goody. I don't like the thought. It sounds prissy to me.

I haven't forgotten that cat. Often over the years, he has popped into my mind and I feel bad all over again about it. Now, I wish we had found out his fate. Wondering goes on forever - head under the doona doesn't lead to peace of mind.

* * *

I park my car near the office and walk to Café Yellow to get a second cup of coffee.

Kylie's there. She's grinning 'I heard from Nic last night. He's going to be at the Lido after work. Says he couldn't resist a drink if Emily's paying.'

'So it's not you he's coming for it's…'

Kylie frowns and interrupts, 'It's that too. He says he's looking forward to catching up. He just put it that way for a joke and because I said it that way. Do you know what's up with Emily?'

'No, I don't, but Vince thinks she's pregnant.'

'No. She couldn't be. What would he know? She's not seeing anyone. I wonder if she's got a new job. She's good you know. Another company would snap her up.'

'You think so? Sort of head-hunted.'

Jono finishes the coffees and we head to the office.

'Could be. She's the best manager I've had. Definitely not pregnant. She's not seeing anyone.'

'That's what I thought. If she is, she's very secretive about it. Could be a one-night stand?'

'She'd get an abortion,' Kylie says this with conviction.

We arrive at the office and say hello to Vicky at reception. Her face is smooth and when she smiles there is little facial movement. She is rather like an ice maiden who is keeping us all at a distance.

'Botox!' Mandy tells us when Kylie and I reach her desk. 'I'm going to get some before my wedding. It takes out all the lines.'

'Why not now?' I ask her.

'Expensive.'

'Oh!'

'Yes. It's just my frown lines I'm thinking about. You can't really see them with my fringe but I don't want them in the wedding photos.'

I think of Vicky's frown lines. She hasn't got any and the lines between her nose and mouth aren't there either. Perhaps it is the way to go.

'No,' I tell myself. 'You've got a mortgage! You don't need Botox.'

I go back to reception to look at Vicky. Her unwrinkled face is still wrinkle free. 'This is your first Friday.' I say, as if she wouldn't know. 'It should be quiet. Fridays are usually a bit quiet.'

Vicky's mouth moves into a smile, 'You shouldn't say that you'll tempt fate.'

'Thinking of fate, Vicky, if Bruno rings or comes in, I'm not here. I don't want to speak to him until his tenants have signed up.' I am thinking positively that the ball is firmly in goal and no one will have to open that villa unit again for at least a year. I don't want to jinx it by having some negative vibes from Bruno.

'What if he asks for Lauren? He's asked for her before.'

'She's not here either. No one is to talk to Bruno. I'll ring him when his tenants have signed. Don't tell him that though.'

'What shall I say if he insists?'

'Out. It's Friday and we're all out at appointments. Take a message if he insists.' 'Okay. I'll be firm.'

'You may need to be. He thinks we have nothing to do but attend to his needs.'

Vicky's mouth opens and she laughs, but she'll learn that it is more than funny; it is accurate. I move past The Monster and toward my desk. I notice Kylie wobbling a bit on the high wedge heels of her shoes as she heads towards the kitchen.

To me the wedge looks a bit heavy for the thin straps, but that is just my opinion and I don't voice it. There are a lot of stairs in this job and I wonder for the millionth time how Kylie copes in her beautiful shoes. I don't ask her because I am sure she will say, practice.

I'm wearing sandals too but they are more utilitarian. They have low heels with pretty cut-out designs on the front and straps around my ankle. On further thought, I can see that we drive everywhere and Kylie is one of those people who parks outside the office even if it is only a thirty-minute park. I don't know what she does with her parking tickets. She doesn't stick them around her computer as Lauren does. Perhaps she is more careful. She is more organised.

She turns and says, 'What did you think of the crowd at the open last night? Anyone stand out?'

'No, not in particular. Why?'

'I've already had a text from a couple who were there. They're telling me they're going to apply online.'

'That's good,' I say.

'I can't remember them. I wondered if you could.'

I realise now that I wasn't concentrating on the prospective tenants. I was leaving that for Kylie.

'Not really. I remember someone taking an application, but I'm not sure who they were. They all seemed okay.'

'Yeah. That's what I thought. I'd better ring the landlord and let him know. It'll make his day to know there is a possible tenant. He's one of the anxious ones.'

'Aren't they all?' I laugh as I head to my desk.

I check my diary. I highlight and put exclamation marks by my appointment with Joanne and Rod and their sign-up for

Princess Street at five o'clock. This should be the perfect ending to the week.

There are a couple of emails I answer. My inbox is a pale shadow of Monday's. Very laid back. A tenant wants a copy of their signed lease. They say they didn't get one although there is a note on the system saying they did. Now that everything is scanned and saved to the computer it is an easy matter to bring up the lease and email a copy of it to them. I don't write a comment.

A landlord wants a copy of his last statement. That is easy too. It can be emailed straight from my computer. I don't have to bother accounts. In this modern world everything gets easier and easier.

In my first job, we recorded every phone call and all the issues on a piece of paper stapled to the cover of the property's paper file. Those were the days. Although I think even at that time the office was lagging behind the general advancement into the computer age. They had an elderly director who had trouble keeping up and trouble getting the hang of emails. He is likely to be still wandering around in circles not knowing what upgrade he wants. When he does decide, he will be several upgrades behind, and have to make more decisions. These decisions are hard if you don't like spending money. Giving up the old ways and taking on the new can be hard, too.

I type up my early morning inspection and send it off to the landlord. I have filed the photos of the socket and the door hinge. I'm not sending them to the landlord. I don't want him fussing.

Chapter 24

I'm restless. It must be the Bruno Effect. It would be a good time to leave the office. There's a property I need to inspect where there's been a leak. I grab the keys and head out.

The tenants had to wait weeks for the ceiling to dry out but according to them this has happened and the painter has been in and painted it. I need to check his work.

The place was flooded by one of the hazards of apartment living. The upstairs washing machine connection came off and water flowed freely around the bathroom floor and into the hall of that unit and then into the unit below. The unit below is the one I manage.

My tenants said, 'We didn't notice at first because we were watching television so a bit of water had come in before we saw it. The ceiling sagged in the bathroom and dripped, and water came through the light.'

The upstairs tenants were like my tenants, they too were watching television and didn't notice anything until one of them got up to go to the bathroom and found they walked into a flood.

This is a large, red-brick block that dates back to Edwardian times. It is built around a common area with a well maintained garden. We used to manage a couple of units on the other side from where I am going today. I remember doing an inspection there for Emily in the middle of last winter.

The landlord was difficult – almost impossible to please. We no longer manage his properties. There was an issue with the payment of one of his maintenance invoices. He found us incompetent and that our trust accountant didn't know what she was doing. All Emily's charm and trouble-shooting skills couldn't appease him and he took his properties to another agent. I think Emily felt relief that he was out of her hair, but she didn't say so. I said, He's someone else's problem now,' She just smiled.

At the time of that inspection he had two properties in the building, one above the other, both available for lease. He impressed on Emily and me that he was losing money.

'They're no good to me sitting there empty. I'm more and more out of pocket every day.'

We didn't need to be told that. We understand there is no income from an empty property. This landlord kept asking what we were doing about it. We could have asked Bruno to give him some tips on the advantages of keeping your property empty. Instead we worked harder to keep him quiet.

There was nothing wrong with his units or the rent he was asking. Winter is a slow time and places take longer to let. To speed up the process I said I would make private appointments with anyone who showed an interest in viewing them. It was a freezing day when I arranged for two separate groups to meet me there. I wrapped myself up in a huge green scarf and my thick pale-grey jacket. Last winter my car heater was reluctant to pump out any heat. I had the car serviced but that didn't change the heater's take on what heating a car was all about. The mechanic couldn't explain it to the heater either. He said, 'I've done my best'. His best and the heater's best fell well short of my expectations. I spent the winter wrapped up in my grey jacket and teamed it with various large, colourful, woollen scarves. This block is about fifteen minutes from the office and as I pulled up I felt a faint waft of warm air come from the heater. Too late to be of any use.

There were about a dozen people lounging on the fence waiting for me. They looked as cold as I felt. I hadn't expected such a crowd and it looked as if the prospective tenants had brought their friends and relations with them. I imagine the conversations went like this: 'What are you doing today?'

'Checking out a unit.'

'Good, I'll come with you. I'll tell you what I think.'

'Yeah. Well, I have to be out of this one in a couple of weeks so I can't be too fussy.'

'I'll set you straight on it. Something for me to do today. It's so fucking cold.'

They all heaved themselves away from the fence when they saw me and we headed to the first floor. Stairs are good in the winter and some people run up them, warming their feet or just bursting with energy. The first unit we entered reflected its Edwardian beginnings with wide, dark wooden architraves around the doors and windows. The same wood made up the large mantle that framed the now unusable fireplace. The fire surround had little shelves jutting out and an oval mirror in the centre with a bevelled edge. Dark wooden picture rails circled the room. I admired it. I liked the Edwardian vibe but I was alone in doing so.

'Oh, I don't like all that brown wood. It's so dark. Why don't they paint it?' People would say and walk out.

As I checked names and numbers, my phone rang. I scrambled around in my bag looking for it and someone asked, 'Are we going to see the other one that's available?' What's the hurry I wondered as I found the phone and answered it and began to climb the stairs to open the unit above.

'Hi,' said the voice on the phone, 'we're moving into that unit on Raglan Street tomorrow and I'm in the bank getting the bond cheque.'

'Yes,' I answered, 'What's the problem?'

'Who do we make it out to?'

'RTBA.'

'What?'

'RTBA.'

'I don't get you.'

'It's on the email I sent you.'

'I'm in the bank. I haven't got the email with me. Can you spell it out?' I wondered why he couldn't find the email on his phone. He obviously had that with him.

We had reached the second apartment and I gave one of the guys the keys to open the door. He turned the lock easily enough but threw the door open so hard it crashed into the wall behind it. The noise flew up and down the stairwell like a gun blast. Obviously the landlord had not bothered to supply a door stop.

After the noise had subsided and everyone had pushed into the unit, I said into the phone, 'It's the letters for the Residential Tenancy Bond Association.' Then I said slowly. 'R T B A.'

'Oh,' he said. 'The RTA?'

'It's got a B in it. B for Bob.'

'B for boat,' drifted out of the unit.

'No,' said a different voice, 'B for boooooom.' And he laughed as he drew out the 'oo' sound.

Someone shouted, 'B for bog.'

They all were at it.

'B for bum.'

'You can have B for bonk.'

'How about B for bong?'

'Did they get R? R for rabbit! Have you got a rabbit on the phone?'

'No, it's R for rat.'

'What about R for root?'

It had to be the cold. This was like an over-excited group on a school sports trip.

'Did you get any of that?' I asked into the phone.

'No. I just want to know what to put on the cheque. The teller told me to move away and I have to get another number and queue again.'

'Have you got a pen to write it down?'

'Just tell me. I'll remember.'

'It's R for Robert.' I said.

Someone said, 'Give me an R,' and high-fived the guy next to him.

'R, T for Tom,' I said.

'Give me a T,' drifted from the apartment. I could hear them high-fiving again.

'B for Bob,' I said clearly and firmly.

'B for babble', and a loud high-five.

'A for apartment,' and a high-five.

'No. No, you've lost the rhythm. It's A for Ape.' Another high-five. All this drifted towards me.

I said each letter loudly and firmly into the phone, again. 'Have you got that?'

'I think so,' said the voice.

'Good,' I said, 'Because I have to go. I have people with me.'

Back in the unit, everyone was laughing and fooling around – a sports group after a few beers. In this unit the brown wood was painted white. It certainly brightened the place and I could see the advantage on a grey day. All the activity warmed us and lightened the atmosphere. A few people took applications.

I shooed them out, locked up and wondered who the bond cheque would be made out to.

Back in my cold car the rhythm, 'Give me an R, give me a T, give me a B,' ran through my head. I actually wanted to high-five someone. It had to be the cold. I had a moment of nostalgia for my school teaching days. Kids could be fun and I felt a fondness for the group I had had with me although they could hardly be called kids.

When the bond cheque arrived the next day it was made out correctly. I asked the guy about it.

'Oh yes,' he said, 'we were still a bit confused.'

'Really?'

He went on, 'The next teller sorted it out for us. She'd done it before.' Full marks to the next teller. I hope she got a bonus at Christmas.

The memory of that inspection is with me as I walk into the block, today. The silly rhythm starts in my head.

'Give me an R, give me a T, give me a B.' I find I am walking to the rhythm of it. I give myself a shake and readjust my steps.

I had emailed the flooded tenants to say I would check the ceiling this week, so they are expecting me. I knock loudly and as there is no response, let myself in. The repair is perfect. This unit is another that has been painted white. It looks good but with the dark wood gone, the Edwardian vibe has gone. Has the world moved on from fashionable Edwardian? Are we lighter and freer? I agree that all that brown wood can be a bit heavy and of course I have painted my unit white. I lock up and head to my car. This block is near a large supermarket so I decide not to waste the opportunity to do some shopping.

* * *

Why do I buy so much? My trolley is nearly full. It is as if I am buying for a family of four. But the look is largely caused by a huge pack of toilet paper. It is on special at a really good price. I decide I don't have the energy or the desire for do-it-yourself so I bypass the self-service scan and join the queue for the checkout. The queue lengthens. I notice the old man directly behind me is holding only two items. Sometimes I like to do the right thing, so I turn to him.

'Why don't you go in front me? You've only got two things and look what I've got,' I move aside to let him through.

He smiles but he doesn't move. 'I'm not in a hurry. I'm happy to wait. I haven't got anything else to do today.'

'Are you sure? I feel bad making you wait when I've got so much.'

'You'll have something else to do. And as I said this is all I have to do. I'm happy to wait. I'm not in a hurry.'

He's right – I do need to get through the checkout, get my stuff into the car and get back to work. I go ahead of him.

On the way back I keep thinking about him. It knocks that silly rhyme out of my head, and I wonder how many other people in the checkout queue are happy to wait because that is all they have to do for the day – be part of the crowd in a busy supermarket. It makes me sad. Of course he may not be unhappy. Different things make us happy. So perhaps he is fine and likes his life.

I intend to leave everything in the car except for the perishables which I plan to put in the office fridge. Then it occurs to me that there are drinks after work and I may not want to take my car home after my free wine. I'm still restless, or is it anxious. My life doesn't rely on Bruno's tenants signing up. Restless and anxious is ridiculous. I take some deep breaths visualise Joanna and Rod signing and nodding and smiling as I detour and unload everything at home. Then banish them from my mind.

I test the toilet just to listen to it. I flushed it several times when I got home yesterday for the sheer joy of hearing it make the right noises. I hid the bucket at the back of the laundry cupboard right out of sight and out of mind! The plumber has done a good job. I can't see where the old tank was. This one looks as if it has always been there – no unsightly marks on the wall.

It occurs to me since I have been testing the toilet flush, I should ring the plumber and let him know it is all good. I do this as soon as I am back in the office

'How do you like the new tank?' he asks.

'Very stylish and it flushes, flushes every time. It is wonderful to be in the modern world again.' Am I going overboard here?

The plumber gives a bit of a laugh, 'Yeah, I'm sorry about the delay. I really have been under the pump this week. One of my guys is still away. Got some sort of infection. He won't be back until next week at the earliest. So thanks for being so patient.' I did make him feel bad about it.

So I say, 'That's fine. It's good to get it fixed. And it's good not to have marks on the wall from the old one. You were very clever there.'

'Yeah, that worked pretty well. Seeing it's you and you had to wait I won't charge for my labour. I'll just charge you for the new cistern.'

'Oh gee, I appreciate that. Thanks.' I'm embarrassed I made such a thing of the flushing.

'The least I can do.'

'Well, that would be great. If you leave your invoice at reception, I'll get onto it early next week and thanks again.' We disconnect. I still don't know the cost of the cistern. Even so, he's back in my good books now. I knew he was a good guy. I will send all my plumbing jobs his way – well, I do anyway.

I have a few new emails. One is about lunch.

Friday is the day we try to go out for an office bonding-style lunch. Mandy is the one who organises this. I'm not sure why it's her but I think every office needs a Mandy. I can see her when she's married organising dinner get-togethers and later kid's parties. She'll do it well. She's made for it. It's not something I see myself doing. I'm not made for that sort of thing. I need a Mandy in my world.

She emails, *Who's for lunch? How about the Thai place? Any other suggestions?*

The local Thai is a few doors from the office. This charming café introduced me to Pad Thai a few years ago. I am hooked. They cook it the way it should be. It's one of the best. I email my agreement to Thai. Then remember that I had thawed-out Pad Thai last night. I'm still happy to have it for lunch. In fact, I think I could eat it every day. I should test myself sometime. I especially like it with tofu.

More people want the Italian place further down the road that has a special; pasta or pizza and a glass of wine for $14. It is hard to go past that, and the email string is quite clear; the majority want to go the Italian way.

That choice turns out to be the wrong one. The wine is fine, but the cook is having an off-day with the pasta. Very glutinous and there is a lack of sauce. My favourite mushroom gnocchi is stodgy and not nearly enough sauce. We bond over the disappointing food and go back to work earlier than we usually do after Friday lunch.

Chapter 25

There is an email from reception; *Bruno rang. He says it is urgent. Please ring him ASAP.*

What do I do? Do I ring him back? Do I ignore the message? I feel myself starting to panic. Is there going to be a change of heart with his new tenants? Once I've signed them up it's a done deal. There's no turning back.

If I am going to show my leadership and take on Bruno, I have to have some strategies. I can't let myself get anxious every time I see his name. I was in control when it was just getting tenants and I could see it as a game – now I have let him wind me up. Right, I need a rethink. What I've got here is a bit of a skirmish on the sidelines. I can deal with that. I had planned not to speak to him today, but I can't have an email sitting there with ASAP on it and not do anything. Although I don't for a moment think it needs to be ASAP.

'Right,' I say out loud, 'It's just a skirmish. Take control of it.'

'Talking to yourself?' laughs Vince, as he puts a pile of paper in the recycling bin.

'Psyching myself up to ring Bruno.'

'I'll leave you to it.' Then he adds, 'Good luck,' and walks away.

I dial Bruno. Second ring and he's there.

'What's happened to my tenants? I've been waiting to hear from you.'

I do some mental gymnastics while I get with the play. Which tenants are we talking about? Are we in the maze or the ball game? There is a moment's silence while I do this.

Bruno fills that small silence.

'You said they were signing up today.'

Got it! I'm back with the play. He goes on.

'I don't want tenants that are late or don't do what they say.'

'It's all fine. They're not due until five this afternoon.'

'Why didn't you tell me that? I thought it was this morning.' Why did he think that? 'So they're not late then?'

'No, it's all under control.' Did I forget to tell him the time? Why did he think it was this morning? 'I'll ring you. As they're coming at five you won't hear from me until about five thirty, but I will ring you.'

'Yes, do that. I'll want to know when it is all done.'

'I'll talk to you later.' I hang up quickly. There is nothing else to discuss. My chair creaks as I lean back. It always does that, especially on Friday as if it has got weary and sluggish after a week of use.

More coffee! I am half-way to Café Yellow when I realise I don't need more coffee. I'm far too restless for another shot of caffeine. I'm going to have to work out a strategy for dealing with Bruno. I don't want to get like Lauren and arrive at the edge of nervous breakdown territory.

* * *

Friday is downtime in all areas of real estate. Many from the sales department have the day off, leaving just a skeleton staff. It's interesting to speculate on why the property management phones don't ring as much as usual, and why fewer people come into reception. After all these years it still surprises me.

The receptionist is idle. The property managers are clearing the backlog on their desks. Gossip is in the air.

I needed to check in with Emily. I haven't updated her since our Mickey Mouse excursion on Wednesday. She didn't lunch with us today but Vicky tells me she's in, so I wander upstairs to her office. I find her relaxed, that is, leaning back in her chair and gazing into space. Laid-back Friday here too.

'How's it going?' Of course she asks this. What did we say before 'How's it going?' Did we simply say 'hello'?

'Just waiting until five for Bruno's tenants to come and sign up. I've been sort of on edge all day. I need that property to be gone out of my life.'

'What happened about the key? I meant to ask yesterday but the day got away from me.'

'I spoke to her mother. They've changed the lock.'

'I'd have done that too if Bruno was my landlord. You don't want to be coming out of the bathroom and find Bruno's anxious face peering around the door.'

Emily is strangely relaxed. She's criticising a landlord!

I laugh. It is an entertaining picture. 'You're right; he does look anxious – sort of worried all the time. Not the face you want to glimpse when you're just out of the shower.'

'Have you told Bruno about the lock change?'

'He's not pleased. He says he should have a key to his daughter's apartment. There may be an emergency.'

Emily laughs, 'I don't think he'd be the first person we'd call in an emergency. If he became involved the emergency would double in size.' And she laughs again. She is perky today, and she looks well and relaxed. Rather like the old Emily.

'What happens now?' she asks.

'That's just it. When the tenants come back he'll want a key. We'll need a copy too. They'll wish they'd never asked him to fix the heater.'

'We'll have to work something out, but I'm not sure what.'

This is my chance to step up.

'Lauren is over him. Would you be happy if I took him on? Not that I want him, but it is time Lauren had a rest – he really upsets her.'

'Have you spoken to her?'

'No. Not yet. I thought I'd talk to you first – have it official when I talk to her.'

She's silent for a moment then she says,

'Can we talk about it on Monday? Just sit on it over the weekend.'

Why on Monday? What's wrong with now? I feel a bit deflated. I thought I was taking some initiative, showing that I was concerned with the staff's wellbeing. Oh well, Monday it is.

I head back downstairs, wondering why Emily is so relaxed and letting her thoughts on Bruno come through – not like her.

I also wonder if Kylie is right, and that she has been headhunted and is leaving.

Would they give me her job or would they decide a new broom was the way to go? You can never tell with directors.

I want the job of department manager to test myself. Of course I could go to a recruitment agency and look at what is around, but I like working here. That's the problem. I'm happy. I would get more money as a manager somewhere else and I could learn to be an Emily. It is something to think about. The surprising thing at the moment is that Emily is so relaxed. Like someone who is pleased with life, as if something has gone their way or they have made a decision and they are happy with it. I'm glad I managed to speak to her about Bruno. It does show I'm concerned with the staff's wellbeing. She's big on staff wellbeing.

***

I begin to clear up my desk for a clean start on Monday. Lauren wanders to the back of the office to 'get some fresh air', as she puts it. We both breathe in the summer. She says, 'Have you heard about the latest affair?'

'No,' I say, eagerly.

'Actually, I don't think it is an affair.'

'Well, what is it? What are you talking about?'

'You haven't heard?'

'No. Tell me.'

'Emily and Sylvester.'

'What are you talking about? They've been friends forever.'

Sylvester is one of our older married directors who is based at our Dennison office.

'Yes, Sylvester. They were caught canoodling in the Bayside office.'

'Canoodling!? What does that mean?'

'Jeremy found them. He said canoodling.'

'I don't even know what the word means.'

'Yeah, well I think he means cuddling.'

'I've just been talking to Emily. She is very relaxed and happy. In a way, I would say pleased with herself. She even made a joke about Bruno. Something's gone well for her.'

Lauren said, 'If they were having an affair, I can't see them doing it in the office.'

'Who told you?'

'Skye. Jeremy told her and she is telling everyone.'

'Of course she is. Like the town crier.'

'Something like that.'

'They're old friends,' I say. 'Why shouldn't he give her a hug?'

'We'll just have to wait and see. Why do you think she's shouting this evening?'

'I don't know.'

I have moved on from Vince's pregnancy thing. I am going with Kylie and the head-hunting. I have heard over the years that Sylvester sees himself as something of a lady's man, that he has had office affairs. He usually picks his someone-on-the-side from the sales department and usually it's a young sales assistant. I have often wondered why they would be happy to oblige. He's not that attractive, but he has charm and lots of it. From what I hear, the affairs don't last long and sales assistants move on to another job. I'm sure they get a great reference.

Lauren and I lean on the back door frame thinking about the gossip. I wonder if I will mention to Lauren that Vince thinks Emily is pregnant and that's why she is shouting drinks. My phone rings. I lean over to answer it and Lauren walks off.

I get caught up in a discussion about a tenant having trouble parking his car in his spot because the person in the next door spot parks so badly. I laugh. I understand his feelings.

'Have you spoken to the owner of the car about it?' I ask.

'No. No, I haven't.'

'Why not? Why not ask him to straighten up and leave you some room?'

'I thought the owners' corporation could put up a notice about parking carefully. It would be more official that way.'

'I think you should speak to him. I have a similar problem in my parking area and I've spoken to the driver.' I say this, but of course he doesn't want to know about me. It also makes me sound the perfect person, always doing the right thing. I don't add that I still have problems.

He ignores me and says, 'It's a 'her' and I don't want to get into an argument. I have to live there.'

I can't resist this. 'Why should you get into an argument when all you're asking is that she shows some consideration when she parks her car? I didn't get into an argument when I discussed it with my neighbour.' I'm sure he wants to hit me. I'm so perfect.

He ignores the comment. 'I'd rather you spoke to her or get the owners' corporation to put up a notice. It would be better coming from the owners' corporation.'

I wonder if he fancies her and she's rebuffed him. She may well park badly to annoy him and a row could happen. That would be entertaining for anyone else in the parking area.

'If I was you, I would try to talk to her over the weekend,' I say this, thinking of him entertaining his other neighbours. 'You can send me an email if it doesn't work out and you want further action. I'll forward your email to the owners' corporation and ask them about an official notice.'

'I'll do that! Thanks.' And he disconnects.

It is Friday, and I want to say grow up and handle your own problems, but of course I don't. His email is going to be another one for Monday Mayhem.

* * *

I wonder about Sylvester. It is easy if you are a real estate salesman to have a bit-on-the-side. The hours are irregular and the salesmen drive around all over the place in the course of their work.

No one is expecting them to be on the 5.45 train from the city. No one rings to check on them if they hear the trains are delayed. Agents work on Saturday and can be flexible with their finishing time. It is strange to me that more of them aren't at it. Rumour says it is only Sylvester in our company.

I decide to tell Vince about Emily and Sylvester. What I really want to do is discuss it because I don't believe it. When I get to his desk, Mandy is there relating a story, most of which I miss. When she finishes she asks, 'What's the most memorable routine inspection you've had?' She's sitting on the edge of Vince's desk while he rocks back in his chair. Work is not calling them! Or the gossip it seems.

Chapter 26

I don't have to think very hard.

A couple of years ago Diane, the property manager who used to manage Kylie's portfolio, and I were doing a number of routine inspections together as we tried to get them up to date. We manage an old rabbit warren of a block and about half of the twenty-eight units in it were due to be inspected. Some were overdue. We sent off the letters for eight of them giving them a time between ten and eleven in the morning.

On the day we collected eight bunches of keys, the office camera and the inspection sheets and headed off. We began at the top of the block and worked our way down to the ground floor. Rather than having a central staircase the block has stairs at each end. We zigzagged down, opening doors, making notes, taking photos and locking up again.

Everything was going well. Most tenants were out. The one who was at home opened the door immediately with a written list of maintenance requests.

'There are a few things that need doing,' he said. 'I've made a list.'

Diane took the list and ran her eye down it. 'We're not going to be replacing the blinds because you want roller instead of Venetian.'

'Those Venetians are old and they get too dusty. There's too much dust.'

We looked around and could see the windowsills were very dusty and that may have been caused by the blinds. The dust on his furniture and on the pile of books by the table could not be blamed on the Venetians.

Diane said, 'We're not getting them changed, so you'll have to dust them. We can get the tap fixed.' We all looked at the kitchen tap. Diane tried to turn it off, but it still dripped.

She studied the list. 'What's wrong with the power socket?' We headed for the bedroom and found it pulled from the wall.

'How did this happen?' Diane asked.

'I'm not sure? But it looks dangerous, I could get electrocuted.'

'Really?' I wanted to say but perhaps he's right and he will get electrocuted. Then whose fault will that be?

Diane said, 'I'll get our handyman to attach it to the wall again when he fixes the tap.' We prepared to leave.

'One more thing, it's on your list.'

We studied the list and saw he had written that he required us to put a notice in the common area about the noise.

'Every time people go in and out they slam their door and it wakes me. I'll show you.' He grabbed his keys, went out and gave the door a good, hard slam. We could see what he meant. The noise echoed around the building. We heard his key in the lock and he came in grinning. 'See.'

We agreed to put up a notice about closing the doors quietly.

We went on our way, carefully shutting the doors so there was no noise.

For the inspection, I wrote notes and Diane took photos so the owners could see how their tenants were maintaining their investment. Eventually we arrived at unit number one, a ground-floor property that sprawled around rather like the building itself. We knocked. No response. Diane knocked again then opened the door.

I called out 'Hello?' Nothing. Just silence. We walked into the unit. A few yards down the hallway that was taking us to the kitchen, we encountered the tenant. The bathroom is on the left and there he was enthroned with his jeans and grundies around his feet. We gasped and he shot to his feet giving us a full frontal.

'Oh! Oh!' we both said, as we backed down the hallway falling over each other in our hurry to leave. 'I'm so sorry,' we both stuttered, tripping over our words, as well as our feet.

'We did knock,' I called as we reached the door and shot out slamming it behind us. There was no sound of an echo from down there; just the slam. He didn't say anything, or if he did we didn't hear him. We bundled into the car, thankful it was our last inspection.

When we got back to the office we discussed who would ring him to apologise. We assumed he hadn't known we were coming.

It fell to me. Diane thought as he was her tenant, it could be embarrassing in the future. He answered the phone straight away, as if he were waiting for us.

I explained about knocking and calling out.

'Well, shit happens,' he said.

Did he really say that? Did he make a joke? I wasn't sure how to take it. I floundered and he said, 'I did get the letter, so

I knew you were coming. You can make another time if you like.' Was he sitting there waiting for us?

'Don't worry about the inspection,' I said quickly 'We'll write it up. We saw enough to do that.' Out of my mouth it flowed and I couldn't believe I said it.

He actually laughed. 'We'll leave it then.' I was delighted to leave it.

When I relayed the conversation to Diane she wondered why he hadn't asked if I liked what I saw.

Did he fancy Dianne? He wasn't expecting both of us. Not the ideal way to get noticed by your desired one if you want to take it further. Dianne didn't want to take if further.

I finished telling Vince and Mandy all this and she said, 'You'd think he'd shut the door when he was on the loo.'

'He was home by himself. Why shut the door if you don't want to?'

'The smell,' she said, 'I would always shut the door.' I suppose she had a point if there was the possibility of a smell. I believe now that display was the reason he was perched there. It would be hard to report his need to flash.

Slow Friday is the ideal day for lounging about and telling stories.

Mandy told us about an experience she had had. She was doing an open for another property manager and had a crowd of people waiting to view the place. She unlocked the door and let them in first.

'Is this place empty?' one of those in the lead called.

Mandy pushed in and looked around. The place was filthy. Rubbish, including old take-away boxes, bits of broken furniture and clothes, was strewn around. There was the smell that goes with dereliction. The beds and large pieces of furniture had gone so she guessed the tenants had actually vacated.

'It looks as if the tenants haven't cleaned yet,' she said. She felt she said it feebly and she was embarrassed showing people the place in that state.

One of the prospective tenants pointed to a lump on the lounge room floor.

'What's that?' They all looked at a person-sized lump wrapped in a grubby quilt and what could have been a sleeping bag. The bedding was pulled up over the chin and the clothes that were serving a turn as a pillow came down to the eyebrows.

There was no movement from the bundle. Mandy said there was a bit of talking among everyone there and if anyone was sleeping they should have woken up. Everyone stood around wondering loudly what to do. There was still no movement from the lump. Then they all backed out of the room and scrambled to get outside. The prospective tenants rushed away and Mandy could hear them saying,

'Was he dead?'

'Why didn't he move?'

'Can't be dead?'

'Did you see how dirty the place was?'

'Fancy them showing us through when the place is like that.'

Their voices drifted off as they disappeared. Mandy rang the police. No one had stayed to keep her company. She waited by herself feeling miserable.

The police turned up with gloves and shoe covers and all the paraphernalia they use in such cases. They took the key, knocked on the door and as they inserted the key the door flew open and they came face to face with a dishevelled young man.

Mandy found herself exclaiming with great relief, 'So, you aren't dead!' The relief was so great she started to shout,

'What are you doing in there? This property's vacant! You have no right to be here!'

The police seemed rather amused. One of them said, 'You're trespassing, you know. Get your gear and disappear. Count yourself lucky we won't charge you. But make it quick. I'm sure the agent wants to lock up.'

Mandy said the guy grabbed a few clothes and disappeared down the road. She wondered if the police knew him because she had wanted him charged but they said, 'Let it go. What's the point? He hasn't damaged anything.'

Mandy got the locks changed immediately.

* * *

Before I can discuss Emily and Sylvester, Vince's phone rings and he is caught up in something. Mandy mentions a property she has that has just become vacant and how hard it was to let last time. She gives the address and it takes me back several years to an apartment in the same complex that I managed for another company. The place became part of my property management learning curve.

There are times when you are tempted to 'give a tenant a go'. It often happens to new property managers who get their emotions into the equation. It can work out well and you can have a wonderful tenant. Or, it can go badly as, sadly, it did in this case.

The complex Mandy is talking about is a hard-edged industrial style place that used to be an old factory. It features industrial metal stairs that everyone clonks up and down to get to their units. Inside the apartments, the water and sewerage pipes and metal support beams are all visible. Some owners have painted these, but others have left the silvery lagging over the metal. The shower walls are some sort of metal and the fittings industrial grey. The balcony has an industrial metal base that you can see through so you can look down to the ground. It is safe, but disconcerting. I never felt secure stepping onto it. My landlord described his unit as *über* cool. Cool, if you like industrial grey.

When it became vacant it was invariably winter and people were looking for something warm and homely. It was not popular. One comment made several times was that there was no storage in the bathroom, no shelf, no cupboard under the basin or wall cupboard. The stainless steel basin was on a stainless steel pedestal.

We got an application from a young woman who I had seen at an open, and who was very pleasant. I had given her a tick on my running sheet. She applied with a covering letter that left us all gasping.

There is a first for everything. Suzie's simply written and lucid letter was a first for me.

Please consider my application. I want to be up-front about my job. I am a prostitute and work in X, a gentleman's club in the city. It is like any other job. I am rostered on, work my shift then go home. I do not take clients home and I never work from home. My home is my oasis.

I checked out her application.

She had a rental reference from a private landlord, always a little tricky, because they could be a best friend. The gentleman's club gave her a good reference and explained the hours she worked during the day. They said she turned up on time for her shift and was reliable. They were happy to keep employing her as long as she wished to work there. They also confirmed what her income was likely to be. It was more than enough to cover the rent several times over and far more than a property manager earns. In the office we discussed whether we were in the right job. Judged on income, the answer was a clear, 'No'.

I put the application to the landlord. He said he would think about it, and talk it over with his partner.

Suzie came into the office looking rather like the girl next door to see how her application was going. A couple of our sales guys briefed by Demi, the receptionist, came out of their offices and strolled past to look at her. They didn't believe she was a prostitute. They had seen prostitutes, they said, and that was not what they looked like.

She said she wanted to meet face-to-face because with her job it was difficult to get accommodation if she owned up to what she did. She wanted to be honest. She also explained again that she never brought clients home.

'It's rather like an office job. I'm rostered on and work my shift then go home just like everyone else. It is just a job.' She made it sound like a shift at McDonald's.

After she had gone the sales guys were back again.

'You're joking, aren't you?' said Steve. 'She's no pro.'

'That's what she told me,' I said. 'Why would she say it, if it wasn't true? Anyway I've checked her out.'

'Where does she work?' Steve again.

Mark chipped in, 'I bet it's not on the street. You're not going to see her on a street corner.'

Steve couldn't leave it alone. 'Are you sure she's a whore?'

'Working girl,' chimed in Demi.

'What?'

'The word's working girl Steve. That's what they call themselves.'

'Whatever. They're all pros or whores to me,' said Steve, proving that real estate can be a very conservative profession. No liberal thinking or political correctness here.

'Where does she work?' asked Mark. 'As I say, I can't believe it's on the street.'

'Thinking of going there?' I asked.

He laughed a sort of, 'haw haw, don't be ridiculous' sort of laugh and said, 'You'd have to be joking.'

Steve started to move away and Mark asked again, 'You didn't tell us where she worked.'

I named the gentleman's club in the CBD.

'Oh that place!'

'Know it, do you?' asked Demi with a grin.

'Not personally. No.'

'Fancy her do you?'

'There's the phone Demi. That's your job. And for your information I've got a girlfriend.'

'What's that got do with it?' Demi answered the phone and Mark went back to the sales department.

Demi and I wondered if he ever did visit the gentleman's club. It is not something he would be likely to let slip. Mind you, when he got there someone else may take his fancy, but he did seem to fancy Suzie when she was in the office. If she had any sense as a working girl she would have a working name. She did seem to have sense then.

I liked her. The landlord and I decided to take her at face value and put her into the unit. No one else applied and that helped our decision. For a few months everything was fine. Her rent was paid and we didn't hear anything from her. I conducted my first routine inspection to find the place tidy and clean. There appeared to be no problems. Then a neighbour contacted us to say they had heard a fight in the unit in the early hours of one morning. We rang Suzie. She was upfront.

'An old boyfriend turned up,' she said.

She had told him she didn't want anything to do with him. He got angry and she had trouble getting rid of him.

'I told him not to come back and that if he did I wouldn't let him into the complex.'

A few nights later someone did let him into the complex so he could pound on her door and shout obscenities at her. The neighbours called the police but when they arrived he had gone.

A couple of weeks past, then Suzie called the neighbours herself. She had met her old boyfriend waiting at her door and he had beaten her up. She spent a couple of nights in hospital.

When she was released she came into the office, looking bruised and emotionally beaten – nothing like the girl next door. He had taken her rent money. Demi didn't alert the sales guys this time. I was glad.

'He's a heroin addict,' Suzie explained. She then confessed that when she had been with him a couple of years ago she had been too. She was clean now. He was back from Sydney and he wasn't pleased that she had turned her life around. She was working double shifts to earn the rent money. A few days later she came in and paid the full rent in cash.

Again Demi didn't alert the sales team.

A couple of months went by without us hearing anything from her. Then the neighbours called us to complain about noise from her unit.

The second routine inspection was due. I took another property manager with me.

Suzie was on site. Skinny, with a couple of sores on her face and the property was dirty and untidy; nothing like it had been at the first inspection. She apologised and said she was going to clean it up when her daughter visited and that she had been working double shifts to earn extra money. She wanted some time off when her daughter stayed.

It was obvious to us that she was on smack again. Sometime after that she stopped paying her rent and we evicted her. She didn't challenge the process. We had a warrant of possession and when we turned up with the police and the locksmith the place was empty. Not clean but vacant.

Some months later I saw her in the street. She had cleaned up a bit and was less gaunt. She stopped to talk.

'I want to thank you for giving me a chance. You were all so nice and I blew it.' She had tears in her eyes, 'My boyfriend's back. He's not good for me. I know that but, well…' and she shrugged. I asked how her daughter was.

'I don't see her anymore. My parents think its best. They've taken out an injunction.' She was silent for a moment. Then she said, 'I think it is for the best, but I miss her.' She thanked me again, looked straight at me and said, 'I'm sorry I let you down.'

With that she disappeared into the crowd. I have never seen her since. I wanted to say, 'It was yourself you let down. It doesn't matter about us.' But she was gone before I had the chance. I don't suppose it would have been helpful. She probably knew it.

I'm glad I gave her a go, but I do regret she blew it and caused distress to everyone, including herself. Her landlord felt differently. He thinks it was a mistake but then he was out of pocket. The bond didn't cover all the money he was owed.

No other 'working girl' has applied for one of my properties. Or if they have, they hid the fact and slid in under the radar with a series of lies. On balance that would be a profession I would avoid. The landlord berated himself for accepting her.

'Never should have done it,' was his comment. 'I don't know what came over me.' He didn't meet her so wasn't influenced by the girl-next-door look. I think he did it out of kindness. He wanted to give her a go – to prove she could be a good tenant and not judge her by her job. He didn't deserve the result and the distress that went with it.

Chapter 27

It's getting on for five o'clock and everyone is packing up. I go down to reception where Vicky is sorting out the mail to post on her way to the Lido. We always invite our temps to after-work drinks. Emily likes them to feel part of the team.

'Hi Vicky,' I say. 'I've got some tenants coming in at five for a sign up. I hope they're here a bit before that but I'll come down so don't you lock up. I'll do that.'

I'm sure Lisa has told Vicky to lock up the moment five o'clock appears on her computer screen. There is no way I want that to happen and Joanne and Rod go away because they think we are shut.

'Are you sure? Lisa said it was my job to lock up. I could wait if you like.' Lisa has not got the full process across to her. There is no way Lisa would wait.

'Don't you worry! I'll be here at five. You can head off to the Lido with everyone else.'

As there is no solution, yet, on who will continue to manage Bruno's properties, I remind Lauren that her new tenants will be in. I suggest she might like to meet them. She thinks she will do that at a later date. What she needs is a drink.

'I'll line up a wine for you. You can have it when they've signed. How's that for positive?'

I'm getting nervous. I start wondering what I would do if they were a 'no show'. No sooner has that thought taken hold than I work to banish it. Positive thinking is needed.

I'm at my desk checking that all the documents are in the folder for Joanne and Rod when the place is plunged into gloom. The power's off.

'What the hell!?'

'What the fuck?' reverberates around the office from the few not yet at the Lido.

'I don't believe this!' I say out loud. 'I just don't believe this is happening.'

I get up in the gloom and push the back door wider for more light, and then struggle through the darkened office that is now full of trip hazards, to reception. Someone says she thinks it's a pole failure because the whole of our side of the street is out. We all push onto the street and join everyone else from the other businesses along the strip. A message is passed around saying it is a transformer and they are onto it. Nobody is quite sure who 'they' are. A few speculate but somehow 'they' makes us feel secure – 'they' are doing something. This doesn't make me feel any better. I'm ready for Bruno's sign-up and there is no power.

What to do?

My mind clicks over. I am trying not to think Princess Street is jinxed. Should I ring Joanne and tell them not to come? I stop and get a grip on myself. They must be almost here. I take some deep breaths.

We could sign in a café, although Jono shuts about 4 pm as do others along the strip. The Lido's not suitable, too much noise. More deep breaths and I decide that my desk will have to be the place. I'll have to be careful of trips hazzards. When they're finished I can let them out into the alley behind the office but I can't let them in that way, the gate locks from the inside. Of course I can let them in. I can unbolt the gate and we can walk round. That's what I'll do. I'll meet them out the front and walk round with them. Simple!

I can see a few people heading for the Lido. Why not? There are only a few minutes to go until closing and no computers. Vicky has confirmed that the phones are down too. No power, no phones. So much for modern technology!

I go back to my desk and unbolt the back gate. This narrow area with bins and an old table is not hazard free either, but more so than the dark main office. We're so worried these days about safety and litigation.

I stumble through the main office and hang around at reception.

'It's five,' says Vicky. 'What do you want me to do?'

'Flick the phone to night, grab the mail and go to the Lido. I'll wait. I'll wait by the door. I won't let anyone in.'

What is it about early closing? It suddenly becomes urgent for people to see us. I stand at the door with darkness behind me and people still want to come in. Someone comes with a signed condition report they want to talk to their property manager about, another person wants a rental list. Having got it they want to hang around and discuss it, someone else wants to discuss some urgent maintenance with their property manager. Have they emailed their property manager about it? No. Is it urgent? No. As it transpires it can wait until Monday.

I know now why Lisa locks this door and is away from the reception desk and out the door the moment she switches the phones over.

Joanne and Rod are here. I lock the office entrance door and lead them round the side of the building. As we turn the corner I can hear someone knocking and shouting.

'Is there anyone there?' I behave as Lisa would and ignore it.

I settle Joanne and Rod at my desk and apologise for the lack of power.

'Not your fault,' said Joanne, 'We're just glad we can still sign up. We noticed everything was dark when we came along and we wondered.' I want to hug her for her desire to commit to Bruno's place .

We have a pack of information we give new tenants to take away with them. I go through this with them to make sure they understand everything. It is a good idea to do this before they sign the lease because once they have done that and got their receipt for the first month's rent they want to leave and they stop listening.

I get them to sign a form that explains we have advised them to get their personal items and household goods insured because we are not liable if something happens to them. Occasionally tenants argue about this. They believe that if someone breaks in and steals their laptop the landlord should be liable for the replacement. This is not so and they need to be aware of it.

I'm amazed at how many people don't have their stuff insured.

Joanne and Rod don't have any trouble with this. In fact, they are happy with everything. They have the bond and the first month's rent with them. I take these and the bond lodgement form they have signed and leave them to read through the leases and initial every clause if they are happy with it and don't have any questions.

With no computers there is no electronic receipt, and I have to stumble back to reception to get the receipt book so I can hand write one.

Joanne and Rod are reading, initialling and occasionally discussing. It takes a while to read through the lease. Caruthers adds extra clauses to the standard lease. One is about polished boards and not wearing stilettos on them. Another is about Blu Tack. Blu Tack can make a real mess. It is not easy to get off whatever the packet says. Since I have worked here we have included a clause about putting protectors under furniture when it is on polished boards. The clause also says that tenants will be liable for any damage caused to the floors. I am not getting caught twice.

Joanne and Rod are happy. No questions. They take their pack, the receipts and signed lease and I let them out the back gate. As they leave Joanne says how glad they are they have found something near her father. Rod has said next to nothing to me. The strong silent type.

* * *

I sit for a minute at my desk. Is it too good? If I ring Bruno will I jinx it? Will they rush back and say they've changed their mind? This is nonsense. I dial Bruno's number. The power is still off so no phones. This is the first time I've rung him from my mobile. Now he will have my number in his phone. The call goes to voicemail. That's another first. I leave a brief message to say the Princess Street tenants have signed, paid the rent and the bond. It occurs to me the place will need to be cleaned as it's been empty for so long. I write a yellow sticky note to talk to Lauren about it on Monday. I grab my things and head out. My phone goes as I am locking up the office. Of course it is Bruno. What was he doing when I rang? I don't ask him that – I don't want to know.

'So, they've sighed have they?' he says.

'Yes,' and I repeat everything I said in the voicemail and finish with, 'So, good news all round. Have a good weekend.' And I disconnect. For a moment I thought I would mention the cleaning then I thought better of it.

I arrive at the Lido and give the thumbs up to Lauren who calls out.

'Well, why's Bruno ringing me. His name came up. Didn't you tell him it was all signed and sealed?'

'I left a voicemail. So he rang me back. That's twice I've told him. There is no need for you to talk to him!'

'What? He always answers.'

'Not this time but he rang back straight away. Forget him. Where's my drink?'

Lauren waves her hand at a glass of red wine on the table near her. The place is filling up and the noise is rising. I head to my glass and squeeze in near it when Emily taps someone's glass and says, 'I assume that everyone who's coming is here.'

We all stop talking. We are desperate to hear what she is going to say.

There is a pause and we become quieter.

'I know I've been under the weather lately and not giving you all as much help as I would like. I owe you all an explanation.'

Another pause and we lean forward. There's a hush. It's as if the people at neighbouring tables have also quietened to hear her. I'm thinking, 'My God, I hope it is not cancer, obviously not a new a job. You do not start that way for an I-am-leaving-speech.' Emily takes a deep breath as if to give herself courage.

'I'm…I'm pregnant. Twelve weeks. So far it hasn't been an easy road.' There is a hush. I'm looking at her and I see that she has rehearsed this. I can see her taking a breath to carry on. 'I wasn't sure when to announce it. I've felt bad not telling you all, but I wanted to wait for the twelve-week scan to make sure everything was okay. I'm relieved that I'm telling you now. It's a weight off my shoulders. I needed to let you all know.'

There is more silence as we absorb this. Then she goes on.

'I'm not discussing who the father is at the moment, so I would be grateful if no one asks me. At the moment it's my secret.'

I catch Vince's eye and he gives me a smug smile as if to say, 'See. Pregnant'.

Emily stands up. 'I needed to tell you all. It took me a while to get my head around it and this seemed a good opportunity while we're celebrating Bruno's new tenants.' She looks at me. I give her the thumbs up and say, 'A done deal!'

She smiles at me as if we are conspirators and I suppose we are, when you think of the key debacle.

'I have left money at the bar for you all. So drink up. I'm not staying, because obviously I'm not drinking.' She stops for a moment.

'About the pregnancy,' her voice gets a little louder, 'I just want to say I am really pleased. I know I always said I didn't want children and that my nieces were enough. Now it has happened…' she stops. She looks as though she's going to cry.

'Congratulations,' shouts Vince. We are great at congratulations and it fills that gap when it's hard to know what to say. We all echo Vince and people scramble up and hug Emily and she does start to cry. She has built a good team and we all know that we'll stand by her, support her and cover for her.

But we'll not rest until we know who the father is. She's going to have to let it out sometime.

Vince says he'll walk her to her car.

As they go out, our table starts to buzz. Even though Vince suggested she may be pregnant, I didn't believe him.

Was this an accident? Or was it intentional? Did she find that her nieces were not enough and she wanted her own child? Perhaps loving her nieces made having her own more desirable.

What was all that about eating Granny Smith apples? A pregnancy craving? Did she hope we would see it in that light and guess? If she thought that about the apples she didn't realise how strongly she had made the case for No Children.

A secret father? She knows how we love to gossip. She can't expect us to leave that alone. I can hear Kylie running through a list of possible candidates including her old boyfriend.

Just then, Skye swings through the door.

'What's all this? What have I missed?'

'Emily's pregnant!' shouts Lauren as she hands me a second glass of wine. 'Enjoy this. You won the bet but don't expect me to buy you another one anytime soon.'

'Two's fine and Emily's buying. It's a win-win for me tonight.'

'Whatever. And now I think about it, I shouldn't have got you that second glass. Bruno keeps ringing me.'

'Don't answer,' I say then add, 'You can if you want to but there is nothing more to say. His tenants signed and paid the bond and rent. It's after hours.'

'I know he's not going to stop. I'll have to answer next time.'

'Over to you,' I shout above the noise which has increased since Emily left and Skye turned up. 'He's all yours.' I take a large gulp of wine. ' Forget him for the evening.'

'I think you should speak to him. You organised the tenants. It has to be something about them.'

I nearly agree. I'm such a pushover. I gulp some more wine. It steadies me, 'I've done enough. There's nothing to say. It's a done deal. Perhaps he wants to talk about something else.'

'On a Friday night! He has to be joking. Of course he's going to keep ringing. Why doesn't he get a life? I need another cocktail and when he rings again, I'll answer it. He won't hear much over the noise.'

'Ask him why he didn't answer his phone. I'm curious.'

'If you want to know that, you'll have to ring him.' She pokes her phone in my direction.

'I'm not that curious.'

She shrugs and heads in the direction of the bar. There is table service but it is usually quicker to get your own drink.

Skye comes over with a bright blue cocktail. 'I hear I won't have to open Princess Street, tomorrow. Has it really gone? I can't believe it. I'm going to have withdrawals.' She laughs.

'Signed, sealed and paid for,' I say. 'They've paid everything.' I'm beginning to feel smug about this success. 'If anyone turns up tomorrow just let them know.'

'I'll sit in my car with my air-con on full blast. It's going to be hot.' She takes a large gulp of the bright blue liquid. 'Emily's pleased. Yes?'

I nod. 'She said she was.'

'Great. Who's the father?'

'That we don't know and she's not telling.'

'I bet it's Sylvester. Did you know that Jeremy saw them together?'

'Yeah, I heard.'

'Where is Jeremy? He left before I did.'

'I haven't seen him.'

Vince is back.

'How is she?' I ask.

'Emotional. I bet everyone's saying Sylvester's the father.'

'I am, for one,' says Skye. 'It has to be someone. This isn't the Immaculate Conception. And Jeremy saw them together. Where is Jeremy? I'm going to ring him.' She disappears into the crowd.

Vince says, 'It is going to be a bit complicated if it is Sylvester. Another drink?'

'Two house reds. I'll line them up. It'll be hard to move in here soon, let alone get a drink.'

'I'll do the same. I'm getting picked up so I may as well drink up,' he laughs at his tame joke and heads to the bar.

I'm in shock.

I sit in the midst of all this noise and for a moment I'm envious. I can't understand why. I don't want a baby. Well, I don't think I do.

We say, 'No children,' but that does not really answer the question. There's always something at the back of our minds that knows there is time to change our thinking. The door has not shut and these days it is staying open longer and longer. Emily made the decision. She has said 'Yes'. I can hear Kylie talking about a one-night stand, and I think if that is the case she could have had an abortion – instead she said yes to a baby.

No one will ever say to her again, 'Oh no children? Don't you want them?' And that particularly stupid comment my grandmother's generation makes, 'Don't leave it too late. You're not getting any younger you know?' As if you didn't know that.

I wonder if underneath it all I do want children. Is that where the envy comes from? Well, a child perhaps, not children. I've spooked myself. I can't understand that pang of envy.

Vince pushes through the crowd, struggling with four glasses of wine. We manage to get them on the table without spilling any.

'A night for wine? You're not having a cocktail?' I ask and take a sip from my glass.

'No. No cocktails tonight. I don't really like them. They're too sweet and I drink them too quickly. I thought of beer but decided on wine.'

Lauren comes up and crouches beside me so her mouth is right at my ear.

'Bruno. He wanted to know what we're doing about the advertised open for tomorrow. He didn't want people turning up and no one being there. He said he rang you too but you didn't answer.'

'Phone's in my bag. I wouldn't have heard it.'

'No problem,' said Laruen waving a glass of some yellow liquid around, 'I've dealt with it.' She takes a drink of the yellow cocktail. 'This stuff's really good.' She drifts off smiling.

I turn to Vince. 'The frustrating thing about Bruno is that under that annoying surface, he's kind.'

'Why's that frustrating?

'It makes it impossible to really dislike him.' Vince smiles and I drink some more wine and say, 'I've let Bruno's place and I'm drinking to that. But it's more than that. I think I'm drinking to Emily. She's made a decision about motherhood. She could have had an abortion but she chose motherhood. There's no turning back now. I feel a little disturbed by it. I'm drinking to her courage.'

'Do you think it takes courage?' he asks.

'I don't know, but I think so. What do you think?'

Vince doesn't say anything. Mind you, it is so noisy he may not have heard.

I look at him and wonder if he and his partner want children or have discussed it. I don't ask. It's not a question you ask at the top of your voice in a noisy bar. Instead I say, 'Let's just drink up and get onto our next glass.'

No one comes up with a suggestion other than Sylvester for Emily. If we hadn't heard that silly gossip today, we would never have thought of him. Who would we have had in the frame then? There is no one else. A one night stand as Kylie is suggesting? Someone, and I think it is Mandy, suggests a donor. That idea does not get much traction. We still believe Emily didn't want children. She said it often enough for us to believe her. You have to be desperate to go the donor route. I can't imagine Sylvester wanting this one if it is his. It is more than just complicated for him. You would think he would have had a vasectomy if he is going to keep playing around. His kids must be teenagers.

Vince's partner turns up and after a couple more drinks I leave with them. There is no way I can pass a breath test.

* * *

As I unpack my bag at home, I notice a text from Emily, *Let's meet for coffee on Monday about 11. I want to have a chat.*

'My god,' I think, 'is she going to confide in me? Could I ask her why she's decided to keep it?' Or how she got it in there in the first place? Well, the obvious way of course, but there has to be more to it than that. A shaft of reality appears out of the wine haze. We had planned to discuss Bruno's management. That may be all it is. But would she text about that?

When she takes maternity leave I'm going to want her job – acting head of a department is a good step up on the career ladder. I wonder how long she will work for. I bet she doesn't give up her job. If she doesn't ask me, I'll put it to her. I'm buzzing with the wine but I can't stop thinking about it.

I've the weekend to plan for the meeting. I'll be proactive. I want to step into her role. I start drawing down pictures of myself in her job, successfully trouble-shooting, getting the business I pitch for. I see my career zooming upwards. I see myself exchanging my apartment for a bigger and classier one. Another picture shows me buying another apartment so I have a second one and the beginnings of a property portfolio.

Maybe I've got well ahead of myself but you have to dream and have goals. When I let my mind race down a track like that I need a destination with stepping stones on the way. I am glad Emily didn't get an abortion.

This week has been unlike any other. Emily and I will laugh about the Mickey Mouse key excursion – although that problem is not resolved. Could we even laugh about her throwing up now I know why? It could be a good meeting.

* * *

I have the weekend to psyche myself up and prepare my pitch to her. I'll need to work out what to wear, too. Something that shrieks positive. Something that tells who I am. Lemon? Green? Yellow? Definitely not Melbourne-black.

I check my phone again and notice I have a voice message. Half asleep I log into it. Bruno's voice shocks me awake. I'm so stunned I miss the beginning but I catch him saying,

'So I will go and do the cleaning in the weekend. I want them to move into a clean place. I want it clean when they leave. So I will make it nice for them. That's what I was ringing you to tell you. You don't do anything I will do it.' And he's gone.

'Well that makes Monday easier and I scored the goal. The game's over. I've won!

So much to think about! I step onto my balcony to look at the night lights and breathe in some city air. It is still and the air's soft. I am glad I drank all that wine. I need something to help me sleep.